Remember Me at Willoughby Close

A Return to Willoughby Close Romance

KATE HEWITT

TULE
PUBLISHING

Chapter One

"THIS PLACE *STINKS*."

Laura Neale kept the smile on her face with cheery determination as she turned to face her fourteen-year-old daughter. Maggie had yanked the earbuds from her ears as an expression of her discontent and now stood scowling in the centre of their new home, her smartphone clenched in one hand.

Carefully Laura closed the door on number three, Willoughby Close. The moving van had just left, the place was full of boxes, and their almost ten-year-old golden retriever, Perry, was making small whimpers of agitation. He didn't like change. Neither, apparently, did her daughter. Yet here they were, and Laura was determined to make it work. Make it *good*.

"What about it stinks?" she asked lightly as she gave Perry a comforting stroke. The grief counsellor had told her to reflect emotions back to her children, and make sure they understood she was actively listening to them. The concept, which sounded so helpful in theory, tended to fill Maggie with rage, but Laura persevered because she didn't know what else to do. Surely it would start working at some point.

"Everything," Maggie stormed, case in point. "What *doesn't* stink about it?" She flung her arms out to encompass the open-plan living area, which Laura thought was rather nice, if a bit small: a galley kitchen of granite and chrome in the corner, French windows overlooking a little terrace and garden—now covered in a glittering January frost—and a living area with a woodburning stove that promised to be cosy when lit, their two sofas framing it.

"Maggie, I know it's different," Laura said, pitching her tone somewhere between bracing and sympathetic. "And it's smaller than our house back in Woodbridge, certainty." She gave a commiserating smile, which made Maggie fume all the more. "We'll get used to it," she said as something of a last resort, and Maggie threw her arms up in the air before stomping off, except there was nowhere really to stomp off to. She stood by the cooker, her back pointedly to her mother.

Laura didn't know whether to laugh or sigh at this pointless show of defiance. She decided to do neither as she turned to her other child, eleven-year-old Sam, with as much optimism as she could muster. "What do you think, Sam?" she asked, injecting a slightly manic note of cheer into her voice that she found herself often adopting, to make up for Maggie's mood.

Sam didn't even glance up from the screen of his iPad,

where he was constructing some kind of trap for cows on Minecraft. "Um…it's okay." He'd walked into the house without looking at anything, and had been sat on the sofa, amidst a mountain of boxes, ever since.

"High praise, indeed." Laura bent down to fondle Perry's ears. "It's all right, Per," she murmured. "This is your new home."

"Even the dog doesn't like this place," Maggie proclaimed in a tone of ringing contempt. This time Laura couldn't hold the sigh in.

"He'll get used to it, Maggie."

"Well, I won't," her daughter declared, and then, for want of anywhere else to go, flounced upstairs.

Laura decided to enjoy the moment's peace rather than worry too much about her daughter's theatrics. There was, she knew, no point in reminding Maggie that they'd all agreed to this move two months ago, when Granny and Grandad had suggested they move closer to their house in Burford, and life in Woodbridge had started to feel so bleak, none of them able to clamber out from under the cloud of grief they'd been living with for just over a year.

"We miss Tim so much," Pamela had told Laura, the threat of tears thickening her voice. "Having his children close by would be such a comfort." No mention of what a comfort it would be to have their daughter-in-law close by as well, but Laura chose not to mind. Her in-laws were grieving. Tim had been their only child. And in any case, her relationship with them had always been slightly prickly.

When Laura had suggested the move to Maggie and Sam, they'd looked surprised, and then thoughtful. A new start might have been what they all needed, and her children were aware enough to know it.

"We could see Granny and Grandad more?" Sam had asked eagerly, because her in-laws tended to spoil them with presents, sweets and unlimited screen time. The other grandparent option was slightly less appealing—Laura's father lived in a semi-squalid caravan in Cornwall and was an indifferent host at best, and her mother had died before they'd been born, when Laura was only in her twenties. She still missed her, missed having her wisdom as well as her humour. Her dad, unfortunately, offered little of either.

"Yes, loads more," she'd told Sam firmly.

"And we'd start new schools?"

"Of course we'd start new schools, doofus," Maggie had interjected scornfully. "We'd be moving hundreds of miles away."

"That's the tricky part," Laura had explained with a sympathetic look for both of them. "Leaving everything and everyone we know here, to start over. How would you feel about that?"

Sam had just shrugged, surprisingly nonplussed; he was leaving primary at the end of the year, and would have been starting a new school anyway. And, Laura knew, he didn't have too many friends, preferring his own company and the world he constructed on a screen than the potential bullies who teased him because he was a little different, a little shy. Leaving Woodbridge would, she'd acknowledged sadly, be no hardship for her quirky son.

"What about you, Maggie?" Laura had asked. She knew her daughter had several close friends at school, but she also knew since Tim's death Maggie had contemptuously declared them all fakes. No one, it seemed, had been there when she'd truly needed them. Laura could hardly blame a bunch of fourteen-year-old girls for not knowing how to deal with death, but it still hurt her daughter. A lot.

Although, she suspected, whatever her friends' reactions, Maggie would have been angry anyway. Her daughter had been in a near-constant state of fury since the police had rung her mobile just a week before Christmas and informed them that her there had been an accident. Words to freeze the blood in her veins, for her heart to still, and yet it hadn't. It had kept beating on, relentlessly, long after Tim's had been stopped by a skid into a tree on the side of the road.

When Laura had asked her daughter her opinion about moving, Maggie had, at least, not been angry. She'd merely shrugged, chewing her thumbnail. "Maybe. I don't know."

"You can think about it, of course. It's not a decision any of us should take lightly."

Maggie had nodded, and then, to Laura's surprise, there had been a soft knock on her bedroom door two nights later. She'd startled awake, as she often did since Tim's death, her heart thudding in her chest, her body twanging into tense alert, sure something was wrong; it was just a question of what…

"Mum?"

"Maggie? Is everything okay?" She glanced at the clock on the bedside table; it read two o'clock in the morning. Her heart rate ratcheted higher, panic her default setting since her husband's death.

"I want to move."

"Oh." Laura had eased back against the pillows, filled with relief that nothing was wrong, or at least more wrong than it already was. "Okay, sweetheart. I'm glad you've made a decision. We can talk about it more in the morning."

And when they had done so, Maggie hadn't changed her mind. But apparently she had now.

Laura moved to the kitchen where boxes were piled on the worktop. She'd had the foresight to pack one with the essentials—kettle, teabags, and a carton of UHT milk. Unfortunately she'd forgotten to mark what box it was on the outside.

It had been typical of her, in the last year, to make such a hash of things. Her brain still felt as if it were fuzzy, as if everything was happening in slow motion, but she was the one who needed to catch up.

Her best friend Chantal, who lived in London, had told her that was normal. "Grief messes with you," she'd told Laura seriously. "You have to give yourself a lot of time."

Except how did one do that exactly, especially with two grieving children to shepherd and support? Time wasn't a commodity you could buy in the shop; neither was it elastic, something you could stretch and expand to suit your needs. It simply *was*, and in her low moments Laura wondered if she'd ever have enough time to feel normal again. Time one day not to feel so sad…or so guilty.

Forcing these uncomfortable thoughts into a dark corner of her mind that felt as if it was getting bigger and bigger by the hour, Laura reached for the first box and tore the tape off the top with a satisfyingly loud rip. Sam looked up from his iPad, and then back down again, thumbs moving in concert over the screen.

"Ten more minutes on that thing," she told him, "and then you can help me unpack."

Sam merely grunted, and Laura wondered if she'd have the energy to enforce the ultimatum she'd just given. Goodness but it could be hard to parent solo. There was never anyone else to take up the slack, to step in when you needed a breather, to play the bad cop when you needed a moment or two to shine as the good one. Thirteen months on and it still felt so very hard.

The first box she'd opened was all the nice table linens she hardly ever used. Naturally. Laura opened another, to find her standing mixer and all her wooden spoons and spatulas. Why hadn't she marked her box of essentials? For heaven's *sake*.

Four boxes later she'd finally found it and was gratefully plugging in the kettle. Maggie was still upstairs, no doubt telling all her so-called fake friends back in Woodbridge how much she hated it here. Never mind that she'd said they were fake, they were the only ones she had right now, and Laura understood her need to cling to what was familiar.

Far from the first time, she wondered if moving across the country was actually a good idea when your life was already in such upheaval. When you were still grieving, or at least trying to, except over a year on and you still weren't sure how it was supposed to feel, what life was meant to look like.

The kettle boiled and she tossed teabags into two mugs and then poured boiling water over them before Perry, true to form, came over and snuffled against her thigh, hoping for something to eat, even if it was just biscuit crumbs.

Speaking of biscuits…Laura ripped open a packet of rich tea ones. "Sam," she said gently. "It's been fifteen minutes. Time to get off that screen."

With a groan that seemed to come from the depths of his lanky form, Sam tossed the iPad aside and went over to grab for a biscuit—or three. "Okay, what?" he asked, spewing out some crumbs.

"Shall we sort your room out?" Laura suggested. The kitchen was more important, but she wanted her son to be involved. Excited. And she thought she should go upstairs and check on Maggie, even if her daughter wouldn't appreciate what she'd see as interference. She'd bring her a cup of tea as a peace offering.

"Okay." Sam gave her an uncertain smile that made Laura's heart ache with both love and worry. Since their dad's death Maggie had been full of fiery theatrics, while Sam had gone very quiet. It was tempting to focus more on putting out the fire rather than making sure her youngest was okay, but she did her best to take moments with him when she could—to enjoy simple pleasures as well as to simply *be*, letting the sorrow spin out.

Now she ruffled his hair and he leaned in for a quick hug; that was something else that was new since Tim's death. Her son had become cuddly. While she savoured the connection, it also worried her. Sam would never say he was afraid, or sad, or just plain unhappy. But what if he was? What was he struggling with, that he never told her about?

"Come on," Laura said, and together they headed up the narrow, open flight of stairs that led to the cottage's first floor. Admittedly, it was significantly smaller than their house in Woodbridge, which had had four bedrooms and two receptions, plus an eat-in kitchen. It hadn't been a mansion, but it had been nice enough, and number three Willoughby Close was, at least in terms of square footage, a definite downgrade.

But the view was gorgeous, and the cottages were wonderfully quaint, with their wooden beams and statement stone wall. Not that her children would necessarily appreciate that kind of quaintness.

Maggie was camped out in the back bedroom, which was smaller than her room at home, but still, Laura told herself, perfectly adequate. She had enough of a guilt complex going on not to add to it with the fact her daughter had a slightly smaller bedroom than she was used to. First-world problems and all that.

"Hey, Maggie," Laura said in the same bright voice she'd used with Sam. "I brought you a cup of tea."

Her daughter did not reply. She was sitting hunched under the window, a curtain of dark hair obscuring her face, her fingers flying over the screen of her phone.

"So this is your room," Laura said unnecessarily as she put the cup of tea next to her. The cottage had, unfortunately, only two bedrooms, but the caretaker Jace had offered to put up a temporary wall in the master to turn it into two. Maggie had the back one, with the window, while Laura had, in typical maternally sacrificial fashion, taken the smaller, windowless one. Sam had the front bedroom. It would do; it would have to, because it was the only property they could afford in the whole area.

"Shall we start unpacking?" Laura suggested. Boxes were stacked along one wall and the furniture from Maggie's old bedroom—bed, bureau, chair, and desk—were all in a jumble against each other, leaving very little room to manoeuvre.

"Can my stuff even fit in here?" Maggie demanded, her

gaze still on her phone.

"Considering it's already in here, I should think so." This time Laura couldn't keep a very slight edge from her voice. She was tired, she had a headache, and the last thing she wanted to do was unpack everything. She'd much rather take a bubble bath and sleep for about twelve hours. She'd been in a state of perpetual exhaustion for a year.

Maggie just jerked one shoulder in the semblance of a shrug, and Laura decided to help Sam instead. Maybe if she left Maggie to it, she'd start to unpack a little on her own. Maybe she'd even get into a better mood.

When Laura came into the other bedroom, Sam was standing by the window that overlooked the little postage stamp of garden.

"Dad would have hated this garden," he said matter-of-factly.

His words gave her heart a little twist. "Perhaps," she agreed, "but he would have been able to do something magical with it." Their garden back in Woodbridge hadn't actually been that much bigger than this one, maybe twice the small size, but Tim had managed to fit a tree house, a zip wire, and several raised vegetable beds in it, although when he'd died the veg beds had been full of weeds, the zip wire broken. But that was Tim to a tee—infectious excitement veering to weary indifference and back again.

Another thought to banish to that dark corner of her mind.

Laura joined her son at the window and put her arm around his narrow shoulders. He leaned into her as they both looked out at the view—the tiny garden covered in frost, the wood and the wolds beyond, the glint of the Lea River no more than a promise on the horizon. It was a perfect wintry scene.

"It's beautiful here, isn't it?" Laura said quietly. "I'm looking forward to exploring."

Sam didn't reply, and she didn't force a response from him. She felt sorrow emanating from him in a rolling wave, and she understood it. Everything about this house—this life—was different than what they were used to. It wasn't what any of them had wanted it to be, and yet here they were.

"Shall we get started?" she asked gently, and he nodded.

They worked in quiet companionship for about half an hour; Laura located sheets for Sam's bed and made it up while he organised all his books—mainly *Horrible Histories* and Minecraft annuals—in the wooden bookshelf Tim had built for him a couple of years ago. There were reminders of her husband everywhere, which was, Laura had come to realise, both a good and bad thing. She didn't want to forget, of course she didn't, and yet it could hurt so much to remember.

"This is a good start, isn't it?" she told Sam, dusting her hands on her jeans, just as the doorbell rang.

"Who's that?" Sam asked and Laura shook her head. The

only person she'd met in Wychwood-on-Lea was the caretaker Jace, and then only briefly.

Feeling cautious for some reason, she headed downstairs, Perry lumbering up to follow her to the door with an expectant sniff.

"You must be the new tenant!" The woman at the door let out an embarrassed laugh. "I mean, obviously you are. I saw you guys move in. But don't worry, I'm not a stalker." Another laugh. "Goodness, I sound mad, don't I? My name's Lindy."

She stuck out a hand, which Laura shook with an uncertain smile. "Laura Neale."

Lindy nodded enthusiastically; she seemed that sort of person, practically pulsing with energy. About six feet tall with long, tumbling golden-brown hair, she definitely seemed larger than life. Next to her Laura felt more diminished than usual. She suspected she should invite her in, perhaps for a cup of tea, but with Maggie still pouting upstairs and boxes all around, the thought exhausted her. She had not been very good at all about socialising since Tim's death.

"Sorry," she said while Lindy kept looking at her expectantly. "I'd invite you in, but we're in the middle of unpacking."

"Oh no, don't worry about that," Lindy said quickly, although Laura sensed her flicker of disappointment and felt worse for it. "I just wanted to say hi. And bring you these."

She thrust a plastic container towards her. "Chocolate chip cookies. You're not allergic?"

"No, no, we're not. Thank you." Quite suddenly, Laura felt as if she could cry. She hadn't expected such kindness from a stranger, and it touched her almost unbearably. "Thank you," she said again, and then revealingly, sniffed.

"It's no problem. Moving can be so hard, can't it?" Lindy gave her a look of sympathy, and Laura wondered if she somehow knew about Tim. She hadn't told anyone in Wychwood that she was widowed—not the head teacher of the primary school where Sam would be attending, or the one of the comp in Burford where Maggie would. She knew she would have to eventually, but she didn't want either of them to be marked by tragedy from day one. They didn't want it, either.

As for anyone else…the only other person she'd met in Wychwood-on-Lea was Jace Tucker, and she certainly hadn't told him.

She knew she would have to tell people here eventually— of course she would—but sometimes it was nice not to have to live every moment under that heavy knowledge and its ensuing expectation.

"Yes, I suppose it is a challenge," she replied, managing a smile as she hugged the container of cookies to her chest. "Thank you for these. They look lovely. Proper American-style cookies."

"That's how I like them." Lindy gave her an uncertain

smile, as if wanting to say more, or perhaps still wanting Laura to invite her in, but she couldn't, not when the cottage was a jumble of boxes and Maggie was still in a mood, and…she just couldn't.

"Thanks," she said yet again. "We'll have to have you round soon, when we're all sorted." Lindy nodded, and then, with a semi-apologetic smile, Laura closed the door.

"Who was that?" Sam asked as he clattered down the stairs. "And what are you holding?"

"That was our neighbour," Laura told him as she turned around. "And cookies. Do you want one?" She pried off the lid of the container, and with greedy gladness Sam stuck his hand in. Laura blinked back the last of her tears.

Moving *was* hard, especially when you still felt raw and wounded with grief, and you weren't sure you'd done the right thing in the first place. Did she even *want* to be closer to Tim's parents? Sometimes she wasn't sure.

And what about leaving Woodbridge and all their friends, not that they'd had that many. They'd only lived there for three years, not quite long enough to feel truly settled, but long enough for friends from the last place they'd lived—outside London—to more or less forget you.

Not that everyone had actually *forgotten* them, of course, Laura reminded herself, not wanting to marinate in self-pity, as tempting as it sometimes seemed. Just the casual friends and school gate acquaintances, the people you rubbed along with well enough without realising quite how much you depended on them on a day-to-day basis. But they still had *friends*. Of course they did. Just not all that many. But enough. Chantal, for one, who had been, and continued to be, an absolute lifesaver.

Stop with the self-pity.

Laura took a deep breath and then reached for a cookie. She took a big bite; it was chewy and delicious and the gooey chocolate soothed her soul enough to smile at Sam and mean it. "So," she asked, "shall we have a takeaway for supper tonight?"

"Yes, please!" Sam crowed enthusiastically, and Laura finished her cookie, dusting the crumbs from her fingers.

"Let me see what restaurants I can find on my phone." Never mind that Maggie was still sulking upstairs, or everything was still unpacked, or Perry was whining by her feet, agitated again by this strange turn of events. It was going to be okay, she told herself. Eventually. She'd make sure of it.

Chapter Two

"**Y**OU'RE GOING TO have a *great* day."

Sam let out a beleaguered sigh as he looked at her with impatience mixed with a pity that belied his years. "Stop saying that, Mum."

"But you are," she insisted. They were walking up the high street towards the little school at the top of the village for Sam's first day, the first day of winter term after the Christmas holidays. "I've heard it's a lovely school. Everyone's really, really friendly."

"You heard that from *one* person."

Jace's wife, Ava, who was eight months pregnant and waddling like a duck yet still managed to look both sexy and beautiful, had stopped by yesterday to say hello. Although they were obviously unpacked by that point, Laura still hadn't been able to invite her in. Her throat had closed on the words and she'd just smiled instead, while Ava told her she just lived 'down the path, through the wood, in a cottage that looks like it's inhabited by elves.'

Ava had also assured her that everyone in the whole village was positively brimming with goodwill and eager to be her friend, so Laura felt as if she'd stumbled onto the set of *Postman Pat* rather than a normal English village. Ava had proclaimed that the school was lovely, although her son William was only two and a half and hadn't started yet.

"But Harriet's got a boy in Year Six—Will, just like my William. He's full of energy, I will admit, but underneath he's got a good heart." She made a laughing face to show Laura what she meant, and she'd smiled a bit tightly in return because Sam had had a bellyful of energetic boys with good hearts. He'd been bullied by several of them at Woodbridge.

She hadn't said that, of course; she'd just thanked Ava and then said she still had bits and bobs to put away but she'd be sure to have her and Jace over soon, and then, just as with Lindy, she'd closed the door more or less in her face.

Sooner or late people were going to think she was rude, but Laura wasn't sure what she could do about that. She knew she simply wasn't up to making more than the obligatory chitchat; she wasn't ready for the quid-pro-quo exchanging of life stories that comprised that first crucial get-to-know-you conversation.

Back in Woodbridge, people knowing about Tim had felt awful, because no one had known what to do or say. Their attempts at sympathy had been clumsy, if well meant, and after a while everyone had just avoided them instead, like Maggie's fake friends. Grief seemed as if it were catching.

People *not* knowing about Tim, Laura was coming to realise, was in its own way, just as bad. It felt like the enormous elephant in every room, except only she knew it was there. Perhaps she should have reconsidered the whole moving thing, but too late now. Obviously.

"And Ava said the Year Six teacher was a really cool guy," Laura continued, determined to sell Wychwood Village Primary to Sam even though he hadn't complained about anything so far. It had been Maggie who had offered a litany of discontent—the uniform for the comp was 'hideous,' never mind that Laura had had to spend over a hundred quid on it all. Her GCSE subject choices 'sucked,' never mind that they were the normal ones for Year Nine. The village was boring, even though Maggie hadn't actually explored it yet.

Laura and Sam had taken Perry on a walk through the wood, skirting the elvish-looking cottage where Ava and Jace lived, and gazing at the manor house where Lord and Lady Stokeley resided from afar. Apparently they were lovely too, according to Ava, but Laura had yet to have so much as a glimpse of them, which was fine by her. She'd met enough people for the moment. She still needed to recover.

They'd reached the gates of the primary, joining the steady stream of pupils and parents who were heading into the neat little schoolyard. Laura kept her head down, not wanting to meet anyone's eye, but soon enough she realised no one was looking at her anyway.

It was the first day back after the Christmas holidays, and everyone was jabbering excitedly about trips abroad and presents and family dos, and not paying any attention to them at all—a prospect that should have only brought relief, but managed to cause a little contrary sting of hurt, as well. So much for everyone in the village brimming with friendliness. Laura practically felt invisible, which was what she wanted, and yet…

She didn't, not really. As she and Sam stood off by themselves among all the happy clusters she felt a lonely sweep of sorrow rush through her. Back in Woodbridge, she would have had a few other mums to have a natter with. No one she'd call a best friend, admittedly, but people she could chat to easily enough, go for a coffee with on occasion. Here there was no one. She caught the eye of the mum of a girl who looked about eight or so and tried for a smile, but the woman's gaze skated over her without so much as an upward twitch of her lips.

Chantal had warned her that people in the Cotswolds could be a bit snobby. "All those Londoners deciding they want a page out of *Country Living*, thinking a Land Rover and an Aga turn you into a farmer."

Laura had laughed at that, thinking her friend, who was London born and bred, a free-spirited potter teaching GCSE Art in a massive comprehensive in Wandsworth, was exaggerating. She wasn't laughing now, but, she told herself, it was early days. It was only the *first* day, after all. There was plenty of time to get to know people, make friends.

The head teacher, a friendly looking man in his forties, came into the schoolyard and rang an old-fashioned brass bell, and everyone started lining up according to their year group. Laura put a hand on Sam's shoulder, fighting an urge to wrap her arms around him and never let go.

She'd had the same urge when Maggie had left for the bus, refusing Laura's offer to walk her to the stop on the road into the village. A nameless terror had clutched at Laura's insides and she'd fought not to pull her prickly daughter into the biggest bear hug she'd ever had. *Anything* could happen to her between now and three twenty, when she'd return home. A bus accident, a bully, a mean teacher, a trip on the stairs. When had she become so afraid?

When her husband's truck had crashed into the only tree on a straight stretch of road, she supposed. When she'd realised that life didn't come with guarantees or promises, when anything, actually *anything*, could happen and, in her case, had at least once.

"All right, then. Guess it's time to go." Thankfully her voice didn't wobble. Sam gave her a fleeting, uncertain smile that made Laura's arms twitch at her sides, so desperate was she to hug him. She wouldn't, of course. Whatever street cred Sam hoped to have as a Year Six would be completely destroyed by a cuddle from his mummy in the schoolyard.

Still, she ached with longing and worry as he took his

place at the end of the queue, his backpack already sliding off his shoulder, his fringe in his face. He glanced back at her, and she managed a smile and a wave, even though her heart felt as if it were breaking in half.

Weren't things supposed to get easier, with time? It had been a year. Almost thirteen months. And yet she still felt unbearably raw, almost as wounded as the day she'd woken up after Tim had died and she'd stared at the ceiling and thought, *This is the rest of my life.*

No, Laura decided as the children trooped inside the school and the parents began turning away, heading back out to the street. She wasn't actually that bad. She had healed, a little, in increments, almost without realising it. And despite Maggie's anger now, the three of them had had some good times over the last year.

They'd splurged on a holiday to Tenerife over the summer that had been really quite fun, even though they couldn't actually afford it. Tim's parents had helped, which had been incredibly kind of them, but made Laura feel uncomfortably in their debt. Without Tim as a buffer, she wasn't quite sure where her relationship with them stood. They'd never considered her quite enough for their only son, although they'd never actually said so. Tim had always told her she was being too sensitive, and perhaps she was, but sometimes it was hard not to be.

Still, life wasn't all gloom and doom. Things were slowly getting better, day by day. She didn't cry on a daily basis, for example. Sometimes she even laughed. And some days slipped by without her even thinking about Tim once, which felt both good and guilt-inducing.

In any case, she told herself as she started out of the schoolyard, it was just that starting over was hard, and coming to Wychwood-on-Lea had brought all those old feelings and insecurities to the fore, so she was having to deal with them all over again now.

As she started walking back down to the village, she couldn't help but notice how the other mums paired off happily, making plans. Half a dozen headed into a cute little café, Tea on the Lea, with gales of laughter, shedding coats and scarves as they settled themselves at a table in the window.

Laura dug her hands deeper into her pockets, the wind funnelling down the high street seeming to cut straight through her. It was hard not to feel entirely and quite miserably alone, and, impatient with herself, she tried to extinguish those treacherous flickers of self-pity.

All right, she was alone. But she knew full well she wasn't fit for company at the moment, and anyway, she'd make friends eventually. She always had before. As she turned off the high street to the lonely, wooded road that led back to Willoughby Close, Laura decided what she needed was a cup of coffee and a chat with Chantal before she took Perry for a walk to blow the cobwebs away.

Chantal answered the video call on the second ring, as

Laura curled up in the corner of the sofa by the crackling wood burner, Perry at her feet and a cup of coffee in her hands.

"Well? Got the kiddos off okay for their first day?"

"Yes, I think so, but I almost cried."

"You didn't, though, right?" Chantal looked alarmed. "You know that would seriously spoil Sam's street cred."

"I know, I know, I thought the same thing." Laura let out a laugh. As usual she and Chantal were on the same page mentally. They'd met during freshers week at uni, and lived in London together for a couple of years after graduating—before Laura had met and married Tim.

Even after she'd had Maggie and Sam, and her life had become so much about naps, nappies, and all things infant-related, Chantal had done her best to stay connected. She was godmother to both children, and never forgot birthday and Christmas presents for them.

Determinedly single and childless, she lived for her art—and for her friends. Laura wished they lived closer, but at least the Cotswolds was a bit closer to London than Wood-bridge in Suffolk. "I just hope they have a good day," she told her now, taking a sip of coffee to hide the tears that were once again threatening.

"Well, first days are always hard," Chantal reminded her bracingly. "If they don't have a good day, it's not the end of the world. You don't have to assume life there is going to be a disaster after one so-so day."

"I know." It was a good reminder though; Laura had had a panicky predisposition towards overreaction even before Tim had died. Since his death, her instinct to assume the worst had become finely and unfortunately honed.

"And I'm glad you're there," Chantal continued. "It's only a little more than an hour by train. So when are you visiting?"

"Well, Tim's parents have us booked in for this weekend, but maybe the next?" Maggie and Sam loved visiting Chantal's cool flat in a converted warehouse in the funky Camden Town neighbourhood.

"How are Tim's parents?" Chantal asked, her tone cooling slightly. Laura knew she thought they were snobby; they *might* have looked askance at her outfit for Maggie's baptism—a lace minidress and purple Doc Martens. Laura didn't think they were snobby, just traditional—and a bit reserved.

"I haven't actually seen them since we moved," she confessed. They'd offered to bring a takeaway over the day after they'd moved, but Laura had, rather guiltily, put them off. Tim's parents could be lovely, but they also needed a certain amount of managing, and it took more energy than Laura had at the moment. "I did talk to them on the phone, though, and they seemed okay."

Chantal was silent for a moment, no doubt thinking of something positive to say. "Well, hopefully they'll be some support," she said at last.

"That's the idea," Laura agreed.

"And what about you?" Chantal asked. "Any nice mums at the school gate?"

Laura thought of the women in Tea on the Lea, laughing and chatting. "Maybe, but I didn't talk to any of them."

Chantal tutted in sympathy. "It takes effort, remember."

"I know. More than I have right now, I'm afraid."

"One day, though."

Laura nodded rather mechanically. "Yes. One day." One day soon, hopefully, or she might miss her window.

"You will get there, Laura," Chantal said, her voice full of earnest conviction. "I know it's hard now, and it's been hard for a long time. But things *will* get better."

"Yes, I know." What else could she say? Chantal was no stranger to grief. Both her parents had died in the last few years, along with an ex-boyfriend. Admittedly it wasn't quite the same as a husband, but she understood loss.

"It does take effort, though," Chantal continued a bit severely. "It's not going to just *happen*. A mum isn't going to walk up to you and say, 'Hey, want to be my friend?' This isn't nursery, after all."

"Well, she *might*," Laura said with a smile. "I can hope, anyway."

"You have to *do* something," Chantal insisted in her usual much-needed brand of tough love. "Like I said, it's going to take effort. That's why it's hard."

"Right."

"All right, I'll back off now," Chantal told her with a laugh, reading her repressive tone correctly. "But I expect regular updates."

"Okay," Laura agreed somewhat reluctantly. "Although I'm not sure I'll have that many to give."

"Yes, you will," Chantal returned robustly. "Anyway, what about work? Are you going to register with a supply agency? I think it would do you good to get out there, meet people that way as well as by the school gate."

"It's on my to-do list." Before Tim's death, Laura had been a teaching assistant. Before kids, she'd taught history at a large secondary school in London. Both felt like a long time ago now; since Tim had died the money had been dwindling down and Laura knew she needed to get a proper job. She'd started back with supply in the autumn, but then they'd decided to move and she'd only managed a few days of cover, all of which had been more difficult than she'd hoped—the staffroom chitchat, the nine to five, the actual teaching. Just a day of it had exhausted her, and yet she knew Chantal was right.

She was planning to register with a supply agency here and then look for a full-time job for September—she just had to muster the energy. When, she wondered, was she going to stop feeling so *tired*?

"It would be a good way to meet people, Laur," Chantal persisted. "I know you've always had a dread of the school gate."

"It just feels like Year Seven," Laura admitted. "With the popular girls all flicking their hair and giving superior looks."

"Not everyone can be a popular girl," Chantal reminded her; they'd had this conversation many times before. "Look for the outliers."

I'm the outlier, Laura thought, *and I'd like someone to look for me.* Even if, like with Lindy and Ava, she'd shut the door in their faces. She really was a contrary person. Chantal was right. She needed to get out there and make an effort, even if it was hard. No one was going to come up to her and ask to be her friend. At least, it was unlikely. She needed to jump in first.

"Thanks for the pep talk," she told her friend. "I needed it."

"You know I'm here for you, anytime."

"Yes, I do." Thank heavens for Chantal. She'd come and stayed with them in Woodbridge for a week to help with funeral arrangements; she'd had Maggie for the weekend in London when Laura had been feeling able to cope at home. She regularly sent the kids emails and little presents in the post, and she was always, always available at the end of a phone. Chantal was more than a good friend, she was a godsend. Laura only wished her friend lived in Wychwood, or that Laura could afford to live in London.

"Now let me know how you're doing," Laura said as cheerfully as she could, conscious that Chantal did so much for her. She wanted to keep her end of their friendship up, but as usual Chantal wasn't having it.

"I'm fine, Laur, don't worry. And when I really am having a wobbly, you'll be the first to know."

"Any romantic interests?"

"No," Chantal said on a sigh. "Sadly, forty-two-year-old women who could lose at least a stone aren't being scooped up by eligible bachelors. At least, this one isn't."

"There must be someone who sparks your interest. A teacher at school?"

"No." Chantal pretended to shudder, although on second thought Laura wasn't sure it was pretend. "Definitely not. The only single man at my school is a creepy science teacher who wears his socks pulled up to his knees when he's wearing gym shorts."

"He doesn't wear gym shorts to school," Laura exclaimed with a horrified laugh.

"He likes to volunteer for football club. Trust me, there's no one. And actually, that's okay." Chantal was quiet, and Laura knew she was thinking about her ex-boyfriend who had died suddenly of cancer a year and a half ago, a few months before Tim's accident. Although they'd already broken up, Laura knew the loss had hit her hard.

"Like you said, it does get better," she reminded her friend gently. "Eventually."

"Yep, it does." Chantal blew out a breath. "Some days are better than others, you know?"

"Yes, I know."

"Of course you do. Love you, Laur."

"Love you, too."

Her conversation with Chantal, as it almost always did, made her feel better, and as Laura headed outside with Perry there was a slight spring in her step.

The dank clouds that had blanketed the sky that morning had given way to pale blue skies, the air fresh and damp and tinglingly cold. Willoughby Close looked even more charming with the sunlight lighting up the mellow golden stone; it was very quiet at ten o'clock on a Monday morning. All her neighbours must be at work.

Laura took the path through the woods and then around the back of the manor, its huge, gabled roof visible over the dark fringe of trees. Jace had told her all the residents were permitted to have a wander through the landscaped gardens, but she resisted the urge to explore the hedges and flowerbeds as Perry was getting tired, his shaggy head lowered as they plodded towards home.

He'd turn ten in the summer and had definitely been slowing down; Laura had a terror of him getting ill and dying. She didn't think she or the children could cope with losing their dog on top of everything else; Maggie had only been four when they'd got him as a puppy, Sam one.

Still, that was a worry for another day. The vet had said he was very healthy for an old dog, and today the sun was shining, the children were hopefully having a good day at school, and she was going to make more of an effort. There was no point feeling left out and lonely if she wasn't going to at least *try* to put herself forward.

And so, resolutely, Laura marched up to Lindy's front door and knocked. She probably wasn't home, and as she stood there Laura realised she was at least partially counting on that. This was more of an exercise to prove something to herself, and maybe to Chantal, than to actually reach out to somebody. So it was something of an uncomfortable surprise when, just as Laura was turning away from the door, Lindy opened it.

"Laura!" She looked delighted. "How are you?"

"Oh, uh, fine." Laura summoned a smile, having to abruptly switch gears. She really hadn't expected Lindy to be home. "I just wanted to say thanks for the cookies. They really were delicious."

"It's no problem. Do you want to come in for a coffee?"

"Oh. Ah." Panic warred with pleasure; could she really make that much small talk? No, she decided, she couldn't. Laura flushed as she struggled to find a credible excuse. "I'm just in the middle of something actually, but...ah...maybe another time?"

"How about tomorrow? Two o'clock okay?"

Lindy was like a dog with a bone. Laura smiled weakly. "Sure," she said, and with another smile and a wave, she headed back to number three.

At least, she told herself, she *had* made an effort. And she *would* have coffee with Lindy tomorrow. She seemed perfectly nice, if quite exuberant, but frankly Laura could do with a bit of energy in her life. She needed to move on, she reminded herself, and like Chantal had said, it took effort. Effort she had to be willing to make, and so she would be.

Perry lumbered into the house and flung himself down in front of the wood burner, which had become his usual space. Laura closed the door behind her with a little sigh of relief. Now, she wondered, what to do with the rest of her day? And, she thought, suppressing a sigh, every day after this one?

Chapter Three

"I'VE GOT COFFEE, Earl Grey, chai, or builder's brew." Lindy smiled at her expectantly, her hands on her hips, her golden-brown hair tumbling over her shoulders. "What do you fancy?"

"Builder's brew is fine." Laura stepped into the cottage, which had the exact same layout as hers, but looked a lot more lived in. There were some lovely watercolours of the village on the wall that she duly admired.

"Roger gave me those for Christmas," Lindy said as she caught her gaze. "He's—well, he's my boyfriend, I suppose you'd say, although that sounds kind of juvenile, like I'm about sixteen." She let out a little, breathless laugh; Laura had the sense the relationship must be rather new, and quite exciting.

"Have you been together very long?" she asked, and Lindy shook her head.

"Just a few months, really. Not long at all."

"How did you meet?" As long as she kept Lindy talking about herself, Laura hoped she wouldn't have to answer any questions, although she supposed Lindy would get around to asking them eventually. And she would have to get around to answering them.

"Through my class. I teach ballroom dancing, and Roger came with his mother, Ellen. Not that he likes dancing. Actually, he hates it." She let out another little laugh. "He did it for his mum because it was on her bucket list and—well—she doesn't have long now."

"Oh, I'm so sorry."

Lindy nodded soberly as she poured hot water into two mugs. "She has cancer. She's in hospice now, and she has the most incredibly positive attitude, but it's hard, you know?"

"Yes, I imagine it must be." This, Laura knew, would be a perfect opportunity to talk about her own tragedy. *I lost my husband just over a year ago*, she could say, although that sounded as if she'd misplaced Tim along with her car keys and a mismatched sock. Or: *It is hard, isn't it? My husband died a little over a year ago. Car accident.* She should say it, because she knew the longer she left it the harder it would become—that elephant in the room only she could see.

And Lindy had already, in the first five minutes of her coming over to her cottage, been so open about her own life, its joys as well as its sorrows.

So why was Laura still standing there like a lemon?

"Milk?" Lindy asked. "Sugar?"

"Just milk, please." And now the moment had passed, just as Laura had known it would. She didn't know whether she felt relieved or annoyed, and decided probably a bit of both. Telling someone your husband had died was like hogging the conversation. Everything revolved around that afterwards, and then it became the elephant in the room they both could see, which was worse. Still, Laura knew it had to be done at some point.

"So how did your kids get on at school yesterday?" Lindy asked as she handed her a mug.

Laura took it with murmured thanks. "Okay, I think, although I'm not sure I actually know. They didn't say much. Which I'm hoping is a good thing." She'd spent much of the day in a state of anxiety over how they'd been managing, but when she'd picked Sam up that afternoon he'd just shrugged and loped home, announcing he was starving as soon as they got in the door. She'd made him his favourite peanut butter and banana sandwich while he'd flung himself on the sofa, hugging Perry as he reached for his iPad.

"Just an hour, okay?" Laura had said. "Then we'll play a board game or something."

"Mmm…" was all the reply she'd received.

Maggie had been much of a muchness when she'd breezed in a few minutes later, grabbing a banana from the fruit bowl before heading upstairs.

"How was school?" Laura had called after her a bit desperately, and she'd received a bored "Fine" in response.

Clearly she needed to get her own life, so she stopped

obsessing about her children's. She'd spent the afternoon in absolute knots, and yet here they were, sprawled about snacking, as if the day had just been like any other. Laura was relieved, of course, but she was also anxious. What if they were hiding something from her? What might she be missing?

Because you've missed things before, haven't you?

"That's good, though, isn't it?" Lindy said optimistically, forcing Laura thankfully back to the present. "They would have told you if something had gone really wrong, wouldn't they?"

"I don't know," Laura admitted. "Teenagers tend to be monosyllabic at the best of times. That is, when they're not infuriated with you." She gave Lindy a wry smile as she sipped her tea.

"Yes, I suppose you're right." Lindy nodded thoughtfully. "I think I went through that phase, although I know I tend to idealise my childhood a bit." Now she was the one to smile wryly, a touch of sorrow to the curve of her lips. "My parents died in a car accident when I was nineteen."

"Oh." Laura nearly spit out her tea. Okay, now she *had* to say something.

"I like to get it out there," Lindy said semi-apologetically. "Otherwise it becomes awkward." She held a palm up as if to forestall Laura's stammering commiserations. "It's okay, though. It was a long time ago. Not that that makes it better, of course, but, you know, I've learned to heal. To grieve. It's a process, and Roger has actually helped a lot with it, so it's all good. Or becoming good. Whatever." She let out a self-conscious laugh.

"Actually," Laura said, her cheeks starting to burn for some reason, "I can relate. My husband died just over a year ago. In a car accident."

"Oh." Lindy's eyes widened, and then for a reason she could not possibly fathom unless it was sheer nerves, Laura started to laugh.

She clapped a hand over her mouth, horrified at herself. "Sorry," she gasped. "It's not funny. Nothing's funny about it at *all*. Of course not. It's just...I dread telling people, because like you said it can be so awkward, and then it becomes the defining thing about you, and I just...I just wanted to be normal for a bit. And then you come out and tell me..." She started to laugh again, and to her relief, Lindy did, as well, both of them bringing up deep belly laughs as if the whole thing were completely hysterical, which actually, in a weird way, it sort of was.

"What a pair we are," she said, wiping her eyes. "The Tragedy Twins. Is that awful?" She looked at Laura anxiously. "It's so much more raw for you, I know. I shouldn't joke..."

"No, no." Laura's stomach hurt from laughing. When had she last had a proper belly laugh? Goodness, but it felt wonderful, like exercising all sorts of old muscles. "No, it's...it's so nice. That someone gets it. It makes it so much easier. I mean…" She blew out a breath as the laughter that had seized her so utterly a few moments ago started to trickle away. "It's awful and some days I can barely get out of bed, but I still want to be happy. It's just hard to know how."

Lindy nodded soberly. "I know exactly what you mean. It's like you have to learn how to live again, as if you need an instruction manual."

"Too bad there isn't one."

"No, and I have to say, books on grief didn't help all that much. They were either too painful to read or I wanted to throw them across the room for being so bloody obvious."

"Yes." Laura couldn't help but laugh in relief. She had an entire shelf of books on grief that so many well-meaning people had given her, and she'd barely managed to get through one.

"How are your children doing with it?"

Laura shrugged and sipped her tea. The laughter had drained right out of her, replaced by a familiar flatness. "I couldn't really tell you. Maggie is angry all of the time, and Sam's just quiet. They were both seeing a grief counsellor before we moved, although I'm not sure whether it helped or not. They both went reluctantly, but hopefully it did something."

"A year isn't a long time, in terms of the grieving process," Lindy said after a moment. She smiled wryly. "Sorry if you didn't want to hear that."

"I think I knew it already." Laura smiled back. Despite

everything, she felt better for having told Lindy. Talking *did* help, she realised, especially when it was with someone who understood something of what you were going through. She was glad she'd said something.

"Anyway, I think it will get better. It already has been. You know, more good days than bad ones. Mostly. It's just this new start...we moved to be closer to Tim's—that's my husband's—parents, and starting over has made everything feel fresh again, for some reason, like I'm feeling it for the first time."

Lindy nodded soberly. "I understand."

And Laura had a feeling that she really did. "Thank you for this," she said, hefting the half-drunk cup. "I really appreciate it. It's been hard getting out of the house sometimes, so if I've seemed rude..."

"No, not at all," Lindy assured her. "And don't worry even if you have! You have good reason. But you'll find people here are friendly. Maybe a bit too friendly, if you're looking for some space. They'll be dragging you out for drinks no matter how you feel."

The thought both heartened and terrified her. "Perhaps that's what I need."

Lindy smiled with a sort of benevolent approval. "Perhaps it is. Olivia in number four is on her honeymoon at the moment, but when she's back we'll all have to go out for a drink. Emily's in number one—have you seen her?"

Laura shook her head.

"She's at her boyfriend Owen's mostly," Lindy admitted on a laugh. "I think they'll probably get engaged soon. Willoughby Close seems to have a little matchmaking magic in it—everyone who has lived here has paired up!" She gave Laura an encouraging smile. "Perhaps it will be your turn one day."

"I don't think so," Laura said rather firmly. She wasn't ready to think that way yet. She certainly hadn't, not even once, in the last year, not remotely.

Still she was heartened by the conversation with Lindy, and she thought it was probably best to quit while she was ahead, and she was still feeling good about everything.

"I should go," she told Lindy. "I have to pick up Sam in a bit, and…well…" She laughed self-consciously as Lindy gave her a knowing look.

"You've done your daily quota of socialising? You sound like Roger." Laura raised her eyebrows and Lindy explained with a laugh, "Roger is something of an introvert. Actually, you're nothing like him, but I get you, don't worry." She patted Laura's hand. "Thanks for coming in for a cuppa. I'm really glad you did."

"Thank you," Laura told her, meaning it, and then she headed back to number three. She'd barely made it through the door before a text pinged on her phone.

How was it?

She'd told Chantal about Lindy's invitation, and her friend knew exactly how nervous Laura would be and reluctant she would have been feeling.

It was actually really good, she texted, and was rewarded with a lot of random emojis—a boot, a fish, and a clown face. It had been their little joke for a while now—a competition as to who could find the weirdest emoji to punctuate a text.

Smiling to herself, Laura was just about to slip her phone into her pocket when it started to ring. Surprised, she glanced at the number and saw it was one she didn't recognise. Her stomach hollowed out.

The last time an unrecognised number had called her mobile...

Is this the wife of Timothy Neale?

Laura closed her eyes. She couldn't bear to remember that conversation, the sober voice of the police officer, the words that had filtered through her consciousness without really penetrating. *Accident...critical condition...come now.*

She opened her eyes when she realised the phone had stopped ringing. A shuddery breath escaped her. Okay, that had been an overreaction. The call had most likely been from a telemarketer looking to sell her double glazing or life insurance.

Then, the ping of another text. *Hello, this is Sam's teacher, James Hill. Sorry for the impromptu text—the school's phone system is down. Would you mind coming in to school today a few minutes early so we could have a little chat?*

Laura found herself back up on the panicky ledge she'd been talking herself down from. A *chat?* Why did Sam's teacher need to have a chat with her on the second day of school? The terror of a major disaster morphed into the fear of a minor one, which felt much more real. What was happening with Sam? Was he being bulled again? What had gone wrong?

Already Laura's heart was fluttering like a wild thing and she heard herself taking shallow breaths.

"Calm down," she said out loud. "It might be nothing." And even if it was something, it most likely wasn't something big, or at least *that* big. She could handle it. She had to handle it, because there was only her and this was what life was about—the ups and downs, bumps and jolts of normal existence. Life wasn't smooth sailing, even if sometimes it was an empty stretch of straight road with a single tree...

No. Don't.

Another breath, and then it started to even out. Her heart rate settled down and Laura went to the sink to wash her hands, tidy her hair. It was already ten to three, so if she wanted to get to school in time for this *little chat*, she'd better leave now.

Perry lumbered up hopefully, blinking doleful eyes at her, as if he already knew.

"Sorry, Per," she said as she scratched his head. "Next time."

She normally took him for the school run, but not when she was having *little chats*.

The sky had turned grey again, dusk already starting to

close in, a frigid dampness to the air as Laura started walking briskly down the lane to the road. What could Mr Hill want? Was Sam in trouble? Had there been some sort of mishap? Her fear was he was being bullied; it had happened at his last school, and while it had been fairly low-grade, whispered asides and muttered name-calling, it had still hurt. She wanted Sam to have a fresh start here, but what if fresh starts weren't always possible?

Calm down. Breathe. It was going to be okay. She would make sure of it.

Laura turned up the high street, her arms swinging at her sides, past the little tea shop, now empty of customers, and a pet shop—no, actually a pet *bakery*—then a vintage clothing shop, and then one that sold wooden toys. One day, maybe even one day soon, she'd pleasantly poke her way through them all. One evening she'd take Maggie and Sam to the pub, The Three Pennies, for fish and chips.

One day, but not today.

The school came into view, its crenellated roof and golden stone making it look like a happy, welcoming place, where laughter rang out and children played freely and parents didn't have to be called in for little chats.

Okay. Stop. It didn't have to be anything bad. Maybe, just maybe it wasn't.

"Can I help?" The tone of the woman at the front desk was a little pointed; Laura wondered if she was well versed in helicopter parents. She found herself smiling in apology, as if she'd done something wrong.

"Hello, I'm Laura Neale. My son Sam just started Year Six, and Mr Hill asked me to come to school a few minutes before pickup for a chat." Little or not.

"Oh, I see." The woman's expression thawed as her tone became friendlier. "Let me just go find him. I'm afraid our communications system is down, but it will be repaired as soon as possible." This said as if she'd already had to deal with a litany of complaints. Laura smiled her understanding.

She crossed her arms and tried not to tap her foot as she waited for Mr Hill to appear. Her chest felt tight and her throat was closing and nothing had even happened yet. Goodness, but she was prone to panicking. *Calm down, Laura.*

Did anyone calm down when told to, even if you were just speaking to yourself?

"Mrs Neale."

Laura turned, her heart racing, a prickly, panicky feeling sweeping over her skin—and then her mouth dropped open as she stared at James Hill.

Ava had told her he was a cool guy, but somehow the sight of him was still unexpected. Somehow, ridiculously, it had the power to make her blush, a surprising heat coursing through her body. Because James Hill was almost certainly the most insanely gorgeous man she'd ever seen.

Chapter Four

JAMES STUCK HIS hand out for Sam's mum to shake while she stared at him rather gormlessly, her mouth slack, her eyes wide. She didn't speak; in fact, she looked as if she'd been Tasered. He held his hand out, his smile in place while he waited for the penny to drop, and finally, thankfully, it did.

"Sorry," she murmured. She took his hand and James tried not to flinch because hers was like ice. "I'm Laura."

"James." He turned to the sour-faced receptionist who was watching them with an undeserved suspicion. "Thank you, Mrs Petch." To be fair, the receptionist had a lot of demanding parents to deal with, parents with more money than sense or sensitivity. This morning he'd overheard a mother shrilly insisting the school only serve organic food, and if they couldn't serve it to everyone, then at least they should to her son, because he had a 'sensitive stomach.'

James turned back to Laura Neale. "Shall we go into the staffroom for a moment? The Year Sixes are just finishing off some maths before home time, so I can leave them for a few

minutes without it going completely pear-shaped, I think."
He smiled, but she didn't return it, her dark eyes scanning
his face as if looking for clues.

"All right," she murmured as she followed him into the
staffroom off the school hall. The size of a broom cupboard
with a sofa, a mini fridge and a kettle packed into it, it was
not the most welcoming of places, but like many primary
schools that had outgrown their original Victorian building,
Wychwood Primary was short on space.

"Thank you for coming to see me on such short notice—"

"Is Sam all right?" She spoke abruptly, almost aggressive-
ly, her navy eyes sparking in her pale, almost bloodless face.
Her fingers were trembling before she laced them tightly
together.

James studied her for a moment, wondering why she was
so worried. Coming from London, he was used to both ends
of the parenting spectrum—the ones who were indifferent to
the point of neglect, and the ones who breathed fury or fear
down his neck, sure their little darlings could never put a
foot wrong. But he'd never seen a parent look quite so keyed
up as Laura Neale, every nerve seeming to twang through her
body so she was practically vibrating with tension.

"Sam is fine," James said, smiling in an attempt to put
her at her ease. "Sorry, I should have made that clear in my
text. If I'd been able to ring you, I would have explained
what this is about."

"What *is* this about?" Her voice was high and thin, her

hands gripping each other so tightly her knuckles were bone-white. James was worried she might explode—or collapse.

"Are *you* all right, Mrs Neale?" he asked gently, and to his surprise the tightness loosened from her face as her expression seemed to fold in on itself and she bit her lip, tears turning her eyes luminous as she shook her head.

"Oh…" Her voice veered into a wobble as she slumped onto the sofa and drove her hands through her hair. "Sorry. *Sorry.*" She drew a shuddery breath. "You must think I'm mad. I might be mad, actually. It's perfectly possible at this point."

"No, of course I don't…" But something was clearly wrong, and he had no idea what it was. He felt out of his depth, after just a few minutes. "I'm sorry. I didn't realise you'd be so worried. Sam is doing fine." He was a quiet boy, brainy but with a wit, and James knew he would have to be careful not to favour him in class. He reminded him, he'd realised with bemusement, of himself at the same age.

"It's just…" She looked up, her face still pale, her hair falling out of its ponytail in dishevelled tendrils about her face, her expression now resolute. "Sam lost his father—my husband—a year ago. A car accident. I probably should have said before he started, but sometimes it feels like…well, like a sort of handicap, I suppose. It hangs over you so no one can think about anything else and I didn't want that for him in a new school… Anyway." She gave a little shake of her head. "When I received the call from an unfamiliar number, and then something needed to be discussed about Sam…well, I knew it wasn't anything like *that*, of course, I haven't *entirely* lost the plot quite yet, but I suppose I just hit the panic button. As I tend to do. And now I'm babbling." She let out a little laugh and shook her head for a third time, her eyes now glinting with both humour and tears. "Sorry. You really will think I'm mad."

"No, I'm the one who should be sorry," James said quickly. He was appalled by his own thoughtlessness, even though he knew he could have never guessed the full story. "I'm so sorry for your loss. I should have explained what I wanted to talk about in my text. I just assumed…" That she hadn't experienced a hugely traumatic event. He felt like an idiot, even though he knew it wasn't really his fault. It just was. Sometimes life was hard. Sometimes it felt impossible.

"It's okay." She offered him a wavery smile as she brushed aside his apologies with one slender hand and then slowly stood up. Even standing with her chin tilted and her shoulders squared she was a slight thing, a wisp of a woman, possessing both fragility and a certain steeliness James admired. Her hair was dark, almost black, pulled back from a heart-shaped face in a loose ponytail, a few inky wisps framing it. Large, hazel eyes fringed with thick lashes gazed at him steadily as her bow-shaped mouth curved faintly. "So anyway, what is this about?"

James realised he'd been staring. She was, he had to admit, quite lovely. Beautiful, in an ethereal sort of way, reminding him of hand-spun glass or perhaps *kintsugi*, the Japanese pottery made more beautiful through its lacquered cracks. She seemed breakable, yet strong. Not that he should be thinking along any of those lines about a pupil's mother, and a widow to boot. "Well, ah, it's about starting a club for playing Minecraft, actually. It was Sam's idea, and I thought it was brilliant."

"Minecraft." She laughed softly. "I should have known. I think he's obsessed with that game."

"As far as obsessions go, it's not a bad one for an eleven-year-boy to have," James reassured her with a smile. He was determined to get this conversation—and his own thoughts—back on track. Easy and light, strictly professional. The way he always was with the parents of his pupils. "Some schools have started to use Minecraft in their curriculums to help teach science and foreign languages as well as critical thinking skills. It's proved to be quite helpful."

"What a relief, considering how much he plays it." She gave him a wry smile that had him smiling back, perhaps more than he should have. She tucked the stray wisps behind her ears and then, smile gone, gave him a direct look. "So what does this club entail exactly?"

"Well, as it was Sam's idea, I wanted him to take as much ownership of it as possible. There would need to be a teacher present at the meetings, which I'm happy to be, but if he wanted to work up a permission letter that we could give out to pupils?" He raised his eyebrows in enquiry. "I'll have to have a look at it first, of course."

"Of course. I'm sure he'll find this all brilliant."

"He's a good kid."

Her lips trembled before she pressed them together. "I certainly think so, but…it hasn't been easy."

"I'm sure it hasn't," James said quietly, which had to be a massive understatement, but what could he say? He saw the stark lines of pain on her face, indelible scars formed by grief. "I really am very sorry for your loss." It felt like so many words, but he meant them.

She nodded, and he had the sense that she didn't want to have this conversation, that she was tired of talking about it. She'd indicated as much when she'd said why she hadn't mentioned it before, and he supposed he could understand that. No one wanted to be defined by tragedy, whatever it was. No one wanted to be considered only as a negative inversion, the lack of or the loss.

They stared at each other for a moment, Laura clearly struggling to find something more to say and James, he had to admit, enjoying just looking at her. She really was a lovely woman, with a delicacy to her features and yet a strength to her bones. She reminded him, a bit whimsically, of an otter, with her dark eyes and sleek figure, a playfulness hiding beneath her serious expression. She was also, he reminded himself, a widow as well as the mother of a pupil. Clearly off limits, of course, and yet…

Laura let out a huff of laughter. "You really must have

thought I was absolutely bonkers, coming in here in such an almighty tizz. Although I suppose you get your fair share of crazy parents."

"I do."

Her mouth quirked in a smile and she brushed a hand over her hair. "I'm sure you've got some war stories to tell. I used to be a teacher, a long time ago."

"Did you? Primary or secondary?"

"Secondary. History. But I haven't done any since I had children—just a bit of teaching assistance in our local primary, before we moved here. Still, I remember the parents who marched in demanding this or that. Thinking they were the most important person in the school." She shook her head, smiling, and James smiled back. Yes, there were a few of those at Wychwood Primary, just like there had been in London. "Anyway. I'll talk to Sam about the club. And thank you for encouraging him. Besides, you know, the situation with his dad, he was also bullied a bit at his last school." She grimaced. "Something else I didn't want to mention at the start. I don't think Sam would want me to, but perhaps it's better if you know."

"The more information I have about any child in my class the better, but I do take your point." James paused, cocking his head. "I was bullied as a child, so I can sympathise."

"You!" She looked at him in such disbelief that James couldn't keep from laughing a little.

"Why so surprised?"

"Well…because…I mean…" Rosy colour swept across her cheeks as she stammered her reply. "I just wouldn't have thought it."

"You'd be surprised at some of the children who report being bullied. It's not all the so-called nerds with glasses, or whatever the unfortunate stereotype might be. Although, to be fair, that pretty much was me, minus the specs." He thought back to his fairly miserable early school days—a nerdy kid who loved chess and logic puzzles, preferred reading to football, and had a stammer to boot. It had taken him until Sixth Form to find his feet and spread his wings. Sam would, too.

"Kids are wonderful," he told Laura, "but they can also be cruel. They see differences and they sense weaknesses, and unfortunately they know how to make the most of both."

"Yes, I certainly saw that when I was a teacher. It seems wrong somehow. You expect kids to be good, pure even, and yet they can be even more cruel than adults." She sighed. "Not that the kids at the last school were cruel. They just made a few remarks. It wasn't that big a deal, but on top of everything else… Life is hard enough, you know?"

"Yes, it certainly can be." He gave her a sympathetic smile. She'd certainly had her fair share of hard lately. Perhaps there would be some good, or at least some easy, on the horizon for her, now that she'd moved to the village. He wouldn't mind some for himself, either. Life hadn't been nearly as hard for him as it obviously had for Laura Neale, but he'd moved to Wychwood-on-Lea in September for a change. Not that he'd be so insensitive as to say something about that now. He could hardly compare a break-up to a bereavement.

"I'm glad you're on board with the club idea," he told her. "I think it will really be great for Sam, as well as the whole school."

The bell rang signalling the end of the day, and Laura's eyes widened. "I should…"

"Yes, I certainly should. The Year Sixes will be champing at the bit, trying to get out of the classroom." Even so he had an unwise impulse to continue the conversation, to say something more, although he had no idea what. She was the mum of one of his pupils. She was a *widow*, for heaven's sake. Off. Limits. "Thank you for coming in."

"Yes, of course. Of course. And thank you. For…everything." She flung a hand out towards him and after a second's hesitation James shook it, unsure if that's what she'd intended. It wasn't icy anymore; it was warm and soft and eminently touchable, her fingers small and slender against his palm before she withdrew her hand, her face still rosy. "Well. I should collect Sam."

"Yes."

Still they were staring at each other. This was starting to feel a little bit awkward. With a small, apologetic smile, James went to the door and opened it, gesturing for Laura to pass through first. Her shoulder brushed his chest as she went by, and he breathed in the lemony scent of her shampoo or soap. He straightened to avoid any further contact; he didn't want to embarrass himself any more than he already had, staring at her like some love-struck idiot. What on earth was wrong with him?

With one last fleeting, uncertain smile, Laura hurried out of the front entrance to the schoolyard, where parents were congregating in cheerful knots under a sky the colour of a bruise that was already beginning to darken to dusk.

James gave himself a hard mental shake before he headed back to the Year Six classroom, where the pupils were indeed starting to go a little haywire. Coats were being tossed in the air and someone was using a boot like a football.

"All right, all right, settle down!" James called out in his sternest voice, and the pupils gave him a sheepish look before the coats and stray boot went back to their owners. James glanced out the window at the schoolyard, but he couldn't see Laura anywhere.

SHE WAS *SUCH* an idiot. Laura stood in the corner of the schoolyard, doing her best not to meet anyone's eye. She definitely didn't want any friendly getting-to-know-you chats right now, not when she'd just made such an utter fool of herself in front of Sam's teacher, and she was feeling scorched through with humiliation.

But who would have ever thought a schoolteacher would be so…would be so…well, *sexy*?

She had been completely floored from the start of their meeting, as well as totally wrong-footed, panicked over Sam, and then mesmerised by James Hill's eyes, which were the blue green of the Caribbean, or what Laura *thought* the Caribbean looked like, judging from pictures she'd seen, as well as his floppy, chestnut-brown hair, his tall, muscular physique, the tweed jacket and battered cords he'd worn with confident ease. Everything about him had been relaxed and wry and basically just…gorgeous.

Shocked at the nature of her own thoughts, Laura stiffened where she stood. Why on earth was she thinking this way about Sam's *teacher*? She hadn't looked at another man with anything close to romantic interest even once since Tim had died. She'd barely noticed they were *breathing*, for heaven's sake, lost in her own haze of grief as she was. Yet she'd certainly been aware of James Hill in that way. *Very* aware. Had it simply been because of his rather noticeable good looks, or something else? Something more? Was that buried, deadened part of her coming back to life? How very inconvenient.

"Mum!"

With relief, Laura pushed the disturbing thoughts to the back of her mind as she waved to Sam, who was hurrying towards her, a shy smile brightening his face.

"Guess what?"

"What?"

"I'm going to start a Minecraft Club with my teacher, Mr Hill!"

"Wow, that sounds amazing, Sam." She ruffled his hair even though they were still in the schoolyard, and he let her, grinning, making her heart feel light. She loved to see her son so happy. It made her spirits lift in a way that nothing else could.

"He thinks Minecraft is really good at teaching stuff," Sam continued as they headed out of the schoolyard. "I told you, Mum, it's *not* the same as Fortnite."

"So you've said. Maybe it's time I believed you." She gave him a teasing smile; he was still grinning, bless him. Today had definitely been a good day.

As they walked down the high street back towards Willoughby Close, Laura's thoughts drifted inexorably back to James Hill, and she remembered again, with fresh humiliation, just how ridiculously she'd behaved—panicking over Sam and then at the end shooting her arm out like that…

She wasn't really sure what she'd been thinking in that moment. She'd had some crazy idea of grabbing his hand with both of her own, like some sort of feudal thanks to the lord of the manor. He must have thought she'd really lost the plot by then, and perhaps she had, but the truth was she'd just been so grateful that he seemed to *get* Sam. The idea that something might actually be going right in their lives at last had filled her with teary gratitude.

And as for any so-called sparks she'd felt, well, those had

been due to an excess of emotion and nothing more. James Hill certainly couldn't have felt them. Besides which, he had to be about thirty, a good ten years younger than her, which just added to the humiliation of her own response. *Ludicrous.* Ludicrous. But he was, Laura thought on a sigh, undeniably gorgeous.

Smiling faintly, determined to make herself see the humour in the situation, she fired off a text to Chantal.

Just made a complete idiot of myself in front of Sam's teacher, who happens to be insanely gorgeous. She added a couple of random emojis as she always did with Chantal—a stiletto, an ice cream sundae, and—not so randomly—a facepalm.

Sighing, she slid her phone into her pocket. The next time she saw Mr Hill she was going to do her best to act like a normal, well-adjusted and reasonable person.

As they turned into the lane that led to Willoughby Close, her phone pinged with a text. Already smiling in expectation of Chantal's undoubtedly witty reply, Laura swiped to read the text.

Not insanely gorgeous, surely...and not an idiot, either. What's with the stiletto?

Laura stared at the text in confusion—it wasn't at all Chantal's style—when, with an icy ripple of horror, she realised what she'd done. She'd replied to the last text she'd been sent without thinking, because the only person who ever texted her was Chantal.

But she hadn't sent the text to Chantal. She'd sent it to James Hill.

Chapter Five

J AMES STARED AT his phone, willing a response. When the text had pinged on his phone, clearly meant for someone else, he'd debated for a few minutes about whether to reply. He had a feeling Laura would be mortified that he'd seen it, and yet if he didn't reply, she would know eventually, if not sooner, that he'd received it, probably the next time she looked at her phone, and his silence would be seen as—what? Arrogant? Rude? Indifferent?

And so he'd replied, trying to make light of it, and maybe even being the tiniest bit flirty, because, well, why not? She'd said he was insanely gorgeous, after all. The memory made him smile. No one had ever called him *that* before.

He might have beefed up a bit since his school days, and chess, reading, and logic puzzles all could be seen as, to an adult, if not quite cool, then at least kind of coolly different. Maybe.

But she hadn't replied, and it had now been ten minutes. The schoolyard was empty along with his classroom, which held that salty, sweaty smell particular to Year Six boys on the cusp of puberty. James kept a can of air freshener spray in his desk drawer, and he needed to use it several times a day.

With a sigh he put his phone back in his pocket and headed to his desk. He had thirty maths sheets to mark before he headed home.

Outside twilight was falling as he worked his way steadily through scribbled pages of long division. He usually loved the quietness of his classroom at the end of the day, almost as much as he loved it when it was full of children, cocky ten- and eleven-year-olds who were still young enough to be cute—sometimes—but old enough to be thoughtful and smart—mostly.

He loved seeing their minds awaken, excitement firing up their eyes as ideas took hold. When he'd decided to do a PGCE in primary education after completing his English degree at Durham, his parents had been a bit nonplussed.

"Not a lot of blokes in primary teaching," his father, a Shropshire farmer born and bred, had remarked as he'd rocked back on his heels, his thumbs firmly in his belt loops, his expression one more of blank incomprehension than outright disapproval.

"Nope," James had replied as cheerfully as he could, because, as ever, his father's lack of endorsement had stung. "That's why I'm doing it, at least partly." His father had narrowed his eyes and he'd explained patiently, "Boys that age need male role models. There aren't enough men in primary education, especially with the lack of fathers at home. And I like that age." Secondary school students had too much attitude for his liking. By fourteen they'd already hardened, become cynical and suspicious, a brittle shell already forming around their minds. It was sad, and he admired all the teachers who were willing to take that on, but he liked to teach the younger ones, whose minds were still malleable, their enthusiasm still infectious.

And here he was, seven years into it, and not regretting it one bit, except maybe the lack of romantic prospects. Every teacher at Wychwood Primary was married save for him, and that had been the case back at the school in London where he'd taught until this year.

His uni friends had all managed to pair up since graduation, as had he—although unfortunately his three-year relationship hadn't gone the way he'd hoped or planned. But that was life for you, with all its complicated tangles and turns. Things didn't always get tied up neatly with a bow, or in his case, a wedding ring. Helen had decided they weren't suited, and she'd probably been right, even if it still stung more than a little when he let it.

James slid his phone out of his pocket. Nothing. It was probably just as well. Yet as he thought again of Laura calling him insanely gorgeous, he couldn't help but smile.

"Mum. *Mum.*"

Impatience sharpened Sam's voice as he tugged on her sleeve. Laura blinked him slowly into focus; she realised she'd been standing in the middle of the pavement, staring at her phone in something probably resembling Munch's *The Scream* as she'd absorbed James Hill's text. Dear heaven. Could she possibly have embarrassed herself more? Well, probably, but she didn't like to think about that. The current reality was certainly bad enough.

"Sorry, Sam." She dropped her phone into her bag, half-wishing she could chuck it and all of its texts away entirely. She'd have to reply to James—Mr Hill—at some point, but she didn't have enough composure to do it now. "What were you saying?"

"Mr Hill wants me to write a letter explaining about the Minecraft Club," Sam said in the tone of someone who had said this before and had not been heard. "Will you help me?"

"Yes, of course." She smiled at him, even though her stomach was still cramping unpleasantly at the thought of that stupid text. She'd called him insanely gorgeous, for heaven's sake. "Sounds fun."

Back at the cottage Perry lumbered hopefully to his shaggy feet while Sam dumped his school bag, coat and lunch box on the floor and sprawled next to the dog, putting his arms around him and burying his head in his shaggy coat. Nothing like the easy, unquestioning loyalty of a canine, Laura thought as she picked up the detritus Sam had happily left behind, hanging his coat on the stand by the door and then washing out his lunch box at the sink.

"So good day today, huh?" she said, and Sam made a noncommittal noise. Laura wanted to ask him if he'd made any friends, or met any kids he thought *might* be friends in time, but she knew better than to press him on such a sensitive subject. No child over the age of six wanted to be asked if they'd made friends. "Do you know if anyone else in your class wants to join the Minecraft Club?" she asked instead, and was rewarded with another noncommittal noise. The grunts and groans of an eleven-year-old boy should have their own dictionary.

She fixed him his usual snack of a peanut butter and banana sandwich and then sat at the table with him while they hammered out the text of a letter. It was, Laura thought, wonderfully pleasant to sit in a pool of sunshine, Perry sprawled at their feet, Sam's tongue sticking out of the side of his mouth just as Tim's used to as he concentrated on writing the letter.

If she could just hold on to moments like these—cup them between her two hands—she thought she might remember how to be happy. It wouldn't even be that hard.

But then the front door was practically hurled off its hinges as Maggie stalked into the house, flung her coat and backpack towards the kitchen, grabbed an apple from the bowl, and started upstairs without so much as a hello, or for that matter, a noncommittal noise of the kind Sam had been making.

Still Laura tried. "Hello, darling," she called brightly, hating how artificial her voice sounded, but what else was she supposed to do? "Good day?"

Nothing in reply, just the thud of Maggie's feet up the stairs, and then the slam of her door. Laura sighed and Sam reached over and patted her hand.

"She'll grow out of it," he said, so seriously that Laura couldn't help but smile.

"I certainly hope so," she told him. She'd give Maggie a few minutes to decompress and then go up and try again. Sometimes that was all motherhood felt like—endless trying, few results. You just hoped they paid it forward when the time came.

With the letter finished and Sam happily ensconced on his iPad, Laura decided to brave going upstairs. She made two cups of tea in the faint hope that Maggie might accept one, and then crept quietly upstairs.

"Mags? Sweetheart?" She tapped on her daughter's door. "I've got tea for you." She thought she heard a grunt in reply, and so, her heart beating rather hard considering this was her *daughter*, she pushed open the door with her hip and came into the room.

Contrary to Maggie's first scornful assessment, her furniture did fit in the room, and Laura thought it all looked rather nice, the bed under the window, the bureau by the door, the desk in the corner. Laura had offered to paint the walls, but Maggie had dismissed her with a contemptuous 'why bother?'

"Here you go," she said now as she handed her daughter a cup of tea, which Maggie took without a word. Laura perched on the edge of the bed, her own mug cradled between her hands. "How was school today?"

"Fine."

Of course it was. Laura realised she should have known better than to ask such a pointless, open-ended question. The grief counsellor had suggested specific questions that required detailed answers—unless, of course, your child wasn't ready or willing to talk. Considering Maggie had not been willing to talk for over a year, Laura wasn't sure where that left her.

"Have you met some people?" she tried again. "People you might be friends with, I mean?"

"I dunno." Maggie hunched her shoulders as she blew on her tea. "Maybe."

Well, that was promising, surely. "If you ever want to invite someone round—"

Maggie looked up, eyes narrowing dangerously. "Why would I want to invite someone *here?*"

"Because it's our home?" Laura suggested as lightly as she could.

"It *sucks.*"

"Maggie…" Laura hesitated, unsure, as ever, how to navigate these fraught moments. "We're going to be here for some time," she finally said as gently as she could. "You need to give Willoughby Close—and Wychwood-on-Lea—a chance."

Maggie just shook her head, her lowered gaze focused on her tea. "We could have afforded something better than this place."

"If we could have, we would have," Laura replied, doing her best to keep her tone as sympathetic as possible, and not snap the way she sometimes felt like doing. "This was what was available in our budget."

Maggie looked up, her eyes glinting with fury. "Dad had a good business and we lived in a way bigger house than this one. So tell me why this is all we can afford?"

Laura sat back and sipped her tea in order to stall for time. The last thing she wanted to do—well, *one* of the last things—was go into the family finances with her daughter. Yes, Tim had had his own business doing landscaping design. It was why they'd moved to Woodbridge from London; he'd had enough of the corporate world and wanted to follow his dream somewhere near the sea.

They'd all followed it, and it had led to ploughing all the money from the sale of their modest three-bedroom in Chiswick—a house that had been smaller than this one, incidentally—into getting the business up and running, except it never really had.

Which had left them in the unfortunate position of having to use the proceeds from the sale of their house in Woodbridge to settling debts and paying credit cards bills.

As for the lapsed life insurance policy…well, there was no point going there.

"It's complicated, Maggie," Laura said at last, "but please trust me that we're where we can afford to be and if you just—"

"I don't want to *just* do anything," Maggie snapped, and then reached for her phone, swiping the screen with pointed aggression. The conversation was clearly over.

"Dinner's in an hour," Laura said on a sigh, and then rose from the bed and went into her own bedroom, closing the door quietly behind her.

With Sam downstairs and Maggie right next to her, Laura was conscious of how small the cottage really was. Perfectly adequate, but yes, small. She decided to go out into the garden to call Chantal and tell her about that wretched text, among other things.

It was both freezing and dark out there, but at least it was private, assuming no neighbours were skulking about, which Laura doubted they were, considering the weather.

She rang Chantal, trying not to let her teeth chatter, and as always, her friend answered almost immediately.

"So what's the latest? Meet any non-snooty mums at the school gate?"

"No, but…" Laura let out a gusty sigh, and then tried for a laugh. It sounded more like a huff. "I made a complete and utter fool of myself, Chantal. Properly, I mean."

"Oh, this sounds good," Chantal replied. "Let me get a

cuppa and settle in for the full story."

Laughing properly this time, feeling better already, Laura waited while her friend did just that, and then proceeded to regale her with all the salient details.

"Insanely gorgeous," Chantal chortled. "*Insanely.* And he read that? Oh, I love it. I really do."

"I haven't texted him back yet," Laura said a bit glumly. "I know I need to, otherwise I look like I've taken it all too seriously, but…what on earth do I say?"

"Own it," Chantal replied simply. "And laugh it off. There's no other choice, really. Although…it almost sounds like he's flirting with you, at least a little, which I have to say, is brilliant. Just what you need."

"He isn't," Laura declared firmly. "No way. He's about thirty, Chantal—a mere child."

"Thirty is *not* a child."

"Thirty is young and anyway—no. Just no."

Chantal was quiet for a moment, and then, her laughing manner cast completely aside, she asked quietly, "Why not?"

"Why…" Laura spluttered, surprised by the seriousness of the question. She'd been anticipating Chantal's composing of a light and not-so-flirty text for her, not a question aimed straight at the heart. "Why not?" she repeated dumbly.

"Yes, why not. It's been a year, Laura, and you're only forty-one. You need to get back up in the saddle, or at least within fifty metres of a horse, if you know what I'm saying."

"A year isn't very long."

"But it's been more than that, really, hasn't it?" Chantal said, her tone so gentle that Laura had to close her eyes.

"Chantal…"

"I know we don't normally talk about this stuff, even though we talk about some pretty deep stuff. But this is your no-go area, and I've respected that. I've known you weren't ready, Laur, to face whatever demons it is you're facing. Because there are some, aren't there? Between you and Tim."

The silence between them felt suffocating, unbearably heavy. Laura opened her mouth but no words came out.

"You can just absorb that for a few moments," Chantal said with a small, sad laugh. "But think about what I'm saying, because you're young, Laura, and you can't give up on life just because you suffered a setback. A big one, yes, a bloody great huge one, but still. Tim is—"

"Don't," Laura said quickly. "Please don't. You're right, there will be a time for me to—to consider all that, but it's not yet. Not now. Maggie and Sam aren't even settled here, and anyway James is Sam's teacher—"

"James, is it?" Chantal interjected, her voice full of humour once more.

"Mr Hill," Laura corrected quickly. "Now, come on. Enough with the deep stuff." She couldn't even begin to process what Chantal had said, how excruciatingly perceptive she'd been. "Please help me compose a text that does not reveal how horribly embarrassed I am."

"Okay…let's think. How about 'Insanely might have been an exaggeration, and I'm guessing you realised that text was not meant for you. As for the stiletto…why not?'"

Laura ran the words over in her mind, relieved that Chantal had dropped the more serious subject of conversation. "That sounds too flirty."

"Well, *he* was flirty."

"He wasn't."

"Oh-kay. Whatever. Just text 'Oops' then and call it a day."

"That sounds flirty, too—"

"Oh, *Laura*." Chantal let out a groan of laughter. "You've got to make light of it, otherwise he'll think you're a nutter, and you'll just embarrass yourself even more. I mean, what are you thinking of texting? 'I apologise for my inappropriate comment, which clearly wasn't meant for you'? You'll sound properly stuck-up, then."

"I know, but…" Laura nibbled her lip. "This is so far out of my comfort zone already. When Tim and I were dating, people weren't even really texting that much. At least, we weren't."

"So you admit there is something between you," Chantal crowed triumphantly. "Something flirty."

"Oh, for heaven's sake…" Laura let out another gusty sigh. Chantal was right. She *did* feel a spark, even if she was terrified to admit it. Even if James most assuredly didn't. He probably flirted by text with everyone. He was at least ten years younger than her, after all. Texting was his means of communication. He probably had Snapchat, the way Maggie did, as well, and left people on read—which had taken Laura ages to figure out what it meant, because she'd always thought it was *on red*. "Does the message turn red if it's been seen?" she'd asked Maggie, who had looked at her as if she was incomprehensibly stupid. James was probably down with all the techie, text stuff that she found so bewildering.

"Help me, Chantal," she begged.

"I'm your only hope?" Chantal filled in wryly. She was, Laura knew, a huge *Star Wars* fan, and quoted it, much to Laura's confused ignorance. "Okay. Here we go. How about—'sorry about that' with three exclamation points, a facepalm emoji, and another random one to keep the stiletto thing going."

"I don't want to keep a *thing* going, stiletto or otherwise. Especially not stiletto." There was something sexy about them, after all.

"Shows you're confident, you can take a joke as well as make one, but there's nothing suggestive about it. That's the tone you want, Laura. Trust me. I'm the single one here."

Laura considered this for a moment as she worried at her lower lip before she gave a decisive nod that no one saw. "Okay. What emoji?" This seemed very important.

"Let me have a look." Laura waited while Chantal started to scroll. "Panda?"

"No."

"Dolphin?"

"How about a cougar?" Laura joked, and before Chantal could give that suggestion any credence she said quickly, "No animals. Too cutesy."

"Avocado? Broccoli? An ice skate?"

"If I send him an ice skate, he might think I'm asking him to go ice skating—"

"For the love of all that is holy, Laura, that is taking things too far. He is a man. He is not going to read meaning into your random emojis."

"Something else, please," Laura pleaded.

They finally settled on a plug, which Laura felt was safely innocuous and could not possibly imply anything.

"In all my days I have never seen the need for a plug emoji," Chantal remarked. "If he starts texting you random emojis the way we do, you know he's a keeper."

"Don't…" Laura's breath came out in a wobbly rush. *What if he did?*

"Just saying. So you've got it ready?"

"Yes." Laura let out another shuddery breath as she studied the simple text she'd composed as if it were written in Sanskrit. "'Sorry about that,'" she read. "And then the two emojis."

"How many exclamation points?"

"Two. Three looked excessive, the texting equivalent of one of those annoyingly high giggles."

"Fair enough. Feel good about it?"

"I feel sick," Laura confessed. "I don't know why this is freaking me out quite as much as it is. You'd think at my age I could handle replying to a simple text. This should not be such a big deal."

"It's because you're in sight of the horse," Chantal said simply. "Now get back on that saddle and press send."

Holding her breath, closing her eyes—but not before checking she was, in fact, sending it to the right person this time—Laura pressed send. She let out her breath in a rush as she waited for—what? James to reply instantly? What was she, fourteen, like Maggie, glued to her phone?

"And now you wait," Chantal said cheerfully. "And try not to obsess."

"I'm not obsessing," Laura exclaimed. "I barely know him. And I told you, Chantal, I'm not—"

"I know, I know," Chantal soothed. "You're not ready. But you did say he was insanely gorgeous, and it's not every day you run into one of those."

"I'm really wishing I never said those words."

"Actually, you texted them—" Chantal stopped abruptly as the ping of Laura's phone sounded down the line. "Well?" she asked, and with her heart beating far harder than it should, Laura opened the text that had just come in from James. As she glanced at it, she let out a wavery laugh. "What does it say?" Chantal demanded.

"It's just an emoji," Laura told her. "Of a lizard."

"I love this man already," Chantal said.

Chapter Six

"**M**AGGIE! SAM!"

Slowly Laura climbed out of the car as her in-laws rushed towards her children and swept them up into exuberant hugs. She smiled at the sight, determined to be positive. This was, after all, why they'd moved from Woodbridge to Wychwood…to be closer to Pamela and Steve, who clearly adored their grandchildren.

She went to get Perry out of the boot, and the bag of overly expensive goodies for her in-laws she'd bought at the Waitrose in Witney, before joining everyone at the front of the house. The Neales lived in a five-bedroomed, executive-style house on the outskirts of Burford, which they'd bought as empty nesters, to welcome all the grandchildren they'd been eagerly expecting. Laura had never quite shaken the feeling that she'd disappointed them by only producing two.

"Come in, come in," Pamela welcomed them all with teary-eyed exuberance. "It's so wonderful to see you." She enveloped Sam and Maggie in perfumed hugs before glancing at Laura. "You can put Perry in the utility room."

The endless cream carpets and Perry didn't go all that well together, but Laura hadn't wanted to leave him home alone for most of the day. She traipsed off to the utility room while Pamela shepherded the kids into the sitting room, chatting all the while.

"There you go, Per." She fondled the old dog's head as she steeled herself for the afternoon ahead. There was nothing *wrong* with her in-laws, per se. Really, Laura knew she had no cause to complain, and in point of fact she *didn't* complain. But her visits with them over her sixteen years of marriage to Tim had always felt like something to be endured. Slightly. Only slightly.

She left the utility room for the gleaming kitchen, depositing her bag of goodies—a gold-wrapped box of chocolates, a bottle of wine, and some biscuits for cheese—on the worktop.

"Oh, Laura, you shouldn't have," Pamela insisted as she swept into the kitchen for the tea tray that she had already set up with china cups, milk and sugar bowl.

"It's no trouble," Laura murmured. It was the same every time—Pamela said she shouldn't have, but Laura knew if she hadn't, it would have been remarked upon, in a silent, pressed-lips sort of way.

"I'm doing a roast," Pamela said, almost as an accusation, as if Laura's gifts could not possibly compare to a beef joint and Yorkshire puddings.

"Lovely," Laura replied. She was never sure if she was

being ridiculously oversensitive when it came to her in-laws, perceiving slights where there were none. Admittedly they hadn't got off to the best beginning; when she and Tim had started dating, Pamela and Steve had been decidedly put out. They'd been hoping Tim would get back together with Rebecca, the daughter of their best friends whom he'd dated all through university. Laura had started out as second best, and she'd never quite felt as if she'd moved up a place.

"Are you coming in?" Pamela asked as she hefted the tea tray.

"Yes, of course." As if she'd lurk in the kitchen the whole afternoon. Giving her mother-in-law as genuine a smile as she could muster, she followed her into the sitting room, a room done in about twenty shades of beige and cream, with loads of little porcelain figures, some even on the floor or by the fireplace. When Sam had been little, tripping about in his merry way, Laura had been rigid with tension, springing around the room, desperate to avoid a breakage.

Now, at least, she could relax, or try to.

"So you've had your first week of school," Pamela said to Sam and Maggie as she poured tea. "And it was a success?"

"Yeah, I guess so," Maggie said, which was more information than she'd ever offered Laura.

"Granny, guess what?" Sam chimed in. "I'm starting a club!"

Laura sat back and sipped her tea, slightly tuning out while Sam regaled his grandparents with all the details of the

Minecraft Club that she already knew.

In the three days since James Hill had mentioned the idea to her, Laura had done her best to avoid him. She hadn't replied to his lizard emoji text, and she'd more or less skulked in the back of the schoolyard during drop-off and pickup, to avoid so much as meeting his eye.

The morning after the whole texting debacle, she'd woken up scorched straight through with embarrassment as she'd recalled the whole lamentable episode. The slight fluttery feeling of excitement she'd had, simply because a man who had made her feel alive again, even in the tiniest way, was actually interacting with her, had morphed into sheer humiliation.

He had to be laughing at her—a forty-something mum, going all giggly over her son's far younger teacher! It was absurd. Considering Tim had only been gone a little more than a year, it was worse than absurd. It was, she feared, pathetic. She vowed to stop thinking about him, which was easier said than done, although several days of total avoidance had helped, at least a little.

Instead she'd focused on the rest of her life: registering with a supply agency, meeting her neighbours—Lindy had introduced Emily, a lovely young woman who had been shyly friendly but made Laura feel about a million years old, but in a good way, sort of—and trying to get Maggie to talk to her. The last, unfortunately, had been a failure, as usual.

"So, Laura, what do you think?"

The stridency of Pamela's voice made Laura realise guilti-ly that she'd been tuning out a bit more than she'd meant to.

"Sorry, what?"

Irritation flickered across her mother-in-law's face as she gave her a steely sort of smile. "Steve and I were thinking of taking the children skiing over the February half-term. You know how Tim loved skiing when he was younger."

But not when he was older, which somehow felt like Laura's fault, since she didn't ski, although her husband had never pushed for a skiing holiday. "Too expensive," he'd always said. "And too much faff. I'd rather be on a beach."

"Skiing," Laura repeated now in surprise. "Oh, wow…"

"Can we go, Mum?" Sam asked eagerly. "Please? I've never been skiing."

"We thought you might like a break," Pamela continued. "You could get some jobs done around the house…"

Laura blinked, realising who this invitation was for. The children, not her. Which was fine, of course, because she didn't ski and it was understandable that Pamela and Steve would want some time alone with their grandchildren.

And yet…it still stung, somehow. It felt so *pointed*.

"Wow, well, that's very generous," she managed, scram-bling to organise her thoughts. "Thank you…"

"We've booked a chalet at Les Gets," Steve interjected. "Right on the slopes." He smiled at Sam.

"I see." So her acquiescence had been assumed. But what if she'd had plans with her own children for the half-term?

Not that they could afford to go anywhere, but still. "Well, I'm sure they'll love it." She glanced at Maggie and Sam; her daughter looked more enthused than Laura had seen her in a long while, and Sam was fist pumping the air.

"Lovely," Pamela said in satisfaction. "I can hardly wait."

Later, as they were all taking a walk through the fields surrounding Burford, Perry lumbering determinedly alongside them while Pamela marched ahead with Sam and Maggie remained glued to her phone, Steve hung back to talk to Laura.

"Everything okay?" he asked with a semi-sheepish smile that Laura took to be an apology for not including her in the skiing holiday. This was often how her in-laws worked; Pamela bulldozed through and Steve did a little half-hearted clean up afterwards.

"Yes, I think so." She returned his smile easily enough, because she didn't really have a problem with her father-in-law. "It's early days, of course, but I think a change was good for all of us. It was hard in Woodbridge, with everyone knowing." The sudden silences, the awkward condolences the feeling that everyone seemed to have that she couldn't move past her grief when sometimes it felt like *they* had more of a problem with it…she was glad to leave that all behind.

"I'm sure." Steve nodded in a way that closed that avenue of conversation, which was fine. Her father-in-law never did like to probe too deeply into anything, not that Laura had any intention of telling him anything more about life in

Woodbridge—certainly not about the money problems she and Tim had had. *And what about the marital ones?*

No, she certainly wasn't going to volunteer any information about those. She didn't even like to think about them herself.

"You'll get there," Steve told her with a bracing smile and a clumsy pat on her arm.

Laura smiled in return. "I certainly hope so." Because what if she didn't, wherever 'there' was, some golden horizon where life felt normal and good? It didn't, Laura thought, bear thinking about.

BY THE TIME they got back to Willoughby Close it was dark, and Maggie's brief flare of enthusiasm for skiing trips and roast dinners had, predictably, morphed back into a grouchy silence punctuated by dramatic remarks on how late it was, and didn't anyone realise she had homework?

Laura ignored it all as she unlocked the door to number three and they all trooped into the house. Coming home, no matter where they went, always felt a bit of a let-down. It was in moments such as this one that Laura felt Tim's absence keenly; he would have teased Maggie out of her mood, or asked Sam to play a game of ping-pong—not that they had the ping-pong table anymore. But he would have filled up the emptiness with his energy, his indefatigable good humour—except when he didn't.

When Tim had been on, he'd shone. He'd radiated charm and cheerfulness and everybody wanted to bask in his light. But when he *hadn't* been feeling it, well…then the cosy little world of their family had felt depressingly dark. At least Laura had felt it. She thought Tim had done a pretty good job of hiding his mood swings from the kids, turning on the charm and interest when they were around, and descending into sullen silences when they were alone. But she didn't want to think about all that now.

"So what homework do you have?" Laura asked before Maggie could disappear upstairs.

"Just some biology," came the muffled response before Laura heard the thud of her daughter's feet on the stairs and then the door shutting firmly. At least it wasn't a slam. Small mercies.

"What about you, Sam?"

"I don't have any."

"You could read a book," Laura suggested, somewhat half-heartedly. "Aren't you supposed to read twenty minutes a day?"

"Mmm." Having been separated from his iPad for the better part of the day, Sam was now hard at play. Laura sighed and switched on the kettle. She'd save that battle for another evening.

She'd just brewed a cup of tea when a knock sounded at the door, surprising her.

"Lindy." She hadn't seen much of her neighbour since

they'd had coffee earlier in the week, and despite her tiredness Laura was glad to see a friendly face. "How are you?"

"Oh, fine, fine—I just wanted to stop by to ask if you'd like to go out for a drink next weekend, on Friday perhaps? I haven't managed to get the whole tribe together—there are a lot of us now—but Olivia will be back from her honeymoon, and Emily's keen, as well. Ava might come if she hasn't given birth yet! And Alice, too."

Laura hesitated for the merest second, because the thought of proper socialising with a group of people she didn't know was more than a little bit terrifying. She hadn't gone out in a group in over a year, and Lindy had just listed a load of people, never mind about the whole *tribe*. But then she thought about Pamela and Steve taking Maggie and Sam for half-term, and she knew she needed to make friends. She needed to get a life.

"Sure, that would be great," she said. "Really lovely. Thanks."

Lindy laid a hand on her arm. "It won't be scary, I promise." She gave her a conspiratorial smile. "Harriet's not coming."

"Harriet…?" Ava had also mentioned her, but Laura hadn't met her yet, which seemed just as well, considering the comments that had been made.

"I'm just joking. Sort of. Harriet used to live in number two, with her three kids. Will is in Sam's class, I think—she can be a force to be reckoned with, but she's lovely. Honest."

"I'll take your word for it."

"No, seriously." For a second Lindy almost looked upset. "I shouldn't have said anything. Harriet really is lovely. Just…forceful."

"I believe you," Laura said with a laugh. "Don't worry. And I'm looking forward to Friday night." Mostly.

"Who was that?" Sam asked after Laura had closed the front door.

"Our neighbour, Lindy. She invited me out next weekend."

"That's nice."

"Yes, it is." Laura smiled fondly at her youngest child. He hadn't looked up once from the screen for the whole conversation, but she knew his interest was genuine.

"She mentioned Will?"

Laura hesitated, registered Sam's slightly guarded tone. "Yes. Will is Harriet's son, although I haven't actually met Harriet yet." A pause while Sam continued to play his game, his head bent over the screen. "Do you know him?"

"Mum, there are only thirty kids in my class. I know everyone."

"I know, but…" *Do you like him? Is he nice? Or is he mean to you?* Questions she couldn't—wouldn't—ask. "I just wondered if he was a friend," she said as lightly as she could.

Sam twitched a shoulder in the approximation of a shrug. "Not really," he said, and there was a final-sounding note in his voice that filled Laura with a silent dread, because she'd heard it before, back in Woodbridge, when Sam had been bullied but hadn't wanted to tell her.

But there was no need to get ahead of herself just yet. Sam had only had one week of school and he was starting a club; he seemed happy. She needed to let that be enough. She needed to live in the moment and be glad for what it was, and no more.

Laura glanced out at the night sky, a few stars twinkling like distant promises she longed to believe in. Life could work out here. There was every indication that it would—friendly neighbours, Sam and Maggie happy; well, enough, hopefully—in school, supportive in-laws. She had to see the positives. Perhaps she'd land a proper job soon, or at least some supply work. She'd get back into the land of living, instead of just drifting about, waiting for things to be over—a day, a month, a year. She didn't want to live like that anymore. She wouldn't.

Buoyed by optimism, Laura headed upstairs and tapped on her daughter's door. "Maggie? Cup of tea?"

A sigh, as if she'd asked something absurd, and then a muffled "Okay." Heartened, Laura turned to go back downstairs and put the kettle on again. As she reached the step, she heard Maggie speak again, the words faint, a bit grudging, but a balm to Laura's wounded soul. "Thanks, Mum."

THE NEXT MORNING was one of those brilliant wintry days where the whole world seemed to sparkle—and freeze. Laura did her usual lurk in the schoolyard, although she supposed a week on she could look James Hill in the eye without blushing. She hoped she could, anyway.

She tried to meet a few mums' eyes, at least, and a couple gave her fleeting smiles with a look of confusion on their faces—*do I know you?*, Laura suspected, would be in the thought bubble above their heads.

No one made conversation, and Laura's one attempt with another mum about the weather—*cold*—had been met with a vague smile before she'd turned away to talk to someone else.

Well, that was okay. She'd try again tomorrow. As Chantal kept telling her, it was about the trying. She watched Sam troop inside with the other Year Sixes and wrapped her scarf more tightly around her neck, in preparation for the icy wind that funnelled down the high street.

"Mrs Neale? May I have a word?"

Laura turned around to see the head teacher smiling at her with the kind of sympathy that made her realise he must know about Tim. James Hill must have told him. That wasn't really a surprise, of course, but she still had to steel herself against it.

"Yes?"

"I'm Dan Rhodes, the head teacher here. We've spoken on the phone a few times…"

"Yes, of course. It's so nice to meet you properly."

"And you. I wondered if you had a moment? Nothing serious, quite the contrary…"

"All right." These unexpected chats were going to give her a heart attack one of these days.

Back into the school she went, although this time she had the privilege of being in Mr Rhodes' office, which was slightly more spacious than the staffroom, with a desk, two chairs, a large houseplant.

"I hope I didn't worry you," Dan Rhodes said with a little laugh, and Laura had the uncomfortable feeling that he'd had a complete debrief of her conversation with James, including her over-the-top anxiety. Great. Hopefully James Hill hadn't told him about her text, too.

"Not at all." She gave him a polite smile, the kind that was meant to say, in a friendly way, *Get on with it, please.*

"Mr Hill mentioned you used to teach history," he said without preamble. "And that you worked as a teaching assistant?"

"Yes…"

"Because as it happens, we're in a bit of a bind. Our Year Three teaching assistant has been put on sick leave until the February half-term. We were about to apply to the agency, but it's always better when there's a personal connection, don't you think?"

He smiled winningly at her while Laura stared blankly. "You want me…to provide cover?" she finally surmised, a few seconds too late. He was going to think she was thick.

"Er, yes, if you're free…?"

Of course she was free, and yet…Laura hesitated. Why was Mr Rhodes offering her the position? It was obvious there was little personal connection, considering she knew no one at the school, and it would be just as easy, if not easier, to go through the agency.

"It would only be for five weeks," he said. "And you seem more than qualified."

Did she? How on earth would he know that? Then the penny dropped with a depressing thud. This was pity. He knew about Tim and he felt sorry for her. Laura resisted the notion, even as another part of her thought, *well, so what?*

It was still a job, and they could certainly use the money, and it was only for five weeks. Plus she could keep half an eye on Sam…

And what about James Hill?

Her stomach dipped at the thought, whether in terror or excitement or both Laura couldn't tell. She'd been avoiding him for the last week, and yet now the thought of seeing him again brought a frisson of…something.

"Well?" Dan asked, and slowly Laura nodded.

"That would be wonderful, actually. I've already registered with an agency so you'll have to go through them anyway, though…"

"That's fine. We'll sort out the paperwork and if it's agreeable to you, you can start as soon as we've got it all cleared—hopefully in the next few days."

Laura felt as if her head was spinning. How had she bagged a job so quickly, and without even trying? Whatever the reason, whether pity or Providence, she was grateful. "Great," she told Dan. "Thank you."

Chapter Seven

F OR HEAVEN'S SAKE, the *noise*.

It had been awhile since Laura had been in a classroom—well, a few months anyway—and she'd forgotten just how chaotic they could be. She stood in the doorway of the Year Three classroom while thirty children got their reading records out of their backpacks and went to their tables for twenty minutes of personal reading—an activity that sounded as if it should be quiet, but wasn't.

The clatter of shoes, the screech and squeak of chairs being moved, the shrieks of girls and the shouts of boys… It was a lovely, welcome, happy sound, but it was also giving Laura a bit of a headache. Fortunately her job this morning was to listen to a group of three, who were struggling with literacy, read from their books. Mrs Frampton, the Year Three teacher, had suggested she take them out to the school hall for some quiet while she got on with the rest.

"All right, Phoebe, Jake, Isla," Laura said brightly, adopting the brisk cheeriness she used instinctively as a teacher, "shall we find a cosy place out in the hall?"

Rain drummed against the long, narrow windows as Laura arranged a small table and child-sized chairs in one corner of the draughty and decidedly un-cosy hall. It still seemed slightly surreal, that just three days on from her conversation with Dan Rhodes, she was now ensconced in a classroom, and employed for the next five weeks.

She'd been worried about Maggie and Sam's reaction to her working, which had been clearly unnecessary, because they hadn't been bothered at all. *She* was the one who felt the need to hover, not them.

She'd also been worried about Perry, who didn't like being alone all day; when Tim had been alive, he'd often taken him to work, with Perry blissfully hanging his head out the window of Tim's truck. The memory still made Laura smile, even as it gave her a pang.

In any case, Perry was taken care of, too; Lindy had offered to take him for a walk and check in on him several times a day. Laura would be home by half past three, so it was just about doable.

And then, lastly, she'd been worried about James, which was another non-starter because she hadn't even seen him yet this morning, and she seemed unlikely to do much more than pass in the hall during the course of a school day. Which was, of course, absolutely fine.

"So, Biff, Chip, and Kipper," she said as she glanced at Isla's book. She'd had years reading these books with Sam and Maggie; they were standard across the entire country, and she remembered many of the well-loved stories. "*The Lightning Key*. That sounds exciting."

The next twenty minutes passed peacefully enough, as Laura listened to each child read a page, gently correcting or helping them when needed. Around her the school settled into the day—children heading to the reception area with the registers, the dinner ladies starting up in the kitchen with a clatter and clang of pots.

Laura had forgotten how much she liked this—the hum of a busy, productive place, the feeling of community that could be felt even when she was sitting in a corner with three seven-year-olds. The last year had been, she acknowledged, even more isolating than she'd realised.

"Everything going all right?" Dan Rhodes asked brightly as he paused in the hall on his way to his office.

"Brilliantly, thank you," Laura assured him. She'd once been in charge of a whole department, before kids, but she was perfectly content with the low level of responsibility she had now. This job might be a great way to get back into full-time teaching, but easy did it.

She didn't see James until playtime after lunch, when she was standing on the side of the schoolyard, watching a frenetic game of stuck in the mud and enjoying the fresh, if rather frigid, air.

"So how are you finding it?" The smile he gave her as he walked up to her was entirely easy, which somehow disconcerted her all the more. It was almost as if they'd never spoken before, and all the while Laura had been hyper-aware of the admittedly brief conversation they'd had, the whole semi-flirty texting, although she realised now she'd undoubtedly read way too much into a single emoji. Of a lizard.

"It's fine," she assured him a bit too heartily. "Really fine. I realise how much I've missed teaching."

"I'm glad—not that you've missed teaching, of course, but that you're enjoying it now. I was worried I was overstepping by putting your name forward to Dan, but it seemed almost providential."

"I'm grateful you thought of me." She dug her hands into the pockets of her coat and gazed at the kids careening around the schoolyard, achingly conscious of James standing so close to her and trying not to be.

He was wearing pretty much the same outfit he had before—battered cords, a button-down shirt, brogues. Laura thought he probably wore the same thing every day, and it suited him. When she glanced at him out of the corner of her eye, his own glinted with good humour, and for some reason that made her blush. Oh, dear. She needed to get a grip on this—whatever *this* was. To James, she was quite, quite sure it was nothing. And it should be nothing to her, as well because, oh, for about a million reasons. She kept her gaze on the kids and so did James, although she could see he was smiling faintly.

The playground supervisor rang the big brass bell, and the children, almost as one, began to troop inside. Laura made to move past James, and found he was looking at her, not with that small smile, but with an alarming sort of intensity.

"Duty calls," she said with an uncertain laugh.

"I'm glad you're here," he said, and then, rather abruptly, he turned and walked away, jogging up to a couple of Year Sixes whom he began chatting to with laughing ease.

Laura stood rooted to the spot, going over his words, analysing them for far more meaning than they likely possessed. *I'm glad you're here.* Was that a sympathy sort of thing, or something with more intent? Was she ridiculous to think it was anything but a bit of well-meaning kindness, the sentiment of someone who had felt sorry for her and was glad to have helped?

Of course that was what it was, she thought with a mental facepalm as she headed inside. *Of course.* And she was a fool to think for a second—to hope—it had meant anything more.

THAT EVENING LAURA stood in front of her mirror, exhausted from the first full day's work she'd done in months, gazing uncertainly at her reflection. She'd been unsure of the dress code for a night out with a few friendly neighbours, and so she'd called Chantal, who was eyeing her critically from her phone, which was propped against her mirror.

"Don't look as if you're trying too hard."

"You're the one who says I have to try," Laura replied with a laugh as she pulled at the front of her stretchy top, afraid it showed a bit too much of her admittedly small amount of cleavage.

"Yes, but you're not on the pull," Chantal replied. "Are you?"

"Chantal."

"It was a serious question. What's the latest with Mr Insanely Gorgeous, by the way?"

"Oh my goodness, I wish I'd never texted that to you," Laura exclaimed, shaking her head. She had a feeling she'd be hearing about it for months, if not years.

"Well, you *didn't* text it to me," Chantal replied serenely, "did you?"

Laura rolled her eyes. "True enough." She was just thankful she'd got through the day without James referencing it, although stupidly, that had also caused a little contrary needling of disappointment. Had he *forgotten*? Perhaps he had women calling him insanely gorgeous every day of the week.

"Did you talk to him today, though?" Chantal asked. "I want all the goss, Laur."

"We chatted briefly." That slightly odd exchange in the schoolyard had been their only conversation all day, although Laura had seen him from a distance several times, not that she'd been looking for him. Not exactly, anyway. Goodness, but she was acting like a lovesick teenager. She had to stop that. Really.

"Well, there's definitely potential there," Chantal stated. "Now if there is any chance he might be at the pub to-night—"

"There isn't."

How do you know?"

She didn't, but she couldn't contemplate the alternative. "I just know, okay, Chantal? I don't think he even lives in Wychwood." Actually, she didn't know that at all, but neither did Chantal.

"Well, I was going to say, if he might be there tonight, then, yes, wear the stretchy red top, because *phwoar*. But if not…maybe a jumper?"

"I thought they might go dressy, this being the Cots-wolds. They're all ex-Londoners. At least I think they are."

"Who are now trying to live the country life," Chantal said in the voice of someone who thought she knew what she was talking about. "Maybe you should put on a pair of Wellies."

"Oh, for heaven's sake." Laura pulled off the stretchy top and grabbed an old faithful—a cashmere sweater in dark blue that Tim had bought her one Christmas because he thought it matched her eyes. She remembered how pleased she had been, yet also swallowing down the sense that perhaps they couldn't afford it. "How's this?"

"Boring but suitable."

"Perfect, then."

Chantal was silent for a moment, and Laura glanced at her phone, waiting for the usual acerbic but loving comment.

"You know I just want you to be happy, right?" Chantal asked.

Cue massive lump in throat. Laura's gaze flitted from the phone to her reflection; the dark sweater made her look as pale as a ghost. "I know."

"It isn't that I didn't like Tim or that I don't respect his memory," Chantal continued, and now she had the dogged tone of someone who was going to say their piece no matter what. "It's just...you're still young, Laura. And there's so much life ahead of you."

"I know—"

"And I think sometimes there is a tendency to idealise—or perhaps even idolise—someone who has died." Laura closed her eyes, bracing herself for what came next. It had been a year and Chantal had never talked about this, although she'd skirted alarmingly close to the topic recently. "And it's important to remember your marriage to Tim wasn't all hearts and roses. No one's is."

The lump in her throat was getting bigger. "I know that, Chantal."

"I know you do," Chantal said quickly. "Better than I do, of course. It's just...sometimes I think you want to put Tim on this pedestal, maybe for the kids' sake..."

"He was their *dad*." Her voice sounded thick and she had to blink rapidly several times. "And he was a really good dad.

They don't need to know anything else, Chantal." She'd lowered her voice because Maggie was in the next room, and this was definitely not a conversation she wanted her daughter overhearing.

"Okay…"

"I've got to go." Laura reached for a pair of earrings and stabbed them into her ears.

"You're not angry, are you?" Chantal asked, sounding anxious, and Laura sighed.

"No, of course not." She knew her best friend meant well, but sometimes the truth, even just a little bit of it, hurt. And she didn't need that kind of laid-bare honesty right when she was about to go out with a bunch of people she didn't know. "Just pick your moments a bit better, okay?" she said with an attempt at a laugh, and Chantal gave a grimace of apology before Laura disconnected the call. Showtime.

"You look nice, Mum," Sam told her as she came downstairs.

"Thanks, love." She straightened her top and tried to still the flutter of nerves in her belly. This didn't have to be so hard.

And actually, thankfully, it wasn't. She met Lindy, Emily, and Olivia outside in the courtyard, and was glad Chantal had advised the jumper. Everyone was dressed casually as well as warmly for the weather, and they all seemed remarkably enthused to meet her.

"It's nice to have some kids in the close," Olivia said, her brand-new wedding ring glinting on her finger. "It's been a bit quiet, hasn't it, ladies?"

"Too quiet," Emily agreed. "Except for the dogs." She gave Lindy a teasing smile.

"Toby does tend to bark when I'm not around," Lindy explained. "He's a rescue greyhound."

"And soon you'll have some little ones nearby, as well," Laura said, doing her best to be part of the banter. "Isn't Ava due soon?"

"Next week," Lindy confided. "She said she'd meet us at the pub—Jace is driving her so she doesn't go into labour on the high street."

"Alice was going to come," Olivia chimed in, "but she's still feeling nauseous. That morning sickness. Not that I know what it's like, of course!"

"But maybe you will one day," Lindy said with a purposeful nudge. Olivia blushed.

"Maybe, but I'm forty-one," she murmured. "Leaving it a bit late."

The same age as Laura. Olivia's words caused a sorrowful sweep of unexpected longing to rush through her. When Sam had been little, she'd wanted to try for a third, but Tim had been more cautious, worried about money. Then Sam had come out of nappies, started sleeping through the night and not needing her as much, and the prospect of easy holidays and full nights' sleep had beckoned, putting paid to that broody desire.

Strange to feel it now, when there was absolutely no chance of it happening.

"Shall we head off?" Lindy suggested, and they all started down the darkened lane.

Laura tried to follow the general chitchat as they walked into Wychwood-on-Lea, the names being batted about making her head spin a little. There was Harriet, whom she'd heard of, and Ellie, whom she hadn't, but was now apparently living happily near Oxford with her husband and daughter. Richard was Harriet's husband, and he'd just bagged a new teaching job near Oxford, and Ellie's husband was, amazingly, a viscount. Then there were the children and dogs—Marmite and Abby, Chloe and Mallory—Laura couldn't keep track of them all. She let the words wash over her as she gazed up at the night sky and breathed in the frosty air. *Live in the moment,* she reminded herself. Right now, thankfully, it didn't feel too hard.

The pub was crowded on a Friday night, warmly lit and full of laughter and chatter. Ava had already arrived, bagging a table in the corner, bottles of both red and white already on the table.

"I thought I'd get you all started, since I can't have anything to drink," she said, lacing her hands over her enormous bump. "I can't wait until this one is out in the world, and that's a fact. I'm toasting his or her birth with a glass of Rioja."

Laura was still in the process of shedding her coat when Ava turned a speculative and slightly beady eye upon her. "I hear you're working at the school till the half-term."

"Yes, as a teaching assistant," Laura answered as she took her seat. "It's nice to keep a hand in."

"I envy you," Ava said with a dirty laugh, "getting to rub shoulders with the divine Mr Hill. The whole village has been buzzing about him since he started in September."

"I haven't," Lindy interjected with a laugh. "I've been at the school every week with the Year Sixes and I haven't heard a word."

"That's because you've been completely smitten with the lovely Roger Wentworth," Ava replied. "Trust me, every woman between here and Chipping Norton has her eyes on stalks looking out for Mr Hill. He's insanely gorgeous."

Laura froze as she caught Ava's glinting look. A *knowing* look? Had she said that on purpose? Had someone told her that she'd texted those exact words to James? It felt like far too much of a coincidence, and yet…

"Apparently he's also incredibly charming and funny and nice," Ava continued. "Too good to be true, perhaps, although I'm sure he'll make some lucky woman happy. Laura, what would you like? Red or white? I'll pour."

"Oh, um, red please." She still felt flustered by Ava's remark, although she was doing her best not to show it. Surely it had to have been an admittedly uncomfortable coincidence.

Ava handed her a glass and Laura took a healthy sip, grateful for the comforting burn of alcohol. She had a feeling she was going to need a glass or two to get through the evening, what with Ava's knowing looks—or not. She still couldn't tell if that remark had been pointed or not, although she told herself she was just being panicky as usual. Paranoid, too.

"Well, well," Ava said as she handed more glasses round. "Speak of the devil, or should I say the angel, or how about just the sexy?" She gave another dirty laugh. "Look who's here."

Laura turned, even though she knew she didn't need to. She could tell from Ava's delighted voice who had to be in the pub, just as Chantal had suggested earlier.

And yes, there he was, one elbow propped at the bar, a pint in front of him, laughing at something the bartender had said. James Hill in the insanely gorgeous flesh.

Laura took another gulp of her wine as she wished, fleetingly, that she'd worn her stretchy top after all.

Chapter Eight

JAMES DIDN'T OFTEN go out to the pub. He liked a pint as much as the next man, but he was more of a quiet night in type of guy than a rowdy laugh at the local. He'd let himself be dragged out tonight by his fellow members of the Wychwood Chess Club—yes, he was a card-carrying member—because he fancied a break from his own circling thoughts.

He really needed to stop thinking about Laura Neale. Every time he recalled telling her so abruptly that he was glad she was there, and her ensuing look of bewilderment, he mentally cringed. It wasn't quite on the same level as her stray text, admittedly, but it still had its own particular brand of awkwardness.

And the fact remained that as lovely as she was, Laura Neale should not be on his romantic radar, for the same reasons he'd enumerated to himself several times before. Mother of a pupil. Widow. Off limits. The end.

"Who are you giving the eye to, then?"

Edwin, an eighty-year-old geezer who also happened to be sharp as a tack and a chess master, elbowed James rather hard in the ribs.

"Sorry, what?" He turned to his companion who had already downed his first pint and was well on his way with the second.

"You're giving a lady the eye," Edwin proclaimed with a gleam in his own. "I can always tell. Is it that one in the corner? She might be in the family way but she still looks pretty nice to me."

"What?" Startled, James clocked Edwin's knowing nod towards the woman sitting next to Laura, who looked to be about nine if not ten months pregnant. "No," he said, amusement and irritation warring within him at the old man's obvious appreciation. "No. Just no."

"What about the one next to her, then? The blonde one?"

"Edwin. No. Stop." He shook his head, exasperated as the old man cackled with laughter. "I'm not giving anyone the eye. Honestly." Although he was looking at Laura. Again.

Deliberately James turned back to the bar. "How about another pint?"

The bartender, a slick-looking guy in his twenties, pointed a thumb at his drink. "You've barely touched it, mate."

"Even so," James said a bit grimly. He enjoyed playing Edwin over a chessboard, but his conversation and accompanying cackles left something to be desired.

"Why don't you go talk to her, if you like her so much?" Edwin demanded, and pretending not to hear him, James turned to talk to Jason, another member of the chess club. He was smiling in amused commiseration as he took a sip from his own beer.

"So who *were* you looking at, by the by?"

"I wasn't," James replied automatically, and then gave a sheepish grin. It wasn't as if he could actually deny it. "Just a woman I know. Mum of a pupil. Nothing like that."

"Okay, whatever you say." He shrugged, and then, to James's relief, started talking about the weather. He could talk about the weather. Cold, even for January. Easy.

Yet his gaze kept sliding towards Laura of its own accord, and then, once, her eyes met his and it almost felt as if he'd put his finger in an electric socket, everything in him jolting with awareness. Good *grief.* He needed to get out more. Date more. Something.

Moving to Wychwood had meant being closer to his family, but romantic opportunities were thin on the ground, something that hadn't bothered him too much when he'd been fresh from a break-up, but six months on he was definitely feeling the lack. He forced himself to look away from Laura yet again.

The rest of the club members were talking about Magnus Carlsen, the reigning chess champion's latest shock defeat, and James drained his pint as he did his best to listen in.

Perhaps he should just go home. He'd bought a falling-down cottage off the high street that needed a ton of work—most of which he was ill-equipped to do—but he was slowly making it as cosy as he could and he had Netflix, after all. Still, the thought depressed him. Thirty-two years old and this was what it had come to?

He looked again at Laura and saw she was looking back. Then, an expression of determination hardening her features, she rose from her seat and started towards him.

The hairs on the back of his neck stood up as anticipation fizzed in his belly. Her gaze remained locked on his as she marched towards him, and he gave her what he hoped was a welcoming smile.

"Laura…"

"Did you tell Ava what I said?" she demanded without preamble.

James simply stared as belatedly he realised the determination on her face looked more like anger close-up.

"Ava…" Who was Ava? "Sorry, what?"

She shook her head as she bit her lip, her anger turning to anxiety. "It's just she said…and she seemed to *know*…"

"Sorry, I have no idea what you're talking about." Conscious of Edwin's avid stare, he took her by the arm and gently manoeuvred her towards a more private corner, away from the bar. "Start from the beginning, please."

Laura let out a rushed breath, her gaze lowered as she forced out, "My friend Ava said something about you being…oh, well you being insanely gorgeous." The words were spoken reluctantly, defiantly, and had James grinning anyway. "And it just seemed so strange that she would say the exact same thing…" She looked up, her hazel eyes filled with both accusation and vulnerability. "Did you tell her about my text?"

SHE WOULD NEVER have asked if she hadn't had two glasses of wine in rather quick succession. As it was, Laura's head was swimming and standing so close to James made it spin all the more. He smelled heavenly, like cedarwood. He was also looking at her in confusion, which then cleared to what could only be considered genuine amusement.

"You think I told this Ava person about your text? Do you really think I'm that much of a complete prat?" And then he started to laugh.

"I don't," Laura said quickly, "but then why would she say that?"

He shrugged, still smiling. "If two women are saying it, I guess it must be true."

Whatever determination she had been holding on to left her and she let out a sound that was half groan, half horrified laugh. "And now I've just made this worse, and so I'm even more embarrassed."

"Laura, don't be." He touched her arm briefly and then pulled back. "The text was funny, that's all. It's no big deal." A pause and then he added, almost casually, "If it helps, I think you're pretty gorgeous, too."

She glanced up at him, shock firing through her, along

with a wary pleasure, even though she suspected he was just saying it to be nice. "But not insanely so?" she managed to tease, even though her heart was racing.

"We-ell…" He pretended to think for a moment and then laughed and shrugged. "Look, let's just forget about it, okay? I did not tell this Ava, whoever she is, about the text. I didn't tell anyone. I mean, for heaven's sake, what would I say without sounding, as I said, like an absolute prat?"

"I don't know," Laura admitted. "I suppose I'm paranoid."

"Look, it was funny, that's all. What was with the stiletto emoji anyway?"

She risked a glance at him, finding a smile. "What was with the lizard?"

He smiled back. "It just seemed like the spirit of the thing."

That heartened her a little. "Well, I suppose it was. My friend Chantal—that's who the text was meant for—and I have this running joke about emojis. We once had a conversation about how many there were, and then we started signing off our texts with the most random ones we could find."

"Sounds fun."

She glanced at him, acutely conscious of how unhinged she must have seemed, rabbiting on about that stupid text like some obsessed sixteen-year-old. James had forgotten it, or at least simply saw it as amusing; why couldn't she? Well, from now on she would. Honestly, she was being ridiculous. It was time to stop, and start behaving like the grown-up she really was.

"I'm sorry about all this," she said as she straightened, meaning to head back to her table where—she couldn't help but notice—Ava, Olivia, and Emily were all watching her avidly. She hadn't even told them where she was going; she'd just lurched up from the table like a crazed woman on a mission.

With what she hoped was a cool smile she turned to James. "I'm afraid I've got out of the habit of socialising in the last year, and frankly, normal human interaction of any kind. I promise I'm not really this odd. Forgetting about the text sounds like a fabulous idea, and one I intend to act on immediately."

"I don't think you're odd," James replied, his voice dropping to a murmur that swept across Laura's skin. "But you've been going through a hard time." He paused. "Which is something you can talk to me about, if you wanted to."

The invitation surprised her, because she'd assumed his light manner was more or less a brush-off, not a suggestion of something more. She opened her mouth to reply, but before she could form any thoughts, James continued quickly, "But of course you don't have to. I just meant—as a friend. I'm here. That's all."

"Thank you," Laura said after a moment. "That's very kind." Something flashed across his face and now she felt like the one who was giving a brush-off. "I don't have a lot of friends at the moment," she admitted, and James cocked his head.

"Because of moving?"

"Yes, but even before that." The wine was still making her reckless, it seemed. "Tim—my husband—and I moved to Woodbridge in Suffolk three years ago from London, and it wasn't awful by any means, but I don't think I ever really felt as if I fit in." It was the first time she'd actually said the words out loud. "Most people were from the area, and we never quite got over feeling like newcomers."

James nodded slowly. "So why did you move to Woodbridge in the first place?"

"Tim's job. He worked in marketing in London but he loved gardening and he wanted to start his own landscaping design business. He picked Woodbridge because it was affordable, near the sea, and..." She trailed off helplessly. There had to be another reason, but she couldn't remember what it was.

"That's tough," James said quietly. "I imagine starting your landscaping business would require some good local contacts that he wouldn't have had."

"Yes." *Exactly.* It both stung and vindicated her, that James had been able to see in a few seconds what Tim never had, or at least had never been willing to. "It *was* hard. The business never really got off the ground, as it happened."

The now-familiar guilt poured through her in a scalding

rush. How could she talk about Tim this way? He'd done his best. He'd tried so hard. And he'd loved them all utterly. Of that she was certain.

"Anyway," she said quickly. "That's all water under the bridge. Woodbridge." She laughed at her own feeble joke, but her voice wavered. James touched her arm again. He had to stop doing that; every time he did it tingled.

"I'm so sorry, Laura."

"No, it's okay. We're getting there. Honestly." She had to reel herself back in somehow. "Anyway, I'm glad we've cleared all that up. So...I'll see you at school?"

He studied her face, looking as if he wanted to say something more, but then he simply nodded slowly. "Yes. See you at school."

"What was that all about?" Ava asked with gleeful, undisguised interest as Laura sat back down at the table.

"Just a school thing," she tried to dismiss, and reached for her wine. Not that she needed another glass.

"It didn't look like school stuff to me," Ava replied. "If I didn't know better, I'd think James Hill was into you."

"Pshaw," Laura uttered, which was a sound she had never made before in her life. "Ridiculous."

Ava cocked an eyebrow. "He looked awfully intent there."

"That's just how he is. He's got to be ten years younger than me, anyway."

"So?"

Laura shrugged, disconcerted by Ava's complete dismissal of a rather significant age gap. "Anyway, I'm not on the lookout for someone." She hadn't told Ava about Tim, and now seemed as good a time as any. "My husband died only a year ago."

"I'm sorry." Ava looked as if she meant it. "I was married before Jace, you know, and he died."

No, she hadn't known that. Everyone got their fair share of tragedy one way or another, Laura supposed. "I'm sorry," she said, but Ava shrugged the words aside.

"A year is a long time, and you're still young," she said, which was what Chantal had insisted, as well.

"Not that young," Laura answered, and glugged her wine.

BY THE TIME Monday morning arrived, Laura had managed to talk herself into a more cheerful frame of mind. Despite her slight drunkenness, it was good that she'd cleared the air with James. Now they could interact as colleagues and maybe even as friends, comfortable in their joint gorgeousness, although, as she'd told Chantal in Saturday's debriefing, he'd just been saying that to be nice.

"Why do you put yourself down?" Chantal had demanded. "You *are* gorgeous."

"Chantal, I'm forty-one—"

"So? Do women stop being beautiful as soon as they turn

menopausal?"

"I'm not menopausal," Laura had yelped, alarmed.

"Exactly," Chantal proclaimed, which was just the kind of tangled argument she loved to make. "So enjoy it. Why shouldn't a good-looking bloke think you're something special?"

"But he doesn't, I mean, not in that way. I mean, it's all fine and good, but really, we're just friends."

"Oh-kay," Chantal agreed in the voice of someone playing along with a deluded person. "You're just friends."

But they really were, Laura reminded herself as she headed into the Year Three classroom, waving at her little trio of readers. Phoebe, Jake, and Isla had been with her every morning of the last week and they'd managed to worm their lovely little way into her heart.

In just a week, she realised, she'd come to feel settled and welcomed at the school in a way that was a balm to her battered heart. Sue Frampton, the Year Three teacher, was chatty and fun, and the other teachers—James included— had all been welcoming and friendly. Occasional chats in the staffroom or schoolyard had been low-key and really quite nice, five minutes here or there which was, Laura suspected, about all she could take.

Plus, to add to her good mood, this morning Maggie had gone to school with a bounce in her step, and Sam was excited for the first Minecraft Club session this afternoon. There was, Laura mused, a lot to be thankful for, and she was determined to remember that. It was time to start looking up, to start living again.

"Now," she told her happy trio as they all settled in their usual spot by the hall, "where are we with Kipper, Chip, and Biff today?"

THE REST OF the morning went smoothly enough, as Laura moved between groups in the Year Three classroom, helping and guiding where she could. It was lovely to see so many little ones, their heads bent in concentration, although some had adorable mischief in their eyes.

At lunchtime she headed outside, admiring the carpet of snowdrops by the school gate, as children raced madly around her, enjoying their twenty minutes of outdoor freedom. Laura hugged her arms around herself as she stamped her feet in an attempt to keep warm.

"You know you don't have to come outside during play-time if it's not your turn to supervise?" James remarked as he strolled up to her. "It is your break today."

"I like the fresh air, and what else am I going to do?" She turned to smile at him, trying not to notice how, yes, gorgeous he looked. "Do you have any other clothes?"

James looked rather endearingly startled. "Sorry?"

"You always wear the same thing—battered cords, but-ton-down shirt, brogues. A kind of funky professor look."

He laughed as he glanced down at himself. "Nailed it.

I'm afraid you're never going to see me in leather jeans and a turtleneck."

Laura pretended to shudder. "Thank heaven for that."

"I know, right? One of my sisters is trying to get me to turn into some kind of fashion icon, but I tell her it's not going to happen."

This little glimpse into his family life intrigued her. "One of your sisters? How many do you have?"

He made a funny little grimace. "Four, and a brother, as well." He held up a hand. "I know. I know. Six children in the family, all from the same parents. What can I say? Maybe it's a Shropshire farmer thing."

"Wow." Somehow she could see him in a big, chaotic, happy family. "Where are you in the line-up?"

"Third, smack dab in the middle. What about you? Any siblings?"

"A brother who moved to Australia a few years ago and is living the high life, as far as I can tell." She rarely spoke to Sean. "My parents divorced when I was thirteen, sadly. No big happy family, I'm afraid."

"I've been lucky in that way, although if you had four sisters breathing down your neck, you might not think so."

"Maybe not," she agreed with a smile. She wondered if his sisters teased him, if they were nosy about his girlfriends, then told herself not to think like that.

His gaze turned serious, lingering on her face. "How was the rest of your weekend?" he asked, and his tone reminded her of a doctor asking how she was feeling.

"Fine. Good, actually. You know." She shrugged dismissively. She really didn't like talking about these things, and thankfully James seemed to get it.

"Great. I'm glad." He opened his mouth to say something else, and then closed it, a frown coming over his face as his gaze focused on something over her shoulder. Laura turned around, her stomach dipping at the sight of Mrs Petch, the receptionist, striding purposefully towards them, looking more sour-faced than usual. What was wrong? Should she and James not have been chatting?

"Mrs Neale?"

"Yes—"

"I'm afraid I've just taken a call from Burford Comprehensive. They tried to reach you on your mobile but you weren't picking up."

"I don't get a signal in school—" Already her voice sounded high with panic.

"They'd like you to ring them back as soon as possible," Mrs Petch said flatly. "It's about your daughter Maggie."

Chapter Nine

LAURA PERCHED ON the edge of a hard plastic chair, her mind and body both numb. The head teacher of the comp, Amanda Stevens, was giving her a look that was an unsettling combination of boredom and judgement. Just another difficult child to deal with. Just another negligent parent to scold.

"And so I'm afraid I have no choice but to suspend Maggie for a week."

"A week." Laura felt as if her insides had hollowed out. She touched her tongue to her lips, her mouth as dry as a bone. "That seems…"

"It's standard course of action for an infraction of this nature."

"Yes, but…" Was it fair to play the bereavement card right now? She glanced at Maggie, who was sprawled in the chair next to her, looking out the window as if she were indifferent to the proceedings. As if her life wasn't falling apart all around them. She'd only been at the school for a week and she was already suspended. Laura could barely get her mind around it.

"Naturally, when we welcome Maggie back to school, we will expect her behaviour to be in line with the standards we uphold here at Burford Comprehensive."

"Of course," Laura murmured as she struggled not to break down and weep. She could tell the head teacher had labelled Maggie a bad kid, a troublemaker. She'd swanned into school with too much attitude, and within a week of starting she'd been found with a bottle of vodka—*vodka!*—in her locker, and caught smoking cigarettes behind the bike shed. All before the eleven o'clock break. This was the girl who had last year won the Year Eight history prize, been on the netball team, and been called by the head teacher 'an exemplary student and an encouragement to all.'

"So unless there are any other questions…" Ms Stevens said imperiously, and Laura leaned forward.

"No questions, but…" Laura forced herself to go on despite the head teacher's flinty-eyed look. "It's just we've been through quite a hard time recently." She remained unimpressed as Laura stammered through her explanation. "Maggie's father…my husband…he died very suddenly in a car accident only a year ago and we moved here to—"

"Mum, don't." Maggie's voice sounded like the crack of a whip and Laura stiffened.

"Maggie, I'm trying to explain…"

"*Don't.* This has nothing to do with that." She gave Ms Stevens a defiant look. "I don't care, okay? Suspend me.

Whatever."

Surprisingly, the head teacher's imperious look thawed slightly. "I appreciate you have had your difficulties, Maggie, and we have a counsellor at Burford who can help you work through whatever you are struggling with at the moment. But at the same time, there is no excuse for bad behaviour or breaking rules, and so I'm afraid the suspension still stands."

"Fine. I told you, I don't care." The sneer in her daughter's voice was belied by the tremble of her lips.

Laura rose from her chair. "Thank you, Ms Stevens," she said with as much dignity as she could muster.

"Maggie's form tutor will be in touch with work she can complete during the suspension."

"Right. Thank you." She hadn't even got her head round the fact of the suspension, never mind the practicalities. Maggie would be alone at home for a week while she was at work. Hardly ideal, yet what could she do?

They didn't speak as they headed back to the car, Laura's head throbbing and her heart heavy. Next to her Maggie walked with a defiant tilt to her chin and a swagger to her hips. Her eyes sparkled with anger—or tears. Laura didn't know which; she only knew she had, somehow and in some way, to reach her.

As she slid into the car, she rested her hands on the steering wheel and gazed out at the hard blue sky, everything diamond-bright and glinting under the wintry sunlight.

"Do you want to get a coffee in town?" she asked and

Maggie looked at her in disbelief.

"Seriously?"

"I want to talk, Maggie. I want to know what's going on in there." She tried to smile as she nodded towards Maggie's head, but her daughter didn't soften in the least.

"Oh, right." She rolled her eyes. "Then no thanks. I'd rather just go home."

Laura drew a steadying breath, doing her best not to feel stung. Maggie was *trying* to hurt her. That much she knew, but knowing it didn't make it hurt any less.

"Well, I think I could use a coffee," she said as she started the car. "We'll stop at Huffkins."

Maggie shrugged, turning to look out the window, as Laura drove out of the car park and into town.

Burford was almost impossibly quaint, with its long high street lined with terraced houses and shops, some of them five hundred years old, tumbling down to the single-lane bridge at the bottom of the street that was known as the 'Gateway to the Cotswolds,' although Laura had seen several villages claiming that title.

She found a parking space across from the café and soon they were settled at a table in Huffkins, with a hot chocolate and an Americano on the way.

"So." Laura rested her arms on the table as she tried to give Maggie an encouraging look. "Tell me what happened."

Maggie, as usual, was on her phone, and she didn't so much as look up as she shrugged her reply.

"Maggie, please. I know you're angry with me, and you have been, I think, for some time, but I want to help. I don't want to be your enemy."

Maggie's hair swung down in front of her face as she continued to gaze avidly at her phone. "You're not," she mumbled, which Laura found encouraging.

"I'm glad to hear that. So can you tell me what happened at school today?" Another shrug. "Let's talk about the vodka first. Who gave it to you?"

"A guy."

"A friend?"

Shrug. "Sort of."

Laura was doing her best not to imagine chilling scenarios of strange, nefarious *guys* plying her fourteen-year-old daughter with alcohol. "Why did he give it to you?"

"So we could drink it," Maggie said in a well-duh voice.

Well, yes, obviously, but why? Why was her once straight-A daughter suddenly turning into this angry, reckless rebel, and at only fourteen years old?

"Have you ever had alcohol before?" Laura asked after a moment, having no idea if that was the right question to ask. She was groping in the dark here, but she had to do something.

"Dad used to give me a sip of his beer." Maggie's voice was small and Laura's eyes pricked.

"I know he did," she said gently. "Guinness." He'd been drinking the same stout since she'd met him. She had a strange sensation of homesickness at the thought; she hadn't seen those brown bottles in the cupboard for over a year. "You miss him, Maggie. I know it's hard."

"I don't miss him." Back to the savage retort, the quick glare before she returned to her phone.

Why did she feel she had to be angry rather than sad? Did that somehow seem stronger? Their drinks came and Laura sipped her coffee for a moment, doing her best to organise her thoughts.

"What about the smoking?" she asked after a few minutes. "Had you done that before?"

"What does it matter?"

"I'm just trying to understand what happened today. This kind of behaviour doesn't seem like you, Maggie. I'm trying to understand where it's coming from."

"Mum, most kids my age drink and smoke," her daughter told her with hard-edged matter-of-factness. "You're just naïve."

"But you didn't. Or at least you didn't used to."

"So?" Maggie hunched her shoulder. "I'm getting older."

But Laura didn't think it was just a matter of age. Before Tim's death, Maggie had been focused, smart, steady. Yes, she'd had her fair share of teenaged angst and emotional moments; there had been a number of slammed doors and sudden outbursts of anger or tears. Laura didn't think she was romanticising the months and years before Tim's death; in fact, sometimes she felt as if she were doing the opposite.

It was so hard to remember someone accurately, once they were gone. Everything seemed to veer into sentimentality or regret, each extreme possessing its own temptations and trials.

"You don't seem happy, Mags," she said at last. "That's what I'm concerned about. The drinking, the smoking, yes, those worry me too, as they would any parent. But it's the reason for them that concerns me the most." She reached across the table for her daughter's hand, but Maggie yanked it away before she could so much as brush her fingers. "I love you," she said quietly. "I want to help you get through this—whatever this is. Would it help if I booked you in to see a grief counsellor?" Perhaps she should see one, too. She'd gone to a few sessions about six months after Tim had died, but she'd found them too draining. She could put her own emotions on ice while she dealt with her children's...or so she'd thought.

"I don't need any more counselling. None of that stuff actually helps."

Laura was inclined to disagree, but she knew she couldn't force her to go. "Well, think about it, at least," she said.

Maggie drained her hot chocolate and then pushed the cup away. "Can we go now?"

By the time they got home, the brief flicker of hope Laura had felt at having something of an honest conversation with her daughter had flickered out. Dan Rhodes had given her the rest of the day off, which seemed a bit pointless considering the moment they got home Maggie flounced up to her room and slammed the door.

Laura decided to tidy up, something she hadn't actually been able to do much of lately, and then paid some bills online, one ear cocked for any stirrings upstairs. Sam had Minecraft Club that afternoon, and had insisted he could walk home by himself, something Laura knew he was eager to try out, so with a couple of hours stretching in front of her she decided to take Perry for a walk, knocking on Maggie's door first to see if her daughter wanted to come.

"We could get some fresh air, maybe throw a ball for Perry," she suggested, a bit desperately, to which she received an emphatic no.

"Perry doesn't even like chasing balls anymore," Maggie said through the door, her voice muffled.

"We could try…"

Silence.

Laura went back downstairs, doing her best not to be discouraged. Baby steps. Patience. All that.

She was grateful for the fresh air, anyway, and Perry trotted along faithfully by her side as they wandered through the woods and then out to the landscaped gardens behind the manor house. She still hadn't met the owners, Alice and Henry, although she'd heard from her neighbours how lovely they were.

Laura was just turning back towards Willoughby Close when someone came out on the terrace and started waving frantically.

"Are you the new tenant in number three?" she called, her hands cupped around her mouth, and Laura shouted back:

"Yes, I am."

The woman, whom she assumed was Alice Trent, beckoned her forward. "I've been meaning to come down and meet you. I'm sorry I haven't. Can you come in for a cup of tea?"

Somewhat reluctantly Laura came onto the terrace with Perry to meet Alice. She looked very young, early twenties at most, with white-blonde hair and a porcelain, heart-shaped face. There was a beautiful, tiny bump under her jumper that she cradled lovingly.

"A cup of tea would be lovely," Laura said, "but I really should get back to my daughter. She's home from school today."

"Oh, dear. Ill?"

"Something like that." Laura smiled in a way she hoped would not encourage further questions. "But thank you for the invitation."

"Another time, definitely. I've been meaning to come round but I've had the most dreadful nausea." She said this with pride; clearly she was thrilled to be pregnant.

"It can certainly lay you low," Laura agreed. "But hopefully it will clear up soon? How far along are you?"

"Fifteen weeks." Alice stroked her bump. "Do you ever

stop feeling as if you're walking on eggshells?"

"Maybe not entirely," Laura replied with a smile. "But I think you get used to it." Her own pregnancies had been remarkably easy, with no nausea or much tiredness, and smooth deliveries. She had no real war stories to share, but she remembered the incandescent excitement of being pregnant for the first time, the sheer wonder of it.

"And you're settling in okay?" Alice asked with a touch of concern. "The cottage isn't too small? Jace mentioned you'd divided the master bedroom into two…"

"Yes, it's fine. And so quaint. You've done them up really nicely."

"Oh, *I* didn't," Alice told her with a laugh. "In fact, I lived in number four for a few months before Henry and I were married."

"Oh…"

"I wasn't born to this life, trust me," Alice assured her with a smile. "It still doesn't always feel real. But do tell me if there is anything Henry or I—or really, Jace—can do to make your life easier."

Laura knew she meant it, and she was touched. "That's very kind."

"And we must have you round for dinner—you have two children, right?"

"Yes, Maggie and Sam." There was a pause that somehow felt expectant and so Laura made herself say, "My husband died a year ago, so it's just the three of us."

Alice's expression was both shocked and dismayed at her potential insensitivity, which actually made Laura feel relieved. Lindy hadn't gone round telling everyone, as she'd feared she might do. Not that she wanted to have to tell everyone herself, but she hated the thought of being talked about.

"I'm so sorry…"

"It's all right. We're doing our best to make a life for ourselves here." What else could she say? And she did mean it.

"We will have you round," Alice declared. "I'll talk to Henry and then we can sort out dates."

Laura nodded, noncommittal, unsure whether she wanted to agree to a whole evening, although she knew she probably would. Like Chantal kept telling her, she needed to keep trying.

It was getting dark by the time Laura got back to the house, Perry flopping in front of the fire as she checked on Maggie—still in her room—and then started on dinner. It felt cosy, with twilight stealing over the meadows and hills, to be in the quaint cottage with the wood burner going merrily and bolognaise simmering on the stove. If only Maggie wasn't in such a state, Laura thought, and then felt guilty for not thinking of Tim first.

If only Tim were here. But he wasn't, and he hadn't been for a long time. *It's been more than a year*, Chantal had said, so kindly, and she'd been right. Tim had left their family, or at least her, emotionally well before he'd ever got in that car.

The acknowledgement, even in the quiet of her own mind, caused Laura's breath to come out in a shudder. She never let herself think that, because sometimes she couldn't remember if it had actually been true or not.

Yes, he'd been a bit distant emotionally before his death. Physically, too. But they'd still been married; they'd still slept in the same bed, ate at the same table, raised the same kids. Couples went through rough patches, and looking back, Laura didn't even know if she would have called it rough. It just *was*—day by day, getting on with things and not much more. The fact that he'd died on a day when they'd barely spoken, not out of anger but more out of tiredness, didn't necessarily have to signify anything. It was just hard.

And sometimes Laura wondered if it was, for some contrary reason, easier to remember the hard times rather than the easy ones. Chantal said people had a tendency to idolise those they'd lost, but what if the opposite could be true? What if Laura was sometimes remembering a husband who had been more distant and restless in her mind than in reality? It was so hard to know. In fact it was impossible, and that was something she just had to learn to live with, because Tim wasn't here to ask.

A light knock sounded on the door, and Laura was just turning when Sam burst into the house, a wide grin on his face.

"Minecraft Club was great!"

"I'm so glad to hear it."

"Yes, it really went well. Fourteen kids signed up."

Startled, Laura's gaze flew to the doorway where James was standing, his hands in the pockets of his parka, a lopsided smile on his face.

"Oh," she said rather stupidly.

"I walked Sam home," he explained unnecessarily. "It was pretty dark."

"Oh. You didn't..." Laura began, feeling that familiar mother-guilt. Should she have picked Sam up? Had she been negligent in letting him walk home by himself? He'd wanted to, but even so she started to doubt.

"I know I didn't," James said quickly. "And he would have been fine. But we were having quite an interesting discussion about Minecraft, and I wanted to see how you were."

His eyes, such a vivid blue green, were crinkled with compassionate concern.

"Oh, I, ah..." She shrugged helplessly, glancing at Sam who had already dived onto the sofa, iPad in hand. "I'm okay."

"Good." James didn't move, and Laura left the kitchen to join him at the door, lowering her voice as she spoke.

"Maggie's been suspended," she said, quietly enough that she hoped Sam couldn't hear, although she supposed he would find out soon enough. "For having a bottle of alcohol in her locker, and smoking at school." She shook her head, unable to keep the despair from colouring her voice. "She's only fourteen. She's never done anything like this before *ever.*"

"I'm sorry." Although the words could have seemed rote, James's tone was heartfelt. "Is there anything I can do?"

Laura hesitated, because really there was nothing he could do, and yet...it felt so *nice*, to have a masculine presence in her home, even if he was just standing at her door. It was nice, Laura realised, to know he'd walked Sam home, and that Sam had been able to chat to a guy about guy things for a little bit. It was nice not to feel like she was shouldering it all alone, even if just for a few minutes.

"I don't think so," she said a bit reluctantly, because she wished that there was, "but thank you for asking. I'm sure Sam enjoyed your company on the way home. He doesn't have many men in his life now. Just his grandfather, really."

"Well, I could stay for dinner," James said unexpectedly, and Laura stared at him in surprise.

"Not to invite myself over or anything, although clearly that's exactly what I'm doing," he continued with a grin. "But Sam seemed to enjoy talking to someone who actually knows all about Minecraft, and as it happens, I have a fair amount of experience with teenaged girls. My youngest sister is only sixteen."

"Oh my goodness," Laura exclaimed before she could help herself, "you must be so *young*." Younger than she'd thought. What if he was only twenty-five? *Why did it matter?*

It wasn't as if they were dating. Not at *all*.

"I'm thirty-two, actually," James answered with a laugh. "Bella was a surprise blessing for my parents."

"Oh, well…"

"Tell me to get lost if you want to," he said easily. "I promise I won't be offended. I just thought I'd suggest it, in case having a guy around for a bit could be helpful."

Laura hesitated, torn between the oddity of inviting him in, and the desperate desire to do just that. She thought of Chantal telling her to try, and then she thought about her urging her to get back in the saddle, or at least near the horse. "Actually," she told him, "that would be lovely. If you're free…"

"I am," James assured her. "And besides, do I smell bolognaise? Because that's my favourite."

Chapter Ten

JAMES STEPPED INTO the comforting warmth of Laura's cottage and felt it envelop him like a hug. Yes, it had been rather cheeky of him to invite himself over for dinner, but he was glad he'd done it. As he stood in the centre of the room he realised how much he missed being in a home, rather than a half-empty cottage full of paint samples and plywood, as he attempted to do up a house with very limited DIY skills.

But more than that, he missed the kind of home with a family in it—with something simmering on the stove, a sweater thrown over a chair, a dog by the wood burner and a pile of books tottering on the table. All of it was lovely. *Lovely.*

"I did tidy up," Laura told him with an uncertain laugh. "Not that you'd know it."

"I was just thinking how welcoming everything looks," James replied, "especially compared to my place. I bought a wreck and I've been doing it up *very* slowly."

"Do you live in Wychwood?"

"Yes, just off the high street. A tiny terraced cottage that hadn't been updated in about fifty years."

"Ah." She went back to the kitchen to stir the sauce, and James followed her, his hands in his pockets. And here was the other reason he'd invited himself over—to spend some time with Laura. He'd meant what he'd said about being her friend, but he couldn't deny to himself that he was attracted to her—not just her looks, which were undeniable, but the sense of steeliness and fragility emanating from her, the heartbreak and the humour mixed together. He leaned against the worktop as she turned to him with a nervous smile, tucking wisps of dark hair behind her ears.

"Is this too weird?" he asked, deciding to just put it out there.

She let out a laugh. "No. Not exactly. I told you, I'm a bit rubbish at this socialising thing. You might have to give me some pointers."

"Okay." He took his hands out of his pockets and folded his arms as he gave her a mock-considering look. "I'll give you an easy one to start. How are you finding Wychwood?"

"That's not as easy as it sounds," she answered, her voice both tart and teasing. "I'm finding it okay, but starting over is hard. I had a wobbly the first week, when I couldn't find the Waitrose in Witney. Dripping tears onto my trolley kind of stuff."

"I have a wobbly every time I go to Waitrose and see the bill," James replied. "I'm going to eat myself out of house and home if I keep shopping there."

"So that's why you invited yourself over," Laura said as she turned back to stir the sauce again. "Free meal."

"You've got me sussed." Were they flirting? James wasn't sure. It was definitely banter, but was he the only one imagining the undercurrents? Feeling them?

The dog had lumbered from his well-loved position by the wood burner to sniff hopefully at the bolognaise-scented air. James crouched down to scratch him behind the ears.

"I love golden retrievers. My parents have three dogs—one golden, a Lab, and a springer spaniel. What's this one's name?"

"Perry, short for Peritas."

"Alexander the Great's dog."

Surprise widened Laura's eyes and her mouth curved. "How did you know that? Did you study history at uni?"

"No, but I'm a geek." He grinned. "I studied English, but I love history." He straightened, and something in Laura's look made him feel like grinning. She looked considering, as if he'd just gone up in her estimation, which could only be a good thing.

"I'd hardly call you a geek," she said as she turned back to the stove.

"I lay full claim to my geek status," he replied. "And I am proud of it."

"And what is the evidence of this status? Do you carry a card?"

"I'm the youngest member of the Wychwood Chess

Club by about thirty years." She pursed her lips, considering, and then shook her head.

"Not enough."

"I have not one but three sweater vests in my wardrobe."

Her eyes sparkled. "Seriously?"

"They're warm."

"Even so…"

He leaned forward so there was no way Sam, immersed in his iPad, could hear. "You know, even geeks can be insanely gorgeous," he murmured.

A lovely rosy blush tinted her cheeks as she kept her eyes on the sauce. "You told me you were going to forget about that."

"I know, but it's hard not to remember."

The blush deepened, and for a second she risked a glance at him, and James felt as if the very air between them was sizzling. Okay, the undercurrents were real. And strong. And he was glad.

"Wait," Sam said, clambering up from the sofa and making Laura jump, "are you staying for dinner, Mr Hill?"

James turned to Sam with an easy smile. "Yes, if that's okay?"

"Yeah." Sam looked so thrilled that James couldn't help but feel a little bit like a rock star. A geeky one, of course. "Do you want to play Minecraft?" Sam asked eagerly, and James glanced at Laura who laughed and waved him away.

"Go on, then," she said, and with a smile for Sam, James

stretched out on the sofa and let the boy talk him through his complicated and admittedly genius strategy for building up his herd of cows.

He was so immersed in the game that he didn't hear Laura come over until she was standing behind the sofa, her hands braced on the back, leaning over to look at their game. She was close enough that he breathed in her lemony scent and the tip of her ponytail brushed his shoulder. Not that he should be noticing these things, never mind feeling them so acutely.

"Wow. Cows. Sam's explained it all to me a million times, but I'm afraid I still don't get it."

"You're too old, Mum," Sam said, his eyes still fixed firmly on the screen, and Laura's laughing gaze met James's as she raised her eyebrows.

"Too old, huh?"

"Then I'm too old, Sam," James said lightly. "I was twenty-one when Minecraft came out."

Sam looked up briefly, his nose wrinkling. "Nah, you're not too old," he said before returning to his screen. James turned to Laura, meaning to share the joke, but she turned away quickly.

Was she concerned about the difference in their ages? The thought actually gave him hope, because it meant she was thinking romantically, at least a little. Besides, how old was she, anyway? James would guess around forty, since she had a fourteen-year-old, but not much older, maybe younger. Nothing that concerned him, anyway, although perhaps he was getting ahead of himself.

He rose from the sofa and meandered over to the kitchen area, where Laura was slinging plates around.

"Can I help?"

"I should roust Maggie from her lair, if you don't mind setting the table."

"Sure."

She gave him a fleeting smile, but the relaxed atmosphere and easy banter they'd been enjoying earlier seemed to have morphed into something strained and the tiniest bit chilly. James told himself not to overreact.

Smiling back, he reached for the plates.

THIS WAS REALLY weird. It had been fun at first, and Laura had enjoyed the unexpected novelty of chatting and yes, flirting, at least a little, with an attractive man. If that made her a bad mother, a bad wife, a bad person, well...so be it. She was even willing to consider the idea that it didn't.

But then Sam had made that remark about her being too old and somehow even though she knew she should shrug it off, it had caught her on the raw and exposed all her vulnerabilities, or at least a couple of them.

She *was* too old. She was being ridiculous, flirting with James, in her clumsy, cack-handed way. He was probably just humouring her, the way he had when he'd told her she was gorgeous. Maybe he knew she had something of a crush on him and he was enjoying the bit of ego stroking. Maybe she was just something different.

However it played, it still made her feel foolish and a little bit humiliated, and then she wondered if she was being ridiculous, overreacting because that was what she did, what she couldn't keep herself from doing ever since Tim's accident, and that made her feel even more foolish. It was a never-ending, vicious cycle. One she needed to break out of, and she could only do that with effort. By trying, like Chantal had said.

Impulsively Laura grabbed her phone off the countertop and took a sneaky photo of James as he set the table before going to get Maggie. As she headed upstairs she texted Chantal the photo with the caption: *Guess who's coming to dinner?*

The response was instantaneous—a raft of emojis, relevant ones this time—hearts, fireworks, champagne, stunned face. *He really is INSANE!*

Laura struggled not to laugh out loud. All right, that had been reckless; now Chantal was going to think she was dating him, or something absurd like that. She'd just wilfully stoked the fire of her friend's wild conjecture. But it had been fun, and she realised as she knocked on Maggie's door, that she wanted to have fun. She wanted to enjoy having a handsome man in her house, at her dinner table. Was that so very wrong?

"Maggie, love, dinner's ready."

"Fine."

"We have a guest tonight," Laura said, because she thought her daughter would appreciate the warning.

"What?" Maggie's voice was a near-screech as she opened the door to glare at Laura suspiciously. "Who?"

"Sam's teacher. He walked Sam home from Minecraft Club and I'm thanking him by giving him dinner." Laura spoke as lightly as she could and did her best not to blush. Maggie's eyes narrowed further.

"Oh-kay," she said, sounding unconvinced.

Laura smiled. "It's just about ready."

As she came downstairs, she saw the table was laid; James had even used folded paper towels as napkins.

"Fancy," Laura remarked, and he ducked his head.

"I do my best. It's not often I eat in company. Half of my meals are standing at the sink, the other half in front of the TV, I'm ashamed to say."

"Well, enjoy eating at a table while you can," Laura returned. Her phone, still in her hand, lit up with a text from Chantal. *I want all the details!!!* Plus emojis, including some questionable ones. Quickly Laura swiped it off and put it away where James might not actually see a stray text. They'd definitely had enough of *that*.

As Laura drained the pasta, Maggie sloped downstairs, giving James an uncertain look while he offered a wide smile.

"Hello, I'm James."

"Mr Hill," Sam corrected, and James replied easily:

"Mr Hill to you, Sam, yes, while we're in school, but to your sister I can be James."

Maggie stayed silent. Laura doubted she would call him anything, but she'd seen how her daughter's eyes widened at the sight of James. For better or for worse, he really was that good-looking.

They all sat down, and Laura had a jarring moment as she looked around at their faces. Four people at the dinner table. It felt both good and strange, sad and sweet. She glanced at her children to see how they were finding it; Sam looked delighted, Maggie still wary.

James, fortunately, was an excellent conversationalist, especially with kids, which was a relief since Laura feared they might be fairly monosyllabic, save for Sam who only wanted to talk about Minecraft.

"Sam, you are such a nerd," Maggie said, without any aggression at least, when he started talking about the cows. Again.

"If Sam's a nerd, then I am too," James said lightly, without any censure. His smile, aimed at Maggie, included everyone. "I love Minecraft."

Maggie looked incredulous but a small, reluctant smile tugged at her lips and she dropped the subject, reaching over to pour herself another glass of milk. Laura shot James a grateful look, and was surprised to see his eyes narrow as his gaze scanned Maggie before he quickly looked away. Had she missed something?

Trying not to spiral into that special brand of parental paranoia, Laura steered the conversation to nicer topics— half-term and skiing being top of the list.

"You must all be so excited," James said.

There was a brief, awkward pause, before Sam said, "Mum's not going."

James glanced at Laura. "Oh?"

"I'm not a skier. And, you know, grandparent time." They'd finished eating so she rose to clear the table, and James stood to help her. "Coffee?" she asked when Maggie had retreated upstairs and Sam was back on the sofa. It was not quite privacy, but an approximation of it. "Or do you need to get back?"

James hesitated, and Laura cursed herself for asking. She'd probably sounded hopeful. Desperate. Of course he needed to get back.

"Sure," James said finally, and Laura almost said he didn't have to, before she decided to stop being so sensitive and just go with whatever flow was happening. She turned on the kettle while James scraped plates into the bin. She could imagine Chantal crowing exultantly about this. *He really is a keeper.*

As Laura made the coffee, however, she didn't think she was imagining the slight reserve that had come over him, like a chill. He wasn't offering his usual easy chitchat, and whenever she glanced at him he looked preoccupied.

She handed him his coffee and then leaned against the counter, raising her eyebrows in enquiry as she wondered if she had the courage to ask him what he was thinking about, because it was clearly something.

"Penny for your thoughts?" she asked lightly, and he gave her an abashed smile of acknowledgement.

"Sorry, I was miles away for a moment."

Which told her precisely nothing. Laura didn't dare ask anything more. She probably didn't want to know, anyway.

"So Maggie's been finding it tough?" James finally asked, pitching his voice low enough that Sam hopefully wouldn't hear.

"Mainly she's been angry. She had a nice group of friends back in Woodbridge—at least I thought they were nice. But after Tim died she declared they were all fake and basically refused to have anything to do with them. I hoped we'd have a reset here, but it hasn't worked out that way so far." She tried to smile and almost managed it.

"No," James agreed, and he looked so concerned for a moment that Laura's heart lurched.

"What?" she asked abruptly. "Why are you asking?"

James hesitated, and then he put his coffee cup down. Laura started to feel the icy fingers of panic clutch at her.

"James…"

"Can I talk to you outside for a minute?"

Okay, now she was properly panicked, heart thudding, hands icy. She glanced at Sam, who was oblivious.

"Okay."

They slipped outside, Laura closing the door behind them, in poor Perry's face. He'd been hoping for a wee, no doubt, and then his bedtime biscuit, although it was a bit early.

"James, what is it?" Her breath came out in a frosty puff that dissipated into the night air.

"Look, I don't want to panic you—"

"I'm already panicked."

"I'm sorry, Laura. I might be overreacting, but..." He looked so serious, so sad, that Laura was having trouble breathing. Everything in her clenched with fear. She'd been in this place before, and yet she *couldn't* be in it again now. What on earth could James be telling her? What could he possibly know about Maggie, who was safe upstairs in her bedroom, hopefully doing homework?

"When we were at dinner," James explained heavily, "I happened to see the inside of Maggie's arm, when she was reaching for the milk."

"What..." The word was expelled like a breath as she stared at him in confusion.

"There were some lines along the inside of her elbow. I've seen them before—both in pupils at school, mainly girls, but also on my own sister." He sighed as he met her gaze unhappily. "I think Maggie might be self-harming."

"Self..." Laura's mind reeled as she tried to absorb what he was saying. "You mean, cutting herself? Her *arm*?"

"Yes."

Laura opened her mouth to deny it, but no words came out. Maggie was angry, not depressed—and yet as soon as Laura had the thought, she knew it was wrong. Anger could cover lots of things—depression, sorrow, fear, grief. She knew that, of course she did, and yet somehow she hadn't really seen it in her daughter, not when the anger was so often directed at her.

"But..." she began, and then she found she couldn't say anything more. She felt, quite suddenly, as if she'd been punched in the gut, as if everything in her was crumpling. Then James's arms were around her and he drew her against his chest, and the touch was so intimate, so unexpected, that Laura's senses reeled again, an overload of pain and gratitude, of fear and comfort. She craved this, and yet she didn't want to need it in this moment. *Poor Maggie...*

"I'm sorry, Laura," James murmured. "I know you're already dealing with so much. But I couldn't not say something."

"I know," she whispered. "Thank you." Her cheek was pressed against his shoulder and she closed her eyes, savouring the feel of his arms around her even as her heart ached and ached for her daughter.

"There are a lot of resources out there to help," he continued. "And there's a fantastic counsellor in Witney I've had some of my pupils see."

"Year Sixes are self-harming?" The thought saddened her

even more.

"You'd be amazed, and not in a good way. It's hard to be a kid these days." He squeezed her gently before stepping away. "You're not in this alone," he told her, and teary-eyed, still-reeling Laura slowly nodded. For once she believed him.

Chapter Eleven

"YOU'RE SAM'S MUM, aren't you?"

Warily Laura looked at the woman who was gazing at her with a beady-eyed, brisk determination. It was Monday morning, and the Year Sixes were lining up with everyone else; Laura was about to head into school to start work.

"Yes..."

"I'm Harriet, Will's mum." She stuck out a hand, which Laura shook, mentally bracing herself for whatever came next. She'd heard about Harriet, of course, from several sources, about how she could be a bit much, in the nicest way possible, and how she ran half the committees in the village, and probably could do so with one arm tied behind her back.

She had three children, including the somewhat boisterous Will in Year Six. Laura remembered how Sam had been reserved in his judgement of Will, which had set off the clanging of alarm bells in Laura's brain.

"I was wondering if Sam would like to have a play date

with Will?" Harriet asked, and then wrinkled her nose. "I know they hate calling it a play date at their age, but I don't know what other term to use. A hang out? Will would roll his eyes at that one." She smiled encouragingly and, startled, Laura smiled back. This she had not expected.

"A play date?" she repeated, just to check.

"Yes, maybe later this week? If Sam is free?" Harriet raised her eyebrows in expectation while Laura struggled to come up with a coherent response. She couldn't remember the last time Sam had had a play date.

"Um, sure, yes," she finally managed. "Let me just check with Sam."

"Of course. I think Will mentioned it to him at Minecraft Club this week—he's been loving that, you know. And I love the lack of guilt over screen time." She smiled conspiratorially and Laura smiled back.

"Yes, it's so hard to pry Sam off that thing, but Mr Hill does say Minecraft is educational." She stumbled over his name slightly, so accustomed had she become to calling him James.

It had been two weeks since he'd come to dinner, told her about Maggie's self-harming, and given her a hug—three events that together felt as if they'd changed the shape of her life. After James had left, Laura had gone back inside, still reeling from it all, struggling to know how to talk to Maggie about what she'd learned.

After googling some helpful advice on various mental

health and parenting websites, she'd spoken to Maggie the next morning, when they were alone, having taken a personal day from work.

The conversation hadn't been the heartfelt unburdening she'd been secretly hoping for, but neither had it been terrible. Maggie had been defensive as usual, but not so angry, and when Laura had mentioned the marks on her arm—keeping James out of it—she'd rolled her eyes and said, "Oh, *chill*, Mum. Everybody does it. It's, like, normal."

"Hurting yourself is normal?" Laura couldn't keep the dismay from her voice.

"It's just a dare kind of thing." Maggie pulled up the sleeve of her jumper to show Laura the marks—three straight lines on the inside of her elbow, just as James had said. They weren't alarmingly deep, but neither were they mere scratches. She'd gazed at them sadly, feeling an overwhelming sorrow for all that had brought them to this moment.

"What do you use to make them?" she'd asked, trying to get her head around the whole horrible concept.

Maggie shrugged. "A razor, usually."

"A *razor*…" Appalled shock had hardened into maternal resolve. She needed to take control of this situation, instead of always trying to appeal to some more reasonable side of her daughter that she was no longer sure existed. *She* was the mother. She was going to make the rules.

And so she'd insisted Maggie go to counselling in Witney; the counsellor James had recommended fortunately had space for weekly appointments. She'd limited Maggie's time on her phone—a battle she hadn't had the energy to face in the last year—and made sure it was charging in the kitchen every night at nine o'clock.

Maggie had resisted and raged against these measures, as Laura had known she would, but instead of giving in to the endless guilt and self-doubt she had done her best to stay strong. And Maggie had, amazingly, relented.

Over the last two weeks, through Maggie's suspension and school after it, they'd made steps. Small steps, but progress nonetheless, and Laura was determined to look on the bright side. Chantal had said much the same, when she'd given her the rundown of what had happened, and her friend had been wonderfully pragmatic about it all.

"I haven't even told you the half of what I got up to at that age," she'd said with a theatrical shudder. "And I'm not sure I'm willing to, even now. I'm not saying you should dismiss it, of course, only that Maggie isn't the only one getting up to things. And you're taking the right steps, Laura. That's what is important."

It was, Laura knew, in no small part thanks to James that she'd had the strength to do any of it. He'd shared what his parents had done when his sister had been in a similar situation, and he'd checked in on her every day, sometimes just a smile and a lift of the eyebrow, other times a conversation in the schoolyard while Laura confessed she felt as if she were stumbling around in the dark.

"I imagine that's how most parents feel," he'd remarked equably. "It's a fearsome responsibility, isn't it, to raise another human being?"

"It certainly is." She'd glanced at him, curious, and also bold enough now their friendship had been somewhat cemented to ask, "Do you think you want children one day?"

James had smiled and shrugged. "Well, I've got to meet the right woman first, haven't I?"

Which surely wouldn't be her. She was edging onto the shelf when it came to child-bearing. She looked away, not wanting any of her thoughts to be reflected in her face, because while James had been a brilliant friend, Laura was struggling not to crush on him, which was difficult when he was being so lovely.

But at least she'd got through the week of Maggie's suspension, taking the afternoons off work to spend time with her daughter, and Maggie had gone back to school peaceably enough. She had two counselling sessions under her belt and she seemed a little less angry, although her quietness still worried Laura, if she let it.

"So later this week?" Harriet prompted, and Laura realised she'd been miles away.

"Sorry, yes. I'll check with Sam and get back to you tomorrow."

"Great." Harriet cocked her head, her smile turning sympathetic. "How are things? I heard through the Wychwood grapevine that you lost your husband a year ago."

Laura knew she shouldn't be surprised that Harriet had heard; she'd told enough people for word to get around. Amazingly, she didn't dread the conversation about it as much as she might have even just a few weeks ago. She'd progressed in that way, too.

"Yes, a car accident the December before last. It's been hard, but we're getting there."

"I'm so sorry. I'm sure everyone says that, but I do mean it. And the truth is, I don't know what else there is to say."

"Not much," Laura admitted. "It's not an easy conversation to have on either side, to be honest."

"No." Harriet was quiet for a moment. "I went through a rough time a few years ago—nothing like what you've experienced, of course—"

Laura held up a hand to stop that avenue of apology she'd been down too many times before, with no one feeling like they could share their own griefs, as if that would somehow be presumptuous or inappropriate. "It's not a competition."

"No," Harriet agreed with a small, relieved smile. "Anyway, it was all a bit of a mess. My husband and I separated—he had what I suppose you'd call an emotional affair—we lost our house and the lifestyle to which I had become accustomed." She made a face. "And that is as snobby as it sounds, unfortunately. I had a really privileged position, and somehow I thought it had been all up to me. Anyway." She blew out a breath. "I was humbled in a big way, and that actually turned out to be a good thing. And I don't even know where I'm going with this anymore."

She let out a slightly wobbly laugh that heartened Laura. She had not expected the intimidating Harriet Lang to be so real. "Oh, yes," she continued. "I remember now. The difficult conversation. I did my best to avoid those. The schoolyard felt like the ninth circle of hell for a while." Laura nodded in sympathy. She knew exactly how that felt. "But eventually I realised it was up to me to handle the conversations, to tell people where I was and how I felt about it." She raised her eyebrows, her smile turning self-conscious. "I have no idea if any of that is helpful to you. If it's not, you can tell me to shut it."

"No, it is," Laura assured her. "I've been more or less existing in a fog for the last year, but I'm coming to realise it's up to me to step out of it, into the light. Baby steps, admittedly, but still, I am moving in the right direction. I think."

"That's really good to hear." Harriet briefly laid a hand on her arm. "Let me know about the play date. And perhaps we can grab a coffee sometime?"

"That would be lovely," Laura said, meaning it. She really was coming on in life. Coffee with friends, drinks at the pub, and James, of course. Chantal would be thrilled.

"Hey."

Laura's soft voice had James looking up from the literacy

work he'd been marking, his stomach doing a little flip at the sight of her standing in the doorway of his classroom. It was nearly four o'clock, and the school had emptied out leaving only Dan Rhodes in his office and the cleaners mopping the school hall, the smell of the cleaning fluid they used lingering astringently in the air. Already dusk was drawing in and James thought he should turn the light on. He hadn't quite realised he was sitting in the half-dark until Laura stepped into the room, out of the shadows.

He'd done his best to be her friend these last few weeks, and he'd enjoyed the chats they'd had while trying not to freeze to death in the schoolyard. He'd been heartened to see how Laura had opened up, how humour had begun to replace wariness. Although, he realised, she was looking a little wary now.

"Where's Sam?" he asked.

"Play date with Will Lang."

"That's good. They've bonded over Minecraft."

"So it seems. I almost didn't believe it at first. I can't remember the last time Sam had a play date. Year Four, perhaps."

"Well, this is a new start, isn't it?" James said with a smile. Why was she looking so nervous?

"Yes." She took a step closer to his desk, and then reached into the colourful cloth bag she brought to work every day. "I got you this, as a thank you. For being there for me, these last few weeks." With a self-conscious smile she put a bottle of wine on his desk.

James stared, unsure how he felt about the offering. It felt a *little* bit like payment for services rendered; did friends really have to give each other gifts just because you'd listened?

"I hope that's okay," she said uncertainly, and he realised he should have spoken.

"Of course it is, as long as you drink it with me," he told her, and her eyes widened in alarmed surprise.

"Oh, I…I don't…"

"Or we could just get a coffee," James filled in easily, sensing the need to back off. "I'm done here. Do you have time or do you need to get back to Maggie?"

"Maggie's at art club, actually, so I'm at a bit of a loose end."

"Well, then. Tea on the Lea is calling our names."

She hesitated, and then gave a nod. "All right. That would be nice."

James stood up and reached for his jacket. "How's Maggie, anyway?" he asked, as he had done nearly every day in the last two weeks.

"She seems okay, not that she'd tell me in so many words. I've stopped hoping for some massive, heart-rending breakthrough and am just focusing on the baby steps."

"Sounds wise."

"Well, I suppose a little wisdom is a good thing to come by at my age."

Ah, the age thing again. Sometimes she seemed fixated. "You're not that old, surely," he commented, and she just shrugged. "How old are you?" he pressed. "Forty?"

Laura grimaced. "Forty-one."

"You've still got your whole life in front of you."

"Doesn't everyone?" she joked. "The rest of it, anyway. Although really Chantal says the same thing, but…it's not exactly true, is it? I mean, at some point you absolutely don't have your whole life in front of you. That's a fact." She eyed him almost defiantly; her words felt like a warning.

"That's true," James agreed as he slipped his bag over his shoulder and they started walking out of the classroom. "But at forty-one I'd say you still have loads of things to look forward to."

"Maybe," she allowed grudgingly. James considered that a win.

They chatted about innocuous school stuff all the way to the teashop on the high street, which was mostly empty, save for a table of mums who eyed their entrance with avid speculation that didn't bother James but made Laura blush the colour of beetroot.

"Shall we sit in the back?" James murmured. Away from prying eyes.

"So, I'm actually feeling a bit guilty," Laura announced once they'd ordered their coffees.

James raised his eyebrows, surprised by the look of steely determination in her direct gaze. "Guilty? About what?"

"About the fact that you've been brilliant these last few weeks, asking about my children and my life and always listening to me moan—"

"I wouldn't call it moaning."

"Close enough." Her lips curved wryly and his stomach flipped again. Did she know how lovely she was? How much he ached to skim the porcelain softness of her cheek, or tuck a tendril of dark hair behind her ear? The last few weeks had been wonderful, but they'd also possessed a certain agony, knowing he was only her friend, and that when it came to something more, he had to tread very carefully indeed.

"Anyway," Laura resumed, "I haven't reciprocated at all. I have no idea how you're doing, what your life is like, what's tough about it. So." She laid her hands flat on the table. "Hit me with it."

"Hit you with what, exactly?" He suddenly felt guarded, which was a little strange.

"What's hard in your life? What do you struggle with? What do you wish could change? And how can I help?" She let out an uncertain little laugh. "Because right now this friendship feels pretty one-sided, you know?"

"Hmm." He scrambled to think of something to say. "I'm not sure what to tell you."

Disappointment flashed across her features, and James had the cringing feeling that he'd hurt her. "Nothing's going wrong?" she queried lightly. "Relationships, work, health...all of it pretty much perfect?"

"Well, I do have a slightly tricky knee, from when I fell as a kid." He meant it as a joke—sort of—but it fell flat. Laura just shook her head, and their coffees came, leaving James struggling to know how to fill the silence.

He realised he'd liked being the rescuer, the one who could offer a listening ear, a shoulder to cry on. It had made him feel strong, the hero of the hour, an unusual feeling to be sure, and the knowledge that he'd liked it, that he'd wanted that, was a bit shaming. Laura was right. What kind of friendship was it if he stayed up on his squeaky white charger while she grovelled in the complicated mire and muck of life?

"I had a break-up," he said abruptly, "a few months before I moved to Wychwood. It was one of the reasons why I did."

Laura's eyebrows rose as she sat back in her seat, sipped her coffee, and waited for more.

"Her name was—is—Helen. We dated for three years. She broke up with me when I started talking about marriage." This was a lot harder than he'd hoped it would be. He was over Helen—mostly—but he still didn't like talking about her.

Laura cocked her head, her gaze sweeping slowly over him. "Why did she break up with you?"

"Well, I think that would be fairly obvious." He tried for a laugh, but it sounded brittle. "She didn't want to marry me."

"But why not? Did she give a reason?"

"Not really." He glanced down at his barely touched coffee. "Just that it had been fun, but she didn't see it going anywhere. I wasn't adventurous enough, apparently." But she'd only said that when he'd pressed her, desperate for her to give a reason that he could argue against. "Looking back, I think we were both in the relationship for convenience. You know, you hit thirty, and the thought of having to meet someone new is both tiring and terrifying."

Laura let out a little laugh. "Try feeling that way at forty. Or forty-one, to be precise."

Which gave him the perfect opportunity to turn the tables. "So you want to meet someone new?"

"Nuh-uh." Laura held up a hand. "We're talking about you right now."

"Darn. I thought I was almost away there."

"Nope." The smile she gave him was warm, lingering. Her eyes had flecks of gold in them that made him think of stars. "So you weren't utterly heartbroken, then?"

"No. Heart bruised, perhaps. I saw my older sister and brother getting married, having kids, and I wanted that. I still do." A shadow passed across her face and he wondered if he'd just put his foot right in it. Did she think her age disqualified her somehow? Had he friend-zoned her without meaning to? "All I'm saying," he explained a bit awkwardly, "is that I want to find the right woman. And it wasn't Helen."

"Well, that makes sense," Laura said, a bit quickly. "I mean, it's understandable." A slightly laden pause. "So what made you decide to move to Wychwood?" Clearly she wanted to stop talking about romance and right people, which was both disappointing and a bit of a relief. Honesty was easy to listen to, hard to speak. And James had a feeling Laura would be demanding more of it from him—which was a good thing, but also surprisingly scary.

Chapter Twelve

LAURA SCHOOLED HER expression into one of friendly interest as she waited for James's response. It had been foolish to let his remark about wanting a family to sting. She wasn't in the running. She *knew* that. And yet for some stupid reason she had to keep reminding herself of that very obvious fact.

"Well, I was ready to get out of London," he said as he rotated his coffee cup between his palms. He seemed far less at ease talking about himself than listening to her problems, but Laura supposed that was true for anyone. Vulnerability was hard. It left you raw. "And Wychwood is closer to my family. My older sister lives near Cheltenham, my younger in Monmouth, and then two still at home. All within shouting distance of here."

"Your parents have a farm, you said?"

"Yes, near Shrewsbury. Cows and a few sheep."

"You didn't want to follow your family's footsteps and become a farmer yourself?" She spoke lightly, teasingly even, but James's expression darkened briefly.

"No. My brother does that."

Ah. There was tension there, clearly. It was interesting, and somehow reassuring, to know that his life wasn't as uncomplicated as he'd first made it seem. It made her feel a little less of a wreck. "Older or younger?" she asked.

"Older. And far better at farming than I ever was or could be. So." He smiled, but it didn't reach his eyes, and Laura felt a shaft of sympathy for him.

"That sounds like a bit of a sore point."

He looked surprised; perhaps he'd thought he was better at hiding it. "Yes, I suppose it is. Remember when I told you I was bullied as a kid?"

"Yes…"

"Well, that was in part because I was what I will kindly call a late bloomer. *Very* late. And I couldn't do all the farm chores my brother Jack could, who was a big, strapping lad, at least not until I was about sixteen or seventeen, and my father had more or less given up on me. So I suppose it has always been there between us—that I was somehow a failure, although my brother, who never went to university, feels like I'm a bit smarmy about being educated. I don't think I am, but who knows? We both have chips on our shoulders, I guess." He shrugged, as if to dismiss it all, but the movement, for James especially, seemed a bit brittle.

"It's hard to know if we can ever see another person clearly." She'd meant to be talking about his family, but James was too sharp for that.

"Who can't you see clearly, Laura?"

The way he said her name felt like fingers running over her skin. "Tim, I suppose," she admitted. Talking about him with James still felt strange, like picking at a scab, unsure how red and raw the skin was underneath. How much she might bleed.

"In what way?" James's voice was gentle.

"When someone dies," Laura said slowly, feeling for the words, "it's like you can't criticise them anymore. It wouldn't be fair. Or right." She felt a lump forming in her throat and she did her best to speak past it. "And I understand that. It's important not to speak ill of the dead, of course, and yet…it doesn't always leave room for complicated feelings." She took a sip of coffee, needing to claw back some composure. It felt good, being honest, but it also felt incredibly painful.

"What were your complicated feelings for Tim?" James asked after a moment, when the threat of tears had thankfully passed.

"I was angry with him," she admitted.

"Angry for dying?"

"Yes, but also for things before that. Angry for dragging us out to Woodbridge to chase his dream, never mind anyone else's." She bit her lip, shocked by her own admission. She'd never even let herself *think* that before, and yet here she'd blurted it right out.

"That's understandable," James murmured.

"And more than that," she continued in a rush. She felt as if she'd pulled her finger out of the hole in the dam and now all the messy truth was spilling out. "When his business never took off, I was angry about that. I blamed him, although I never said as much. I felt he should have realised it wasn't going to work, that you can't just plonk yourself down in a strange town and expect people to hire you. Trust you. But I never told him that, because I wanted to be encouraging, and so it wasn't fair for me to resent him doing what I'd basically encouraged him to do." She sighed, old sorrows sweeping through her. "We never actually argued, but we became distant. The last few months it felt as if we were just moving around one another." Laura looked down at her lap, doing her best to stay composed.

Silently James reached over and covered her hand with his own, and that was enough for a single, runaway tear to slip down her cheek. She dashed it away quickly.

"Sorry," she whispered.

"Don't be."

She made herself look up at him. "This was supposed to be about you telling me your troubles and once again I've gone and hogged all the drama."

"I don't mind, Laura." His gaze was warm, his hand still on hers, and Laura felt a yearning in her that was so strong it felt like a force field emanating from her fingertips. Then she caught the transfixed, open-mouthed stare of a school mum from the other side of the teashop and she yanked her hand away from James's.

"We are going to be providing the school gate gossip for the rest of the term."

James shrugged, as easy as ever. "So what if we did?"

"Do you really want the parents of all your pupils thinking you're having some—some *thing* with a woman ten years your senior?" She laughed to show the ludicrousness of it, which hurt her all the more, but she *had* to put it out there. She had to let James know that she realised what this was about. Friendship, and nothing more.

"Nine," James said quietly, "and I wouldn't mind."

Her breath felt as if it were trapped in her lungs as she found herself staring at him, as transfixed as the woman across the room had been. His eyes were the colour of the Caribbean and she *couldn't* look away. She didn't want to.

"James…"

"I like you, Laura. A lot." He gave an abashed smile as he spread his hands wide. "I've been meaning to give you space, because I know you've got a lot to deal with and you're still grieving, but if you're going to put me up against the wall I'll say it. I like you. I'd ask you out on a date if I thought you'd say yes."

Her head spun and her stomach fizzed. She felt a million different things and she didn't know what any of them were. "And you don't think I would?"

"I've suspected you wouldn't, considering how cagey you get whenever the conversation drifts even remotely that way."

She glanced down at her coffee again, having no idea what to say. What to feel.

James leaned forward, his voice dropping to a murmur. "Am I wrong?"

Once again she made herself look up at him. "I…I don't know. There's a lot to consider."

"I know."

"But you've known all along how insanely gorgeous I think you are," she couldn't resist saying, managing a smile. "And in the last few weeks I've learned how kind and caring you are, as well." She drew in a shuddery breath, hardly able to believe she was willing to admit this much. Risk this much. "Altogether it's a pretty tempting combination, I have to say."

James's gaze blazed into hers as his mouth quirked in a small, wry smile. "That's very good to hear."

"I'm not a good bet, James," she felt compelled to warn him. "Even for a date. I haven't dated in nearly twenty years. I don't even know how it's done anymore."

"I'm no expert, but I'd say it's about time you went on one, then."

She shook her head slowly. "You make it sound so easy."

"Can't it be?"

"I don't know," she said honestly. "I really don't."

"Well, we could start with a date, and see how it goes from there. Low risk, then."

Her heart bumped and she pressed one hand to her chest. "That suggestion actually terrifies me."

"Hence why I haven't actually asked you out yet. Officially." His smile was wry but his eyes looked sad. "I don't want to pressure you, Laura. That's the last thing I want right now."

"I know." Her breath hitched and she quite suddenly lurched up from the table. "I should get home. Maggie will have finished art club and I like to be there when she gets back."

"Okay." He was, as ever, unruffled by her sudden need to bolt. Laura fumbled for her wallet.

"Let me get the coffees…"

"No, I will." His tone was uncharacteristically firm. "Then we can consider this our first date." He glanced up at her, eyes sparkling. "Then we'll have already got that out of the way.

"I'M *SO* PLEASED to see you!"

Chantal wrapped Maggie and then Sam in big bear hugs, which Laura was thankful her children submitted to more or less graciously. Sam even put his arms around his godmother. Not that Chantal would have been bothered either way; her hugs were of the bulldozing variety.

She glanced up from Sam to smile at Laura. "And I want to hear everything that's going on in that little chocolate-box village of yours. *Everything*," she repeated meaningfully.

Laura hadn't yet told her friend about the loaded conversation she'd had with James at Tea on the Lea. Four days on and she was still fizzing from it. She'd thought about texting Chantal more than once, but it felt like too much information to download via a few acronyms and emojis. She wanted a face-to-face conversation, preferably over a bottle of wine.

"I'm sure we'll be happy to tell you everything," she said lightly. She glanced at Maggie, who had perked up at the prospect of a trip to London to see Chantal and hit the markets stalls in Camden Town. They'd been planning to visit last weekend, but with Maggie's suspension Laura had decided to postpone it until they were on a more even keel, which she *hoped* they were now, although she wasn't entirely sure.

Maggie didn't seem so angry anymore, but she was still worryingly quiet, a closed book to Laura, her pages firmly shut, although sometimes she lightened, offering Laura a smile like a benediction.

But Laura wasn't going to worry about all that now; she wanted to live in the moment, to enjoy each one as it came, even if it took effort. This weekend they were in London and she intended to enjoy it.

Chantal had made an enormous lentil curry for lunch, which was delicious if somewhat outside of Sam's comfort zone, but he gave it a valiant effort until Chantal, militant vegan that she pretended to be, broke down and made him a bacon sandwich.

"You spoil him," Laura told her with a laugh, and Chantal shrugged.

"I'm his godmother. I'm allowed to."

After lunch, despite the freezing temperatures, they went for a walk along the lock and then through Camden Market, where Maggie happily browsed funky stalls and asked Laura if she could have a belly button piercing—even Chantal looked askance at that one.

"When you're eighteen you can do what you want," Laura reminded her. "No body piercings until then." But she said it with a smile, and Maggie's momentary huff was just that, nothing more. Laura breathed a bit easier.

"So," Chantal said as she dropped back to walk alongside Laura, Sam browsing through a comic book stall and Maggie sorting through a tray of junk jewellery. "What's the latest on Mr Hottie?"

Laura couldn't keep a smile from curving her lips as her heart beat harder just at the thought of James. "Not now," she murmured, nodding towards her children, who had ears like bats, at least when it suited them.

"So it must be something really interesting, then," Chantal said with bright-eyed satisfaction and Laura grinned.

"Maybe."

"Oh, Laura!" Chantal crowed, grinning herself.

Maggie turned back to them suspiciously. "What is it?"

"Just teasing your mum," Chantal told her. "Just really pleased she's settled into life in Wychwood so well."

Maggie eyed them both slowly, still suspicious, and Laura felt herself tense. She wasn't remotely ready to talk about the prospect of dating someone with her children yet. She hadn't even talked about it with James since their coffee at Tea at the Lea, and to his credit he hadn't pressed the matter any further. Their relationship at school had fallen back into comfortable lines, but all the while the possibility of a date had sparked inside Laura.

"We're talking later," Chantal promised under her breath, and Laura nodded her agreement.

Later wasn't until that evening, after they'd had fish and chips for tea from a local shop, and Maggie and Sam were curled up on Chantal's huge leather sofa watching Netflix.

"Right," Chantal said briskly, eyeing her two godchildren rather beadily. "Your mum and I are going to have a proper catch-up at the pub across the street. And you two are going to be good as gold, aren't you?" She cocked a thumb at Maggie. "Nothing dodgy on your phone, my girl. I was fourteen once, even if they didn't have smartphones way back then."

A smile tugged at Maggie's lips and she rolled her eyes. "Fine."

"And don't go cross-eyed, staring at your iPad," Chantal instructed Sam. "Watch a film instead. Much better for you." Sam rolled his eyes just as Maggie had, and Chantal cackled with laughter. "Right. We're off."

The pub across the street was as far from The Three Pennies as was possible—instead of squashy armchairs and an open fire, there was techno music, high bar stools, and crushed velvet sofas in a violent shade of purple.

"I'm going all girly and having a cosmopolitan," Chantal announced. "What about you?"

"I'll have the same," Laura said. She felt reckless in an exciting way, liberated, brimming with possibility. It was both wonderful and fairly terrifying, and entirely new.

Chantal fetched their drinks while Laura bagged a sofa, and soon they were settled, sipping their luridly coloured cocktails. Chantal wasted no time getting to the heart of the matter.

"So, spill. Something's happened. What is it?"

"Nothing's happened," Laura assured her. "Honestly, it's probably nothing." She felt a sudden need to backtrack, but Chantal wasn't having it.

"You wouldn't be looking like the canary who ate the cat, or the cat who ate the cream, or whoever ate what, if nothing had happened. What?" She raised her eyebrows, expectant, impatient.

"Well, James sort of asked me out."

"Sort of?"

Quickly Laura explained their conversation while Chantal listened, rapt. "I like this guy, Laura," she said at the end. "I really like him."

"I think I do too," Laura whispered, and then, to her

surprise and mortification, her eyes filled with tears. "I don't know why I'm crying," she exclaimed, annoyed at herself as she swatted at her eyes. "It must be the alcohol."

"You've barely had a sip." Chantal pulled her into a one-arm hug, both of them managing to hold their cocktails aloft as they embraced. "I know why you're crying. Because this is big. You're moving on, Laura, and that can feel hard but it's okay. It's good."

"But I'm not really moving on," Laura protested with a sniff. "We haven't even gone out on a date yet. He hasn't even *asked* me yet. Not really."

"That's just semantics. He *will* ask you, and you *will* go out. And it is just a date. Not a wedding ring. Not even a commitment. A *date*."

"Right." Laura gave her friend a shaky smile. "Right," she said again, and gulped her cocktail.

"I gather you haven't mentioned any of this to your lovely children?" Chantal asked with a cocked eyebrow.

"Absolutely not," Laura said with a shudder. "I have no idea what they'd think about it. I'm not sure I want to know. And I'm afraid Maggie will get all angry again. I'm not sure I'd blame her."

"They have to know at some point," Chantal pointed out gently.

"Yes, when something is actually happening. I mean, why freak them out? We might go on a date and it's awkward and awful and weird, and that's that." Laura took another gulp of her cosmopolitan. "That's probably what will happen, to be honest."

"I don't think so," Chantal returned. "But the important thing is to find out. *Go* on that date. Start living again."

"I have been living," Laura protested, but her voice sounded weak. She knew she hadn't been, not really, and the baby steps she'd been taking since moving to Wychwood had felt hard but good. Yet this wasn't a baby step. This was big. And also terrifying, thrilling, wonderful and utterly alarming all at once.

Could she do it? Was she ready? What if Maggie and Sam weren't ready for her to date? And then there was a whole host of other complications…like the fact James was nine years younger than her. That he wanted a family, children of his own that Laura probably couldn't provide. That there was guilt and grief and fear she knew she still hadn't dealt with. And, if she wanted to project down the line, she had a middle-aged body with saggy boobs and stretch marks and James was just a little over thirty. *Thirty.*

"Laur," Chantal said gently. "Stop."

Laura looked up from her moody contemplation of her drink with surprise. "What?"

"Stop overthinking. I can hear your brain whirring away from here. Just go with it, Laura. Live in the moment, including this one." She hefted her glass high and clinked it with Laura's. "Here's to you snagging the hottest man in the Cotswolds."

"I haven't—"

"Drink up," Chantal cut across her, and she did just that.

Chapter Thirteen

COMING BACK TO Wychwood after a weekend with Chantal could not help but feel, Laura acknowledged, like a little bit of a let-down. Maggie and Sam were quiet in the car as they pulled into a darkened Willoughby Close on Sunday night; the sharp, freezing cold had given way to something dank and damp that made spring feel even further off.

Unlocking the front door, Laura told them to bring in the bags while she fetched Perry from Lindy's, who had kindly offered to take him for the weekend.

"How was it?" Lindy asked as soon as she'd opened the door, Perry making a mad dash for Laura, or at least as much of a mad dash as a ten-year-old retriever could make. It was more of a hurried amble. "Did you have a lovely time?"

"Yes, really lovely." As Laura had left, Chantal had given her a tight hug and whispered in her ear, "*Go* for it, girl. I love you."

"Perry was wonderful as always, but I think he was pining a bit," Lindy said, laughing as she saw the dog thrust his head between Laura's knees, desperate for affection. "And I made you these." She proffered a plastic container of delicious-looking fudgy brownies. "I made some for Jace, because Ava had her baby last night!" Her voice rang out with excitement.

"Oh, wow—"

"A little girl, Zoe. They're coming home tomorrow and I for one can't wait to have a cuddle. If you like, we could stop by together?"

"If Ava's up for it…" Laura began, slightly taken aback because she didn't actually know Ava all that well, although snuggling with a newborn baby sounded lovely.

"She says she is. I'm sure there will be a parade of people through the house, but I'll let you know when she tells me a good time."

Back at number three, Laura saw that Maggie and Sam had indeed brought in their bags, leaving them in a jumble by the front door, and had disappeared up to their bedrooms. With a sigh she began to sort through the post before starting on the washing, surprised and pleased to see a card from Alice inviting them all to dinner at Willoughby Manor next week.

She'd been slightly dreading a return to a community that didn't know them very well, but she was heartened by all these positive signs—Lindy, Ava, now Alice. And of course James.

Never mind the niggling sense of disappointment that he

hadn't texted, even though she'd told him she was going to London for the weekend. What had she been expecting? A note pushed under her door, saying how much he'd missed her? Flowers?

Shaking her head at her own absurdity, Laura stooped down to unzip Sam's bag and take out a weekend's worth of dirty laundry that had been crammed into it.

She'd put the wash on and boiled the kettle to make a cup of tea for Maggie—forever trying to build bridges—when her phone pinged promisingly. *How was the weekend away?*

Laura couldn't keep the silly grin from spreading over her face as she read James's text and then quickly replied. *Great. How was yours?*

Quite nice, actually. Went to Cheltenham to see my sister's new baby, Hannah. She is very small.

Laura let out a soft snort of laughter at that. *Babies do tend to be small,* she texted back. *I'm going to get a cuddle myself when I see Ava's baby this week.*

Good stuff. Followed by several relevant baby-themed emojis. Laura was still smiling as she considered her reply when a voice, sharp with suspicion, interrupted her thoughts.

"Who are you texting?"

Laura looked up to see Maggie scowling at the bottom of the stairs. "What?" she said, mainly to stall for time.

"I could hear the ping of your phone from upstairs." This said like an accusation. "Who are you texting so much?"

"Chantal." The lie fell easily from her lips, even as Laura

wished she had just told the truth. But then Maggie might have freaked out, because really, what reason could she possibly have for texting James Hill and talking about babies, of all things? A confusing tumult of feeling roiled in her stomach and she put her phone on the charger before reaching for a couple of mugs.

"Cup of tea?" she asked as lightly as she could.

Maggie hunched one shoulder. "Okay."

Laura regarded her daughter quietly as she made the tea. Although Maggie hadn't seemed as angry lately, she still, Laura realised, didn't seem very happy. She only wished she knew how to breach her daughter's bristling defences. From everything she'd read in books and online, she simply needed to be patient and keep trying. She handed Maggie a cup of tea, milky and sweet the way she liked it.

"How's your homework?"

"I've got a little."

"How are things at school?" Laura tried to sound as casual as she could. "With friends, I mean." Shrug. "You know the guy who gave you that alcohol," she said quietly, needing to say it even though Maggie would resist. "He wasn't really a friend, Mags. To ask you to keep it for him—"

"Oh, Mum, can you please not sound like some stupid counsellor for two seconds?" Maggie snapped and with a huff she whirled around and went upstairs. Laura sighed and slumped against the counter, just as her phone pinged again.

She glanced at it wearily, the excitement she'd felt earlier draining away. It was from James. *I can walk Sam home from Minecraft Club tomorrow again if you like.*

Was he angling for another dinner invitation, or just being nice? Both? Laura felt too weary now to wonder or reply. How could she be flirting by text with a man so much younger than her, when her daughter was clearly hurting, and life still felt so complicated? When her husband had only been gone for a little over a year?

It felt wrong, even though she loved the little flutters of excitement James caused her, and how they made her feel alive again, as if she were finally waking up from a long sleep. Then she remembered Maggie's sharp voice, asking who she was texting, and she feared her daughter would have even more of a meltdown if she knew Laura was thinking of dating again.

She put the phone back on charge without replying and headed upstairs.

THE DAMP, DANK weather continued into the week, and Monday morning Laura walked to school with Sam under a heavy grey sky, her mood feeling low despite all the hopeful signs of yesterday—Ava, Lindy, Alice. And yes, James. Somehow she was going to have to tell him she wasn't ready to go out on a date. That she didn't think her children were ready.

"I'm going to whip round to Waitrose after school and then I'll pick you up from Minecraft Club," Laura told Sam as they headed into the schoolyard. "So if I'm a few minutes late, don't worry."

Sam's face fell. "Can't Mr Hill walk me home?"

"That was a one-off, Sam." Even if he'd asked again.

"He said he didn't mind." Sam gave her a sideways look, half pleading, half defiant. "I like talking to him. He's cool, for a teacher."

Laura hesitated, knowing Sam needed a man in his life; the only one right now was his grandfather, who preferred watching the footy to playing a board game, and probably didn't even know what Minecraft was.

"Okay," she relented. "If he offered."

"And can he stay for dinner again?"

"*Sam.*" Laura looked at him, exasperated. She was being railroaded into a set of events she actually wanted, which made it difficult to say no and mean it.

"What?" Sam looked at her innocently.

"Mr Hill probably has plans."

"I'll ask him—"

"Let me talk to him first," she said quickly. She didn't need her son to act as a go-between for this. Although on second thought, perhaps she did. She still didn't know what she was going to say, or how to make it not feel awkward.

Fortunately, James remained as relaxed as ever when Laura broached the subject during their usual lunchtime chat.

"Sam is keen on you walking home," she stated, her tone

one of apology.

James smiled, eyebrows raised. "Great."

"And he'd like you to come to dinner again," she continued in a rush. "But please, please don't feel obligated. He's not a great one for boundaries or social cues—"

"I don't know any eleven-year-old boy who is," James interjected, his smile widening.

"I don't want you to feel pressured."

"I don't." His blue-green gaze scanned her face. "But do you?"

Laura let out a gusty sigh that had James raising his eyebrows again, waiting. "Not pressured, no. But I'm...concerned. Maggie is still in a very uncertain place, and I'm not sure how she'd take to...to anything changing."

"Okay." James was quiet for a moment. "But nothing is changing, is it? It's just dinner, after all."

"I know." Her cheeks warmed. Had she been presuming again? "I just meant...in general."

"You mean if we dated." He spoke so matter-of-factly that Laura almost laughed. There was a certain relief in him simply spelling it out. Why couldn't she do the same? Why did she have to be so twitchy?

"Yes. Or something like that."

"Okay, well I'll keep that in mind." His gaze turned both sleepy and significant as he kept his eyes on hers. "And you can keep in mind that if and when we do go on a date, your children won't be present. Not that I don't like them, because I do. But a family dinner is not a date. Trust me."

Although his tone was perfectly pleasant, it still made something in Laura sizzle, as if he'd said something provocative. Seductive. She looked away as she answered.

"Understood."

"Good," James replied with satisfaction.

IN THE END, Maggie barely batted an eyelid when James came in with Sam that evening. Maybe the idea of her mother dating James was so ludicrous that it had not even occurred to Maggie as a possibility. As Sam and James chatted about video games over dinner, Laura thought it probably was. James seemed far more Sam's friend than hers, although as the evening wore on she wondered if that was intentional, to allay any fears of either hers or Maggie's. Or was she overthinking everything as usual?

In any case, it was pleasant indeed to have James simply in her house, at her table. The presence of a man—a kind, funny, interested and engaged man—was something she thought they all needed in their lives.

As before, he helped clear the table when the meal was over, and Sam and Maggie had disappeared up to their rooms. Laura hefted the kettle, raising her eyebrows in silent enquiry, and James grinned his agreement.

Goodness, but she'd missed this—the easy camaraderie, the silent communication, the understanding and the companionship. She hadn't had it with Tim in a while, she knew, well before he'd died.

But she didn't want to think about Tim just now.

And yet it seemed she was going to, because he was the first thing James asked about.

"I know Maggie is seeing a counsellor," he said as soon as they were settled on the sofa with their coffees, "but what about you and Sam?"

Laura tensed instinctively. "What about us?"

James smiled faintly, as if he knew exactly how and why she was stalling. "Are you seeing one?"

"I was, back in Woodbridge. I haven't looked for one here. I'm not sure how helpful it is for me, to be honest. Well, it was hard," she amended. "And I'm not sure I was ready to dredge up all my feelings and examine them once a week."

"Fair enough," James replied, and Laura gave a silent sigh of relief that he wasn't going to push. "And what about for Sam?"

"He didn't mind it, but he didn't love it, either." She sighed. "I suppose I should suggest it to him again, just in case. The thing is…" She hesitated as she sorted through the tangle of her feelings. "He actually seems so happy now. Minecraft Club, the play date with Will…things are going well for him. And taking him to counselling feels a bit like dragging him back into the mire of sadness and grief. When do you get to stop?"

"When you feel like that's the right thing to do?" James hazarded. "I don't know. I've never lost someone to death yet. But I see what you mean about Sam. He does seem happy." He paused. "Did he have a good relationship with Tim?"

Laura prickled instinctively. "Yes, of course he did. Why do you ask?"

"I just want to get to know you, Laura. I'm not suggesting anything." James's tone was gentle, and Laura bit her lip. She'd definitely sounded a bit snappish.

"Sorry. It's just…" She blew out a breath. "Yes, he did, when Tim was present."

"Present? Did he travel for work?"

"No, he just…checked out sometimes. He could be really into something—like building a tree house and zip wire in the garden—and Sam would be really excited. And then when it was over Tim would just…go sort of blank. Emotionally. I think the big projects exhausted him, as much as he loved them. He needed a few days or even weeks to recover, and sometimes to Sam I worry it might have felt like a kind of rejection, even though I know Tim didn't mean it that way."

She'd never explained that to anyone before, not even her counsellor. She'd never said how frustrating it was, how hurtful, to feel as if you only had someone's attention about half the time, even when that half made you feel as if you were the centre of his world.

James cocked his head. "I'm guessing Sam's not the only person who felt that way."

"No," Laura agreed, "but please don't turn into my counsellor, James. I want you very much as my friend, but I don't think I can bear you analysing all my emotions. It feels…unbalanced. Unequal."

"Sorry." James grimaced. "Now I feel like a prat."

"No, don't." She laid a hand on his arm, and just that simple touch—the warmth of his skin through the sleeve of his shirt—had sparks leaping within her. "No doubt I'm being oversensitive. I've just reached the point where I want to stop going over the past endlessly, wondering what went wrong or if anything did."

Although the reality was, she knew, that she just pushed all those undealt-with emotions to the back of her mind, like lidless Tupperware in a cupboard—shove it all in and shut the door as quickly as you could. Probably not a healthy response, but that was a problem for another day. "I just want to live my life now, as best as I can."

James's eyes darkened as his gaze remained steady on hers. "I can get on board with that," he said in a low voice.

Laura's breath hitched. James leaned forward, just an inch or two, but it was enough for her to wonder if—to hope—he might kiss her. What would it feel like to be kissed again, after all this time? Lips on lips, faces close, *bodies…*

A shudder went through her. Her fingers clenched on his arm. Gently James uncurled her claw-like grasp and laced his fingers with his, which almost—almost—felt as intimate as a kiss.

"Remember what I said about children not being present," he murmured. As if to prove his point, someone thundered down the stairs and quickly Laura yanked her hand from James's. Her palm tingled.

"Mum, is Mr Hill still here? *Oh.*" Sam paused, a perplexed look on his face as he took in the sight of them sitting close together on the sofa. Laura scooted across to the other side.

"You can see he is," she said in an over-bright voice that made her wince and James smile. "We were just having a coffee. What's up?"

"I wanted to show him this thing on my iPad." Sam was still looking uncertainly between the two of them, and so Laura rose from the sofa, taking James's coffee cup as well as her own to the sink.

She washed them up, her mind a numb haze, as Sam and James talked about Minecraft. Just remembering the feel of James's fingers linked with hers, that look in his eyes…Laura leaned against the sink as she struggled to get her heart rate under control. She had it *bad*.

She'd just finished loading the dishwasher with the rest of the dinner dishes when Sam headed back upstairs and James made to leave. He gave her a rueful smile of acknowledgement as he slipped on his jacket that Laura could barely return.

Her lips didn't feel as if they were working properly; nothing felt as if it were working properly. Her body felt like a jumble of disparate parts, her heart still beating far too furiously.

"Thanks for having me over," he said lightly, his hands dug into the pockets of his jacket. "Is this going to become a thing?"

"A thing?" Laura repeated dumbly.

"Monday night suppers. Because I quite like the free meal. Lasagne is as high up on my list as bolognaise."

"Oh, well." She let out a shaky laugh. "Maybe, then, if you're up for it."

"I am." He gazed at her for another heart-racing beat and then he turned to the door. "See you tomorrow."

"Yes." Laura remained at the door, breathing in the damp air, as James was swallowed up by the darkness so she could only hear the crunch of his footsteps on gravel, and then nothing at all.

She pressed one hand to her chest; her heart rate was only just starting to slow. She wondered how on earth she would survive a dinner each week, as well as seeing James every day, when she was in this high state of tension and awareness. She feared there was a likelihood that standing in the schoolyard or sitting at the dinner table, she might spontaneously combust.

And yet, she acknowledged as she closed the door, she felt more alive than she had in a long time…and she knew she didn't want to go back to the way she'd been.

Chapter Fourteen

"I SN'T SHE SCRUMPTIOUS?" Lindy's arms were already reaching out for baby Zoe as Ava slumped gratefully onto the sofa. "Why do babies seem so *edible*? Honestly I just want to nibble her cheeks, I really do."

Lindy cuddled Zoe close while Laura watched on with a smile. Zoe was indeed adorable—red cheeks, a rosebud mouth, bright blue eyes, and a tuft of hair the same whisky brown as Jace's. Who could possibly resist her? Already she felt her own arms twitching, longing for a cuddle.

Knowing Lindy wouldn't give her up anytime soon, she turned to Ava. "How are you feeling?" she asked, and Ava rolled her eyes.

"Like I've been bulldozed. I don't know how, because it actually hasn't been that long, but I somehow managed to forget just how the whole process *consumes* you—the labour, the birth, actually having a newborn… I want a holiday." She shook her head ruefully, but she was smiling. Anyone with eyes could see that Ava was absolutely in love with her baby daughter.

She'd come home from the hospital three days ago, and already Laura thought she looked as beautiful as ever, if a little understandably dishevelled. Ava was the type of woman who could make a stained hoodie and trackie bottoms—her current ensemble—look sexy.

"And what about Jace?" Laura asked as she perched on the edge of a chair. When she and Lindy had knocked on the door of the Tuckers' house, Jace had greeted them cheerfully and then, with William tucked under one arm, he'd happily disappeared to do 'man stuff' with his son. A brood of clucking women wasn't exactly his domain, Laura could tell, just as she could see he adored his daughter as much as his wife did. Still, she asked, if only so Ava could beam fondly in recollection.

"Jace is over the moon. It's lovely to see him like this, actually. He was the same with William, of course, and he loves him like his own…" She paused, a crinkle appearing in her forehead as she continued quietly, "It's different though, isn't it?"

"One kind of love doesn't cancel out another," Lindy proclaimed robustly as she planted a smacking kiss on Zoe's plump cheek. "Love increases love. The more you have, the more you get. The more you give."

"I'd like to think so," Ava replied. "It's hard not to worry a little bit, especially as they get older. What if William seems really different to Jace when he's a teenager? His half-brother is a right prat, if I do say so myself, not that they've ever met." Laura only knew the gist of Ava's past life, as hinted at during their evening at The Three Pennies—an older husband who had died, two stepchildren who had made her life difficult.

Ava sighed and shook her head. "But here I am, borrowing trouble, when I have a husband who loves me and two beautiful children." She gazed fondly at Zoe, still cradled in Lindy's arms. "Really, right now I feel like the happiest, luckiest woman in the world."

"And so you are." Lindy jiggled the baby as she began to fuss, the soft, mewling sounds tearing at Laura's heart and memory. "Fancy a cuddle, now that she's not cooing adorably at me anymore?" Lindy asked with a wry smile, and Laura held her arms out.

"You might need to get some practice in, Lindy," Ava remarked archly. "Any wedding bells ringing soon?"

"Ava." Lindy blushed rather becomingly. "Roger and I have only been dating for a few months. I hardly think…"

"But you're not getting any younger."

Lindy grimaced good-naturedly. "True."

"And the two of you were made for each other. Anyone can see that. The man adores the ground you walk on, and likewise with you. If it weren't so cute, it would be sickening." Ava grinned devilishly at her. "Why not put a ring on it?"

Blushing all the more, Lindy laughed and shook her head. "Well, when you put it like that, it seems obvious. But you should know that Roger is a slow and steady kind of person. I don't anticipate wedding bells anytime soon."

"Well, you're the one who needs to hurry him up," Ava replied. "Waltz him to the altar, girl!"

"In time," Lindy murmured. "Maybe."

Laura only half paid attention to the conversation, because the second her arms had closed around Zoe she'd felt her senses go into adoration overload. The lovely warmth of a baby, the comforting weight, that sweet baby smell…she'd forgotten it all, and yet she remembered it exactly as soon as Zoe was in her arms. Laura drew her close to her chest and pressed her lips to the top of her soft, downy head as her own eyes fluttered closed.

"Someone's broody," Ava remarked dryly, and it took Laura a few stunned seconds to realise she meant her.

"What?" She opened her eyes and blinked a smug Ava and a smiling Lindy into focus. "Oh, but…who doesn't love a baby?"

"Loads of people," Ava returned. "Trust me. I wasn't all that fond of them until I had William, to be perfectly honest. Fortunately he grew on me." She slid Lindy a laughing glance. "What do you think? Is Laura pining for another?"

"You seem like a natural," Lindy admitted with a smile.

Laura rested one hand on Zoe's back, savouring the steady rise and fall of her tiny chest. "It's like riding a bike, I suppose," she answered. "You never really forget."

And yet it was true, she realised as she continued to rock Zoe. She *was* a bit broody. She missed this—the tiny snuffling into her neck, the sweet small breaths. *The love.* She still had so much love to give—and not just for a baby. Her arms tightened almost possessively around Zoe as she considered the matter.

She'd been wobbling and waffling about whether to go on a date with James and after Maggie's overreaction about her even texting someone, she'd thought she ought to take a big step back. Yet now, with a baby in her arms, she realised that what Chantal had said was true. She was young, and her life wasn't over. She wanted another chance at the whole shebang—husband, maybe even another child. Did that have to be selfish or wrong? Why did some contrary part of her continue to insist it was?

"You are going to have to give her back, I'm afraid," Ava said, interrupting her whirling thoughts. "I'm leaking." She gestured ruefully to her top, which had two revealing damp patches.

"Oh, sorry." Laura handed the baby over and Ava took her to her breast. Her empty arms were a good reminder that a single date with a much younger man did not, actually, translate into a husband and babies. James would probably be appalled by the spiralling nature of her thoughts. He wanted dinner; she was already onto the happily ever after. Goodness, but she was ridiculous. Chantal would give one of her great big belly laughs if Laura told her how she was thinking, but she also knew her friend would understand. *I want another chance.* It was the first time she'd let herself say it; it was, she realised, the first time she'd actually felt it. She really was waking up.

"SO YOU WILL come?"

James suppressed a sigh as he heard the hopeful and slightly wheedling note of his mother's voice. She was desperate to have all six siblings under one large roof for a weekend, and out of all his sisters and brother, James knew he was the most reluctant to return home. As much as he loved his family as individuals—and he did—when they all got together, particularly back at the family farm, he felt...what?

Resentful, he supposed, at his core. And a bit angry. And a little left out. It wasn't a good combination, and so he avoided the occasional get-togethers, preferring to see his siblings one at a time away from the farm, rather than all together when the need, particularly for his father, to compare the children and their successes became overwhelming. Or so James supposed, since his dad never seemed to be able to resist making a comment or two.

How much does a teacher make these days? Or *I thought teaching little 'uns was a woman's job.* Yes, his father was carved from the 1950s, fortunately in a fairly lovable way, but he was a traditional, taciturn farmer whose father and grandfather had been farmers, and James knew he couldn't expect a man such as that to be anything but a product of his times and culture. Even so, those barbs, made with a faint look of disappointed befuddlement, still held the power to wound.

"James?" his mother prompted beseechingly.

The sigh James had been suppressing came out in a gust of resignation. "Yes, of course. I'm happy to come. When is it? The first weekend of March?"

"Last weekend of February, at the end of half-term. And if you'd like to bring someone…" his mum continued, trailing off meaningfully. She'd had high hopes for Helen, especially since James, in a moment of optimistic excitement, had confessed to his parents that he was going to ask her to marry him. Too bad that hadn't worked out, although nearly nine months on James could admit he and Helen really hadn't been suited.

She'd been a city person, focused and ambitious and a bit brittle, whereas he was too laid-back, too unmotivated, at least according to her, and too geeky. Well, fine. He could handle all that. Besides, there was Laura to think of now, to hope for, although recently he wondered if that was really going to go anywhere.

Every time he felt as if he was getting somewhere with Laura, she backed away, both physically and emotionally. There had been that charged moment on her sofa when he'd been so tempted to kiss her…and then her skittish behaviour the next day, skirting around him in the schoolyard, her face on fire. James understood this new frightening new territory for her after her husband's death, and he considered himself a patient man.

But if it wasn't going to go anywhere, maybe patience was just another way of wasting his time.

"There's nobody to bring, Mum, sorry," he said apologetically. "But I'll be there."

He ended the call and stared out the window of his classroom at the dusky afternoon, trying not to feel dispirited. The prospect of a weekend home always dented his spirits a bit, although he tried to hide it, even from himself. Still, with that in mind as well as Laura's recent seeming avoidance of him, it was hard not to feel the tiniest bit down.

When he went home his father was undoubtedly going to ask, in about five different ways, what he was doing with his life, and right now James was wondering the same thing.

The move to Wychwood-on-Lea nearly six months ago now had been a bit impulsive, but it had also felt right. He was tired of city life—the commute, the small flat, the rush everywhere, the lonely sense of anonymity. He'd also been watching *All Creatures Great and Small* on the telly at the time, which might have had something to do with his rose-tinted view of a thirtyish man making his home in a picturesque village.

Now he couldn't help but wonder if he'd been a naïve idiot, moving to a village with a population of two thousand

and literally no single women, as far as he could see. The only one he'd met so far was Laura. Perhaps he should join one of those dating sites, but he resisted the notion instinctively. At heart he was a pretty old-fashioned guy, a lot like his dad in that respect. In only that respect.

Outside the shadows were gathering and James knew he wasn't in the right headspace to mark another twenty lots of homework on formal and informal language in Michael Morpurgo's *War Horse*.

He slid the workbooks into his bag and reached for his jacket. It was chess club that evening, but he didn't think he was in the right headspace for that, either, what with Edwin's off-colour remarks and some of the members' super-competitiveness. Their pedantic insistence on touch moves could annoy him if he let it.

Even so, the prospect of another night at home, eating alone, watching telly or doing work, filled him with a weary sort of despair. He wanted more from his life than this. The evenings he'd spent with Laura and her kids had been the highlight of his week lately.

He knew she was worried she was presuming too much, but in truth James felt as if she couldn't presume enough. If she appeared in front of him right now, asking if he'd like an evening of talking about Minecraft with an eleven-year-old and weathering a fourteen-year-old's moody sulks, not to mention coffee on the sofa with Laura herself, he'd say *yes please* in a heartbeat.

But she wasn't asking. She'd been more or less avoiding him since Monday night, when they'd had that coffee on the sofa and for a few seconds it had all seemed so promising.

"James?"

He looked up, startled, as he stepped outside his classroom. He'd thought the school had emptied out save for the cleaners, but there was Laura, smiling nervously as she stood in front of him, almost as if he'd magicked her up by the power of wishful thinking.

"Hey. I was just thinking about you," he said, even though he suspected it was unwise and would turn her skittish again.

To his surprised delight, it didn't. "And I was just thinking about you."

"Were you?" A grin tugged at his mouth as his mood started to lift. This evening was looking better already. Much better.

"Yes...I'm sorry I've avoided you the last few days. Although maybe you haven't noticed." She let out an uncertain laugh.

"I have noticed," James replied. They began to walk down the corridor towards the front doors; he sensed Laura needed a moment to gather her thoughts, or perhaps her courage.

Outside twilight had settled softly over the village, lending it a cloak of wispy violet. They started together down the high street.

"Where's Sam?" he asked after a moment, when Laura had remained silent.

"He's at William's again. And Maggie has art club. So I have an hour free, and I'm not sure what to do with it." Another one of those little laughs. "I went home and walked Perry," Laura continued, "and then I came back to school...to see you."

Now *that* sounded promising. "And why did you want to see me?" James asked, striving to keep his tone friendly and light when part of him felt like taking her by the shoulders and demanding she tell him what she was on about. Or maybe taking her by the shoulders and kissing her.

She looked so lovely, swathed in a bright red parka, her hair in a dark cloud about her face, her cheeks and lips rosy from cold.

"Well...to apologise for avoiding you," Laura said, and the hesitant note in her voice told James that she was backtracking again. James decided to wait her out, and didn't reply. "Where are we going, anyway?" she asked after a few minutes. They'd walked the length of the high street and were by the village green, the gazebo and new play park ahead of them, along with the road towards Chipping Norton. After the village green there was nothing but a nursing home and a petrol station.

James glanced at her and shrugged. "I don't know. You tell me."

"Nowhere, I guess," she said after a moment. "Or maybe

anywhere. Shall we walk back up?"

"If you like." He'd walk up and down the high street all evening if it meant she'd actually say what she wanted to say. What he wanted her to say.

Up they went, past all the shops now cosily lit—the toy shop, and one for vintage clothes, Tea on the Lea and Waggy Tails. Past the school again, and still Laura hadn't spoken.

She turned left, towards the river, and James followed her onto a quaint little wooden bridge that spanned the river at the top of the village, the buildings tumbling down before them now softly cloaked in darkness.

"Sorry," she said as she turned to face him. "You must think I'm losing the plot. I just didn't want an audience." She eyed him nervously, her fingers pleated together.

James slid his bag from his shoulder as he watched her. "An audience for what?"

"I…" She took a breath. "I'm ready for you to ask me out."

He eyed her for a moment, knowing how much courage this had taken her, and yet still not able to resist teasing her. Wanting to lighten the moment a little, because Laura was looking at him as if she'd just signed something in blood.

"Well, you know, *you* could ask *me* out," he said. "If we want to be all equal rights about this."

Her eyes widened and she gave a breathless laugh. "I'm ashamed that idea never even occurred to me."

"Well?"

"All right, fine. I'll ask you out. Will you go on a date with me?"

James could feel himself grinning. "Yes, I will."

"It has to be the last week of February, when Sam and Maggie are on their skiing holiday. I'm not ready to tell them about—well about anything yet. Not until…"

"Not until you decide if it's worth it?" He sounded light, but her reticence stung a bit. He understood it, of course, but he didn't like being someone's secret.

"You might decide it's not worth it," Laura fired back. "One date and you might be running for the hills."

"I don't think so." James took a step towards her. Laura's eyes widened a little but she held her ground.

"Nothing too fancy, either, and preferably not in public. Sorry—I know that sounds rude, but this is a small village and I don't want to be fodder for gossip."

Another sting to absorb. "Okay."

"So I thought maybe dinner at my cottage. *Just* dinner," she emphasised. "I'm not…I don't want you to think…"

"Laura," he interrupted her with a soft laugh, "trust me, I don't. And enough with the caveats. We're going on a date. That's all I need to know."

"Okay." She let out her breath in a rush, the tension easing from her shoulders, which had been inching up to her ears. "Okay."

James took another step towards her. He wanted to kiss her badly, but he didn't know if it was the right moment.

Another step, and her lips parted.

"What are you doing?" she asked uncertainly.

"Honestly? Thinking about kissing you. I want to, but I don't want to rush things."

Colour flared in her pale face. "I thought that was for after the first date."

"Well, that might seem like the more accepted time," he agreed, "but what if we just got it out of the way now? So you're not stressing about it for the entire date?"

She laughed softly. "I probably would be, to tell the truth."

"Exactly." He tucked a tendril of hair behind her ear, letting his fingers skim her cold cheek. She shivered under his touch.

"I haven't done anything like this in a long time, James," she whispered. "Married kisses, especially fifteen-year-married kisses, are something else entirely."

"I've been told," he murmured as he rested his hands on her shoulders, "it's like riding a bike."

"Okay." She closed her eyes and screwed up her face as if preparing for an injection. James laughed softly, although the truth was he was nervous too. They had chemistry, he was sure of it, but it still felt complicated. Fraught. And he hadn't actually kissed anyone in a while, either. In fact, the last person he'd kissed had soundly rejected him, so...

"Laura, you look as if you're steeling yourself against something painful."

Her eyes fluttered open. "Sorry. I'm nervous."

"So am I."

"Are you?" She looked so surprised he had to laugh.

"You seem to think I'm this confident Casanova, but I'm really not."

"I suppose it's just because of how insanely gorgeous you are," she returned with a smile, and then, because he couldn't keep himself from it any longer, he leaned forward and brushed his lips against hers.

Chapter Fifteen

*O*H. SOMEHOW, IN the last year, Laura had forgotten she had lips. She'd forgotten how soft and well, *lovely* another person's could be against hers, how having her cheek cradled by a big male hand made her feel so precious and treasured, and how much she'd craved this kind of connection.

And then James deepened the kiss, just a little, so they were definitely moving out of the brush territory, and heat flared low in Laura's belly and broke out along her skin. Oh. *Oh.*

His hands dropped to her waist and he pulled her just that little bit closer, so excitement raced along her veins and short-circuited everything—she couldn't think, could barely breathe. How was she supposed to do this again? She reached one hand up to his shoulder and sort of pawed him, looking for purchase, feeling as if she might explode or faint or cry or laugh. Maybe all four. One kiss was utterly overwhelming.

James stepped back, and to Laura's bemused gratification she saw he was affected too—*thank goodness.* She didn't think she could have borne it if he'd looked coolly unruffled, given her a charming and slightly smug smile and said something like: *See that wasn't so bad, was it?*

Instead he looked as gobsmacked as she felt. His hair was ruffled and his cheeks were pink and he was breathing hard. *Good.*

"I don't foresee any problems in that area," he said after a moment, his voice slightly hoarse. Laura realised she was grinning. And breathing as hard as he was.

She tucked her hair behind her ears, her mind still spinning. Half of her wanted to grab him by the lapels of his jacket and haul him closer. Kiss him again, and more.

But she didn't, because she knew they needed to take things slowly, for her sake as well as for her children's, and already just that one kiss had just catapulted her into a whole other stratosphere of hoping, dreaming, *wanting.*

"Well," she said, because she couldn't think of anything else to say.

James nodded as if she'd said something extraordinarily profound. "Well," he agreed.

They turned from the bridge and started walking back towards town, both of them silent and, Laura thought, spinning. At least she was.

"Are Sam and Maggie looking forward to their skiing holiday?" James finally asked as they passed by the school once more, and for some reason Laura couldn't keep from bursting into laughter. He looked on, bemused, a smile tugging at his mouth. "What?"

"It's just…I don't… My mind is still back on that bridge."

"Mine too," he agreed, giving her a look of such, well, *heat*, that Laura's stomach fizzed. She really hadn't expected this level of attraction, of chemistry, between them. It felt as if she'd swallowed a firework. She was *buzzing*.

They parted company in the middle of the high street, where James was to turn onto a narrow lane of terraced cottages where he lived.

"Someday I'll show you my house," he promised, "when it doesn't look like a construction zone." Laura nodded her agreement, and they both stood uncertainly on the pavement for a moment; Laura suspected James wanted to kiss her again, and the truth was, she wanted to be kissed.

But there were people hurrying by, including a gang of schoolchildren Maggie's age, and she wasn't ready for that level of publicity, so she gave him a funny little wave and continued down the street. Her lips were *still* tingling.

As she walked back towards Willoughby Close, Laura felt as if her mind—and body—had been blown right open. It was just a kiss, yes, of course it was, but it felt like so much more. She'd turned a corner, started a new chapter or maybe even a whole new book… Her life felt wide, wide open, and the realisation brought a sudden hard clench of anxiety. She needed to ring Chantal.

"We're going on a date," she blurted as soon as Chantal

had answered. "And…he kissed me. I kissed him. I mean, we kissed."

"*Girl!*" Chantal's crow of exultation was exactly what Laura had expected, and made her smile, although she suddenly felt quite weirdly emotional. "How was it?"

"It was amazing," she said honestly. "Far more amazing than I expected. I felt like I'd put my finger in an electric socket, but in a good way."

"That sounds promising. Very promising."

"It was." Laura let out a shuddery breath. "And he was so lovely and sweet, Chantal, honestly I think…I think I could…" No, she couldn't say it. It was far too soon. "I think I'm hyperventilating," she said instead as her head started to swim.

She stopped right there on the dark road, her phone pressed to her ear, as her breath came in shallow pants. "I think I might actually pass out."

"Put your head between your knees," Chantal instructed, utterly unfazed as always.

"I'm on the side of the road—"

"*Do it.* And take slow, deep breaths."

Obediently Laura bent over double, her head hanging between her knees, her phone still camped to her ear, as she did her best to breathe slowly. She felt ridiculous, but at least it was working.

"What's wrong with me?" she moaned to Chantal. "I was so excited, it was the best kiss I've had in ages, and now I'm practically having a heart attack here."

"The two are obviously related. The best kiss you've had in ages? You feel guilty, Laura."

Laura squeezed her eyes shut as her head started to swim again. "And you think I should?"

"No, of course I don't, but it doesn't matter a flying fig what I think! It's what you think. What you feel. And right now you feel guilty."

Slowly, as if an invisible hand had pushed her right over, Laura sat back onto the damp grass by the side of the road, her knees drawn up to her chest. "I do," she whispered. "I really do."

"Why do you think that is? This is, by the way, something you should talk to a therapist about, but I'll give you an impromptu session right now because I love you."

"I don't know why," she said slowly.

"Do you think Tim wouldn't want you to be happy again?"

Laura closed her eyes as Chantal's questions hammered at her head—and her heart. "I don't know. I suppose I don't think he'd mind."

"Then what?"

She squeezed her eyes shut harder, unable to avoid thinking about—and answering—the questions she'd been avoiding since Tim had died, and mixed in with the overwhelming grief had been something else. She'd touched on it briefly, ever so briefly, with James, but she knew she needed to be honest with Chantal now. Honest with herself.

"I feel guilty," she said slowly, squeezing each word out from a too-tight throat, "because I wasn't a good wife to him. I wasn't happy with him, especially not at the end. And he died…he died knowing that, or at least suspecting it, I think." The last came out in a gasp; tears were running unchecked down her face.

"He also knew you loved him," Chantal said after a pause, her voice both gentle and firm. "And that you supported him. Were you thinking of divorcing him?"

"What?" A shocked hiss of breath. "No."

"Laura, marriages go through good and bad patches. It's normal. It's natural. Or so it seems to me, from the outside. You and Tim ended on a bit of a bad patch. It's sad that it happened that way, but it doesn't invalidate fifteen years of love and faithfulness. It doesn't make you a bad wife."

Laura couldn't respond, because she was crying too hard. She made a few gasping, mewling noises that she hoped Chantal took for assent.

"Are you in a safe place?" Chantal asked. "Because you told me you were on the side of the road, and the last thing I need is something terrible to happen while I'm talking to you on the phone. That would seriously set back my mental health."

Laura managed a little laugh as she mopped her face. "I'm sitting on wet, muddy grass on the side of the road, bawling my eyes out," she finally managed to choke out. "If anyone comes by, they are going to think I need some serious help."

"And maybe you do, but that's okay," Chantal returned. "Right?"

"Right." Laura let out a shuddery breath. She felt utterly drained, both emotionally and physically, as if she'd run a mental marathon, but it felt good. From the outside this looked like grief, but it felt like healing.

"Thank you," she said softly. "I don't know what I would do without you."

"And I don't know what I'd do without you," Chantal returned robustly. "Because I know if our positions were reversed, you'd be talking me down from the ledge *and* baking me some banana bread, too. Sorry I don't bake."

Laura laughed and mopped her face some more. "I love you, Chantal."

"Love you too, sweetie."

THE NEXT TWO weeks seemed to hurtle past, as Laura finished up her half term of teaching at Wychwood Primary, and prepared to get both Maggie and Sam ready for a skiing holiday, which required the purchase of a lot of expensive kit that Pamela and Steve had not offered to pay for and which Laura felt she couldn't ask about.

"Two hundred quid for a parka?" she'd yelped when Maggie had shown her the one she wanted. "What about the one you have?"

"It's not meant for *skiing*, Mum," Maggie said in her well-duh voice. "It's going to be freezing up in the Alps."

"Right, well let's find one that's slightly cheaper, shall we?" A few weeks ago Laura might have caved in just to see her daughter smile, but she was doing her best to take a harder line now, out of love.

So far she had no real idea if it is working; Maggie was less stroppy, it was true, but she wasn't exactly exuding warm fuzzies, either. When Laura had worked up her courage to ask again about the self-harming, Maggie had just rolled her eyes. But Laura hadn't seen any new marks on either of her daughter's arms, which she took as some encouragement.

In between the silences and the flounces there were a few good times to be had; after the usual Monday night dinner, James stayed for an epic game of Monopoly that had both Maggie and Sam more animated than she'd seen them in a long while.

They'd also gone for a long walk along the river with Perry, just the three of them; it was the first time Maggie had agreed to go on a dog walk in ages. And all right, she'd been on her phone for most of the time, but she'd still been there, walking alongside the river, the ground carpeted with delicate snowdrops.

As the days counted down towards the February half-term, Laura felt an increasing sense of excitement about her date—and one of dismay about leaving the school. She'd become used to seeing James each day, to having their friendly chats in the schoolyard, or even a quick, knowing smile in the corridor. They hadn't shared another kiss since the one on the bridge, but it almost felt as if they had.

She'd also enjoyed the chats with other teachers, the jokes and camaraderie in the staffroom that she hadn't yet taken part in, but she'd still felt included. It was going to be hard to go back to staying home alone.

The second Monday night dinner, right before Sam and Maggie left for their holiday, didn't go quite as well as the first. Maggie had a meltdown about having nothing to wear for the trip, despite all the new winter things Laura had bought, and Sam was whinily demanding James to pay attention to him and his iPad. Laura suspected they were both feeling anxious about a week alone with their grandparents, never mind how fun it was meant to be. She could hardly expect James to understand that, and yet somehow he did.

"That's how life is sometimes," he'd replied with a shrug when she'd stumbled through an apology at the end of the evening. "It's okay, Laura."

His relaxed acceptance of the mayhem in her life both touched and unnerved her, because it seemed so easy for him, and she feared that one day it wouldn't be. One day he might decide he didn't actually like having two teenagers—well, one almost-teenager—hanging around, cramping his style. One day he might decide she wasn't worth the effort, the complexities.

When she'd confided as much to Chantal, her friend had given her the usual tough-talking advice. "Let's get past the first date before you start worrying about the break-up, okay? Meanwhile I'm trying to remember the last date I had. I think it was in the Palaeolithic Age."

"I don't even know when that was," Laura had replied with a laugh.

"A long time ago," Chantal replied tartly.

"Maybe you should join a dating app," Laura suggested hesitantly, to which Chantal snorted.

"Which one haven't I tried?" She paused. "I know Tim dying was rubbish but you were lucky, Laura. You found someone. You might be finding someone again. I'm not envious—well, I *am*, but I'm happy for you, as well. But realise you've been lucky."

"Oh, Chantal." Laura had been overcome by an entirely different kind of guilt. "I'm sorry. I feel like a cow now. You're right, of course—"

"And I didn't mean for you to feel like a cow. Just...realise. That's all."

"I do," Laura whispered. "I do, really." She sniffed and added in a brighter voice, "Do you know, there is a single guy out here who might be up your alley."

"Oh? I'm all ears."

"His name is Dan Rhodes. He's the head teacher at the primary, and I'm pretty sure he's single."

"Divorced?"

"I don't know, actually, but he's mentioned that he lives alone, so... And he's really nice."

"Is that code for ugly?"

"No," Laura said with a laugh. "It's for real. And he is good-looking, in a chilled, bearded sort of way."

"I like a guy with a beard," Chantal replied musingly. "Let me know when you want to set me up."

"Deal," Laura agreed. "Let me get through this date first and then we'll all have dinner together, okay?"

"Sounds good."

FINALLY, THE DAY—AS well as the evening—came. After school had broken up, Dan Rhodes had given Laura a bouquet of flowers, thanking her for pitching in for the half term, and Laura had, haltingly, mentioned having him over for a meal, something that had surprised but delighted him. Laura drove Maggie and Sam to Burford to spend the night at Granny and Grandad's before they were to take an absurdly early flight to Geneva the next morning.

They'd had a couple of Saturday afternoons or Sunday dinners at her in-laws over the last month and a half, and they'd all gone as they always had, with Laura doing her best not to react to the little barbs and stings, even as she couldn't help but count them up in her head.

To her surprise, Pamela gave her a rather effusive hug

when Laura was about to say goodbye. "I really appreciate this, Laura," she said, her eyes suspiciously bright. "I know it's not easy for you, in so many ways. Thank you."

Laura had returned the hug, her arms closing around her mother-in-law with clumsy unfamiliarity. She couldn't remember the last time they'd embraced. She was glad Pamela had thanked her, grateful that she'd acknowledged what Laura was giving up.

"Have a fabulous time," she told them all, her throat tightening only a little, and then they were all waving, and she was in her car, feeling fragile and hopeful and excited all at once. She had an entire week on her own, and dinner with James tomorrow night, and she missed her children already.

Laura spent all of Saturday blitzing the cottage and making food—she'd deliberated far too much, spending a good hour on the phone with Chantal, debating what to make for dinner, as well as telling her about Dan Rhodes, to which Chantal had made approving noises. If they did get together, Laura thought, it would be wonderful. To have Chantal in Wychwood-on-Lea, neighbours even, both of them with significant others or even husbands…

It was a very rosy daydream, as well as a dangerous one. Like she'd told Chantal, she needed to get through this first—or rather, second—date first.

James had, very kindly, suggested he could bring a takeaway so she wouldn't have to cook, but Laura didn't want to eat out of foil containers on their date, first or second. She wanted things to be a bit more romantic than that, and besides, she thought she was actually a pretty good cook.

"But I don't want to try too hard," she told Chantal. "I mean, no oysters or caviar or strawberries dipped in champagne."

"You *have* been thinking about this," Chantal answered with a laugh.

She settled on chicken cutlets in a tarragon cream sauce with roasted potatoes and minty peas, and an apple *tarte Tatin* for dessert. Deceptively simple, considering the tart had taken her most of the afternoon to make.

At four o'clock she nipped out to take Perry for a walk, hoping a little exercise would mean he would be docilely sprawled out in front of the wood burner for the whole evening instead of thrusting his nose between James's knees or worse, desperate for affection.

As she mulched through the carpet of damp leaves in the Willoughby wood, excitement warred with total panic. This was an honest-to-goodness date. They would have hours to spend together, to chat, to laugh, to flirt. They would almost certainly kiss. She was starting to hyperventilate again.

As she came back into the close, she saw Lindy with a tall, good-looking man who held himself a bit stiffly. It had to be the famous Roger. She waved at them both, and Lindy came forward to make introductions.

"We're just off to get a takeaway curry," she said as she linked arms with Roger. They did seem rather ridiculously loved up. "What are you up to, with Sam and Maggie gone for the week?"

Laura didn't know if it was the sight of them so obviously a happy couple, as were her other neighbours, but she heard herself replying, "Actually, I have a date."

Roger looked understandably nonplussed but Lindy goggled at her. "You *do*?"

"Yes, first one." Her laugh was a little manic. "Here's hoping." She started walking towards the door of number three before Lindy could ask any more questions, like who it was with.

"Let me know how it goes," Lindy called, and Laura managed a nod and a wave before she unlocked the door and stepped inside. Time to get ready for her big date. For this she needed Chantal.

Chapter Sixteen

J AMES RESISTED THE urge to tug at his collar as he stood on Laura's doorstep, a hand-tied bouquet of roses and lilies clutched in one fist. He'd debated whether to all go out with the romantic gestures, and then had recklessly decided why not?

In addition to the flowers, he had a bottle of wine in a shiny gold bag looped around one wrist, and he was wearing a freshly pressed button-down shirt and his best pair of cords. Plus he'd worn aftershave. He felt as green as a boy, swallowing nervously, wondering if he'd overdosed on the aftershave. He pressed the doorbell.

Perry gave a half-hearted bark and he heard Laura shush him before she answered the door, looking…well, frankly, looking insanely gorgeous, yes indeed. He could use those words now.

Instead of one of her fairly sensible skirt-and-blouse combinations, or a pair of wide-legged trousers paired with a modest jumper, the kind of things he'd seen her in at school, she wore a dress. A soft, wraparound dress in eminently touchable cashmere, the deep blue colour setting off her eyes perfectly. Her hair was in loose waves about her face and she had, he saw, a flick of eyeliner, a touch of lipstick. He didn't feel so bad about the aftershave now.

"Hello," he said, feeling suddenly shy. She smiled back, looking lovely and just as shy.

"Hello. You scrub up nicely, I have to say."

"So do you."

She laughed and ran her hands down the sides of her dress. "You wouldn't believe how long it took me to decide what to wear. I had a two-hour conference call with Chantal."

"I think the two of you came to the right conclusion."

She dropped her hands from her dress as she gave him a direct look. "I'm nervous."

"So am I. Can I come in, by the way?"

She laughed again as she shook her head. "Sorry, sorry, of course. What a welcome."

"It was a lovely welcome." He handed her the flowers, which she took and buried her nose in, breathing in deep.

"Heavenly. Lilies are my favourite."

"I could pretend to know that, but I didn't. I just like them too."

She glanced up from the flowers, a smile curving lips that looked even lusher than usual, no doubt thanks to the lipstick. "That's even better."

James managed a smile, even though he felt like groaning. He was already longing to pull her into his arms, to kiss her again, to bury his face in her hair, to…

Stop. He really, really needed to stop that line of thinking. Otherwise this was going to be an incredibly long evening, and not in a good way, as much as he was looking forward to Laura's company.

She turned away to put the flowers in a vase, and James took the bottle of wine out of the bag and set it on the table.

"Smells delicious," he remarked, and she let out another laugh.

"That required another long conversation with Chantal. I'm afraid this date has the military planning of—of the Battle of Thermopylae!"

"Thermopylae?" James raised his eyebrows, bemused. "Geek I may be, but I'm not familiar with that one."

"No, I wouldn't expect you to be. I studied ancient history at uni, in case you couldn't tell. And that wasn't actually a good comparison, because the Greeks lost the battle despite their good strategy, although they did take quite a few Persians down with them."

"So in this scenario am I a Persian or a Greek?"

She shrugged, smiling helplessly. "Honestly, I have no idea. The whole analogy breaks down pretty quickly."

"Most analogies do. So do you think you'll look for a position teaching history, now that you're finished at the village school?" A prospect that made regret sweep through him. He would miss her brightening his days.

"I'd like to. I haven't taught history since before Maggie was born."

"Why not?"

She paused thoughtfully, her hands still full of flowers as she arranged them in the vase. "When she and Sam were little, I didn't really have the brain power or the energy. And as they got older it just felt easier to stay in a job that had no marking to bring home, no parent-teacher conferences in the evenings. But I think I'm ready for more of a challenge now." She grimaced wryly. "If I can get a job."

"I'm sure you can."

She smiled and finished with the flowers, and James struggled to find something else to say. Why did he feel so nervous, so awkward, as if every remark jarred, at least a little? He'd been so looking forward to this evening but here he was, standing around, shuffling his feet and wondering what to say.

"I was worried this was going to be weird," Laura said quietly, a wry smile curving her lips although her eyes looked a little anxious.

"What do you mean?" he asked, although he thought he knew very well what she meant.

"We talked about going on a date for so long and now we're actually doing it. It feels weird. Like—*whoa*." She held up both hands in front of her, eyebrows raised, and he smiled.

"Yeah, I know what you mean. But it doesn't have to be

weird."

"The more we talk about it being weird, the weirder it becomes."

"That's a problem."

"Indeed." She slanted him a humorous look. "Why don't I open the wine? I'm sure everything will seem easier once we're slightly sozzled."

"That sounds like an excellent idea."

Laura did just that, pouring them both full glasses and then handing James one before raising her own. "To first dates."

"Technically, this is our second. But yes. To dates, first and otherwise." He clinked his glass with hers and they both drank.

As she lowered her glass, Laura gave him a teasing smile. "Still weird?"

The wine had already snaked its warmth down to his belly. "Getting better."

"Good." She put her glass down and went to busy herself with something at the stove while James took another sip, relaxing that little bit more. "Tell me about Helen," she said over her shoulder, and he tensed right up again.

"Sorry…what?"

"I've told you about Tim," she replied with a shrug as she turned to look at him. "Tell me about Helen."

James didn't really want to talk about his ex on a first— or rather, second—date, but he could see Laura had a point.

"What do you want to know?"

"Anything. Everything." She gave a little grimace. "Well, no, not everything. But let's start easy. How did you meet?"

"At a party." Which sounded so boring. He took a sip of wine as he shuffled through the memories like a deck of old cards. "Thrown by one of my old uni friends. It was summer—one of those surprisingly hot nights." Sultry, even, so the air felt damp. He pictured himself standing in the corner of a crowded kitchen in a tiny flat in Wimbledon, sipping cheap wine and sweating through his shirt.

"And?" Laura continued, a small smile playing about her mouth.

"Someone had put music on, and people were starting to dance in the living room. I wasn't. I am not, and never have been, a dancer."

"I have trouble believing that."

"Believe it." He gave a slightly hollow laugh as he recalled various discos and dances throughout his school days where he had been dragged out onto the floor by some well-meaning—or not—friend. "I am the definition of the white man's shuffle. Rhythm is not my thing."

"And so Helen." Laura put her hands on her hips. "Let me guess. She asked you to dance."

"She didn't ask me, she dragged me onto the floor." Even now he could see the look of laughing challenge on her face as she'd taken him by both hands and pulled him forward. It had charmed him at the time, even if he'd been a bit alarmed to find himself grooving, or attempting to, to 'Dancing Queen.'

"She was like that," he continued. "Determined. I liked it at first. She was—is—the kind of person to get out on a weekend, going to some festival or fair when I would have been happy at home with a book or a movie. Not that I'm a couch potato," he said quickly and Laura smiled.

"I never thought you were."

"But Helen had this drive to do everything. Experience it all. I think, in retrospect, it was motivated by that ephemeral fear of missing out. But no matter how much she did she never seemed to feel like she wasn't missing out, and after a while it started to grate on both of us. I wasn't doing enough, whether it was going to the best restaurants or clubs on the weekend, or trying for a head teacher position before I hit thirty. I don't even want to be a head teacher." He sighed. "I wasn't enough for her, and she was too much for me."

"But you still were going to ask her to marry you," Laura remarked, and James nodded his reluctant agreement.

"Yes, and in retrospect that was a very bad decision on my part. We would have made each other miserable in the long run, and we pretty much already were by that point. But in my family that's what you do—you meet someone, you get married, preferably before you're twenty-five." He took another sip of wine. "My siblings really do make it seem so very simple."

"HOW MANY OF your siblings are married?" Laura asked as she took out the plates that had been warming in the oven. It had been slightly disconcerting to hear about Helen. She wasn't jealous, not precisely, she was too old for that, but she felt...something. A little needling pinprick of discontent, although she wasn't sure why.

"Three," he answered as he put down his wine and helped her lay the table. "My older sister who has just had a baby—her third—and my brother, who helps my father run the farm. They have two kids. Then my younger sister, Elin, married last year, when she was twenty-seven. She left it a bit late," he joked.

"Wow, you'd better catch up," Laura teased back, only to see James smile back briefly enough to make her realise it was a bit of a sore point. Which of course made her wonder how she could possibly fit into this equation. What would his meet-to-marriage family think of their middle son bringing home a woman in her forties with almost two teenaged children of her own? The incongruity of it made her feel like wincing.

"So your family seems quite traditional," she remarked as she brought out the chicken, potatoes, and peas.

"Well, they are farmers and have been for over a hundred years," James replied. "I don't know how they could be anything else. And my parents are staunch churchgoers. I keep promising my mum I'll attend here, but I've only been once or twice." He nodded at the table. "This looks delicious, Laura. Thank you."

"Well, like I said, it was a matter of much deliberation. But don't worry, I won't be crushed if you don't like it. At least not much." She was joking to hide how nervous she felt, how much she wanted James to like everything, especially her. It wasn't quite so weird between them anymore, but the stakes still felt alarmingly high.

"I'm sure I'll love it." Laura refreshed their wine—they'd both already nearly finished their first glasses, which said something about how nervous they were—and then they sat down.

James took a bite of the chicken and pronounced it delicious, making Laura smile. Actually, she thought it was pretty good, which filled her with relief. Except now they had to find something else to talk about, and that seemed hard again. Why did dates have to be so...date-like? Everything became so *deliberate*, and therefore mechanical, and really she just wanted to be with James, the way they'd been before. The way they'd been on the bridge.

Whoa, girl. Easy.

Fortunately James was a bit better at small talk than she was, and he kept the conversation going, asking about the children's ski trip, and which periods of history she liked, and whether they wanted to buy a house in Wychwood or stay in Willoughby Close.

The conversation began to flow along with the wine, and

Laura felt herself relax. By dessert she had that loose-limbed—and loose-tongued—slumberous ease that came from three glasses of wine. If she wasn't careful, she'd say—or do—something stupid, but she hoped she had enough restraint and sobriety to keep herself from embarrassing herself.

After dinner they washed the dishes together, standing side by the side at the sink, and then Laura made coffee and they headed over to the sofa, which they had done several times before, but now there were no kids upstairs and she still felt a bit buzzy from the wine and they'd already kissed once. Surely they would kiss again…

"So what are your plans for the rest of the week?" James asked as he sipped his coffee. "A spa day? Sleeping in? Painting the house?"

"I haven't really thought much about it, to be honest." The week stretched ahead of her, unsettlingly empty. "Catch up on housework, I suppose. Send my CV out at some point. Not much. What about you?"

"Well, if I decide to be motivated, I'll do some DIY. I bought a wreck of a cottage and it needs a lot of work, most of which I haven't yet managed to get around to. So I'll be painting my house."

He smiled wryly, and perhaps because of the wine or just because she wanted to, Laura found herself blurting, "I could help you. With the painting. If you wanted."

"Is that really how you want to spend your half-term?"

He sounded dubious, and Laura wondered if he was letting her down.

"I don't mind." She wanted, Laura realised, not to spend her half-term alone, and more to the point, to spend it with him.

"If you're serious…"

"Sure." She smiled and shrugged, as if this were a friendly favour and not her begging with puppy eyes, *Please spend time with me. Please. Please.*

"That could be fun," James said slowly. "I haven't got any plans other than doing DIY, so…"

He trailed off, but the suggestion was there, shimmering between them. *Let's spend the half-term together.* Laura couldn't think of anything better, and yet, even with the leap of her excitement low in her belly, she already felt herself start to panic. *Where was this going? Where could it go? How and when could she tell her kids?*

"Laura," James said gently as he put down his coffee cup, "stop panicking."

"What…?" She looked at him in surprised confusion. "How do you know I'm panicking?"

"Because you get this deer-in-the-headlights look and a little dent in the middle of your forehead." He reached over and touched the middle of her forehead with his thumb, and even that was enough to make her blood start to sizzle. "Your worry dent." His fingers skimmed her cheek. "What are you worried about?"

"Just, you know." She swallowed hard. His fingers were still brushing her cheek, and a deep, molten yearning was spiralling up inside her. "Dating someone. It feels big to me, and I know it's not the same for—"

"It's big for me, too." He dropped his hand to her shoulder and gently enough so she could pull back if she wanted to, which she didn't, he drew her towards him. "Haven't you figured out yet that I'm kind of a geeky, old-fashioned guy?"

"Well, sort of, I suppose." She was very close to him now, practically on his lap, and his hands were framing his face as he smiled down at her, his eyes glinting like the Caribbean and the firelight from the wood burner catching the golden glints in his hair. Laura's head was swimming.

"I'm thinking about going in for our second kiss," he murmured, and Laura gulped and laughed at the same time, which definitely sounded strange.

"Yes, I realised that."

"Did you? Good."

And then he was kissing her, softly, sweetly, and her head was exploding and her heart was squeezing and oh, it felt lovely and overwhelming and strange.

She couldn't remember the last time she'd kissed someone like this, with such tenderness and yearning and hesitation, taking things so very slow because he knew that was what she needed.

After a few minutes they broke apart, both of them grinning rather self-consciously. Laura's lips were buzzing along with her head; she thought James must be able to feel the heavy thuds of her heart. Every sense was on exquisite overload.

"I should probably go," he said, and disappointment swamped through her, along with just a little bit of relief. This was starting to feel very intense.

"Go…" she repeated, and James smiled wryly.

"Before I get carried away."

In that moment Laura didn't think she'd mind too much if James got carried away, at least a little, but she recognised the wisdom of his words. "Okay."

She clambered rather inelegantly off the sofa and took their coffee cups into the kitchen while James collected his jacket. His hair was a little mussed, and Laura had a vague memory of running her hands through it as they'd kissed. It was enough to send that sweet longing spiralling through her again.

"I'll see you tomorrow?" she asked as she followed him to the door. "To paint?"

"Sounds good. Great, actually." He paused by the door, a rueful smile on his face, and Laura wondered if he was finding it as hard as she was to end this evening. She didn't want him to go, and yet the thought of anything else terrified her.

"I had a lovely time," she told him quietly, meaning it utterly.

"So it wasn't too weird in the end?"

"No, it wasn't."

"Good." He stared at her for a moment, and Laura stared back, and then somehow they were kissing again, a hard, urgent press of lips as he kept his hands on her waist and everything in her fizzed and fizzed.

"Good night, Laura," he said, and then he was gone.

Laura sagged against the door, everything in her spinning now as well as fizzing. She needed to call Chantal and give her a rundown of the evening—well, most of it—but right now she just wanted to savour it all by herself. The conversation, the kisses, just…everything. It had been, despite the initial awkwardness, the most perfect evening. She was sorry it had ended, but at least she had tomorrow—and really, the whole week—to look forward to.

With that thought foremost in her mind, Laura reached for her phone.

Chapter Seventeen

JAMES'S HOUSE REALLY was a wreck. He'd texted her directions that morning and armed with two cups of coffee and some freshly baked blueberry muffins, Laura had walked out of number three with a spring in her step.

Lindy must have been watching for her, because she practically sprinted out of her cottage before Laura had even locked her front door.

"How was the big date?" she'd demanded excitedly, and then she'd clocked the two cups and a knowing grin had spread over her face. "Looks like it must have gone quite well."

"It did, actually," Laura replied. Last night she'd spent two hours on the phone with Chantal going over every aspect—well, almost—of her date with James, and then had had a very mini breakdown as she realised how much she was falling for him, and how much that scared her.

Chantal had, as she always did, talked her down from the ledge and told her she needed to own this relationship, not tiptoe around it. Laura knew she was right, and so she gave

Lindy a direct look as she informed her, "It went really well, as a matter of fact."

"Wow." Lindy looked thrilled as well as intensely curious. "Can I ask who the lucky guy is?"

Laura hesitated, because owning a relationship and blabbing about it all over the village before she'd even told her own kids were two very different things. "You can," she replied finally, "but I'm afraid I'm not going to tell you. I haven't told Maggie or Sam yet, and they deserve to know first."

"Fair enough," Lindy agreed, her eyes sparkling, "but I think I can guess who it is."

Laura went a bit cold at that. She thought of how she and James had practically held hands in Tea on the Lea, walked up and down the high street, kissed on the bridge. Not to mention he'd also been seen having dinner at her house several times. Of course Lindy could guess. The grumpy man with a full sleeve of tattoos who ran the petrol station could probably guess, and the only words Laura had ever spoken to him were "Forty pounds on pump ten, please." That was the kind of place Wychwood-on-Lea was. Which meant she needed to tell Sam and Maggie sooner rather than later. A lot sooner.

"You might be able to," she conceded, "but I'd rather you didn't. This is very new and I really don't know how Sam or Maggie will take me dating someone. Anyone." Especially when the person was Sam's teacher who was ten years younger than her.

"I won't say a word," Lindy promised. "I don't like gossip myself, and there was enough of it when Roger and I were circling around each other." She reached out and touched Laura's arm. "I'm happy for you, Laura. Really."

"Thanks." Laura let out a little laugh. "I'm happy for myself, which is actually a really nice feeling. I forgot what it felt like, in this last year."

"I'm glad you're starting to remember, then."

Laura's good mood stayed with her as she walked from Willoughby Close into Wychwood; it was a fresh wintry day that held the faintest hope of spring, with crocuses poking their bright heads through frost-tipped grass, and the pavement sparkling with the morning's diamond-bright dew.

She found James's house easily enough, because, as he'd said in his text, it was the one that looked as if it should be condemned. A terraced cottage sandwiched between two immaculately kept residences that both had the distinctive sage-green trim known as Cotswold Green, it looked like a very poor relation.

The window and doorframe were clearly rotted through, the paint peeling off in long, dirty, curling strips, and the roof had boards of plywood nailed over where the slate tiles had fallen off. Laura stepped up to the rather battered door and knocked.

"I know, I know," James said before she'd even said hello. "It's a wreck. You were warned."

"So I was." She stepped inside and then felt a frisson of both pleasure and surprise as he took her by the waist and brushed a quick kiss across her lips. Was that where they were now?

"Are we at that stage yet?" James asked, reading her thoughts perfectly. "Kiss hello? Or not?"

"We can be," Laura replied, and he kissed her again.

Inside the cottage was even more dilapidated than it had looked from the exterior. Half the floor was covered in ratty old carpet in a hideous paisley pattern, the other half had been ripped down to very battered floorboards. The walls were a mishmash of ugly colours—burnt orange, dark brown, olive green.

"I started scraping paint and realised that was a lost cause," James explained. "So I thought I'd just paint over it all."

Laura stepped over a hole in the floor where some rotten floorboards had needed to be replaced, to peek into the kitchen, which was a living testament to the 1970s.

"Wow, whoever lived here really liked their olive and orange."

"I know. You should see the bathroom suite. Utterly avocado."

She handed him a cup of coffee and put the muffins on the kitchen table. "Well, let's get started, then."

"Or we could go for a walk," James suggested hopefully. "Since it's such a nice day."

"No, I think we'll paint," Laura told him with a laugh. "Let's get this done."

"All right, if we have to," James answered with a grin, and they got to work.

The last time Laura had painted a room was when she'd redone Maggie's bedroom in Woodbridge, when she'd turned twelve and had wanted something a bit edgier. She'd asked for a black statement wall and Laura had talked her down to deep purple. They'd painted it together, joking and having fun, and the bittersweet memory made her feel both happy and sad. Would they share that kind of laughter again? She hoped so. She hoped they were on their way towards it.

"A penny for your thoughts," James asked, and so Laura told him.

"From what I've seen and heard, teenaged girls are tough, even without a bereavement in the mix. My little sister is coming up on seventeen and she's only just starting to come out of it."

"You mentioned she self-harmed," Laura said hesitantly. "Do you know why?"

James was silent for a moment, his face a study of thoughtful reflection as he carefully painted around a doorframe. He'd chosen a pale blue grey for the sitting room that Laura thought would look lovely when it was done. It would also need about six coats to cover up the dark paint underneath.

"My family is wonderful," he finally answered, choosing his words with care. "And we're all very close. But like any family, I suppose, there are dynamics."

"Around the farm?" He'd hinted at as much, when he'd mentioned his brother.

"Yes, in part. I think I told you last night that the farm has been in my family for a while."

"A hundred years or so, right?"

"Yes. Bought by my great-grandfather. And farmers are proud people. It's hard work, and it's even harder to make a living from it these days, so there's this whole narrative around the farm—keeping it—that keeps us together, as a family. Whatever happens, whatever the cost, the farm comes first."

Laura absorbed this statement silently, along with James's tone. He didn't sound bitter, not exactly, but something close to it.

"And that affected your sister?" she surmised as they both continued painting, the steady, soft slap of their brushes against the wall the strangely soothing soundtrack to their conversation.

"Yes, at least I think that was part of it. There's the sense of tradition too, and we all rebelled against that as we grew up, each in our own way."

"And how did you rebel?" Laura asked with a smile.

"I parted my hair on the other side," James joked. "Seriously, I didn't do much at all. Like I said, late bloomer."

"I'm going to need to see photographic evidence of this."

He pretended to shudder. "Please, no. You'll never look at me the same."

"Now I'm really curious."

They kept painting, and they took a break for lunch, with James making what he called 'epic sandwiches' in the orange and olive kitchen. It was warm enough to sit outside, and he led her out to the garden, a long, narrow strip that ran all the way down to a stream, a tiny tributary of the Lea River. Like the house, the garden was in need of some serious DIY as well as TLC, but as she sat on the cracked stones of the little patio, Laura could already imagine it—the grass neatly trimmed, borders of riotous wildflowers and a wooden swing in the wonky old apple tree at the bottom of the garden.

"This will be lovely, when you're done," she told him, and James grimaced good-naturedly.

"Yes, when I'm about fifty."

Which wasn't all that far away from her own age, yet she remembered how old fifty had seemed when she'd been in her early thirties. Absolutely ancient.

No matter how often she tried to convince herself the difference in their ages didn't matter, in moments like this she couldn't help but feel like it might.

JAMES KNEW EXACTLY when Laura started thinking about

their ages. He'd joked about being fifty and then he saw a shadow pass over her face and inwardly he cursed his stupid blunder. She seemed to count those nine years far more heavily than he did.

He didn't even think about their ages, not really, although he supposed, if things got serious between them, he should. But who was he kidding? Things were already serious between them, at least on his side. He hoped on Laura's too; he knew she hadn't gone on a date with him lightly.

And yet they weren't so serious that she'd told her kids about them, something he wanted to ask about but felt reluctant to do so because he wasn't sure he'd like the answer. He didn't want to be Laura's dirty little secret, a ridiculous toy boy to her determined cougar. He didn't see them that way at all, but he wondered sometimes if she did.

Still, it felt too early to be talking about all that, especially when the sun was shining and crocuses were pushing up through the earth and they still had another six hours or so of painting to be getting on with. He just wanted to enjoy the day—and every day this week—no matter what the future held.

"Shall we keep at it?" he asked as he finished his sandwich, and Laura nodded. James extended a hand to her to help her up, and as she took it, he couldn't resist tugging hard enough that she bumped into him, which gave him another excuse to kiss her. And then kiss her again.

"I thought when you said keep at it you meant the painting," Laura said a little breathlessly when he'd finally, reluctantly, let her go. He was doing his best to take things nice and slow because that felt like the right thing to do, but his blood was raging within him.

"I did, but then I changed my mind." He gave her a lopsided smile, doing his best to tamp down on his libido as they headed into the house.

They spent the rest of the afternoon finishing the living room, which looked much nicer with its blue walls, even if there was still a hole in the centre of the room.

"I hope the upstairs is a bit further on than this," Laura told him with a laugh. She had a smear of paint on one cheek and her hair was delightfully mussed. James wanted to kiss her again, but he didn't.

"The master bedroom is just about liveable," he answered. "The three other bedrooms I can't answer for."

"No wonder you want to eat at mine. You've been living like this for five months?"

He nodded. "I'm not as good at DIY as I'd hoped I was."

"Didn't you know?"

"Not really. Remember I told you how my brother was the big, manly type?" He spoke lightly but as ever talking about Jack made something in him tighten, just a little, and not in a good way.

"I think you're a manly type," Laura told him and with an impish smile she squeezed one of his biceps. "Definitely."

Which emboldened him to ask her if she wanted to get a

takeaway. He'd spend every minute, every second, of this next week with her if he could.

And fortunately Laura seemed to feel the same way, because she readily agreed to a takeaway, and to watching a film on Netflix afterwards, and even helping him paint the kitchen the next day.

"You need to get rid of those colours before you have a permanent headache. It's the least I can do."

James agreed, only if they could go for a walk the day after that, which they did, all the way along the river to Burford, under a rainy sky with puddles like mini-lakes on the low-lying land, but who cared? To him the day was beautiful, as they strolled hand in hand along the river, stopping to kiss every so often, although not often enough for his liking.

"I think Maggie is enjoying flirting with the ski instructors more than the actual skiing," she told him when he asked for an update on the holiday. "And Sam is sticking to the bunny slope. But I think they're happy. My in-laws spoil them rotten, so they'll be enjoying that. Hot chocolate and ice cream sundaes every day."

"Sounds good to me."

"I wish I could give them nice holidays," Laura confessed a bit wistfully. "I know love and attention are far more important than a trip to Tenerife or what have you, but still." She sighed. "But the truth is, I never will on a teacher's salary, and that's assuming I even get a job."

"At least they have grandparents to give them those kinds of treats."

"Yes." She sounded a bit uncertain, which made James wonder about her relationship with her in-laws. The few remarks she'd made suggested it wasn't straightforward, but then what relationship was?

Right now, in these halcyon days when it was just the two of them, their relationship *did* seem straightforward, but James suspected that was simply because they didn't have to deal with any of the usual complicated mess and muck of life—like difficult children, awkward families, demanding jobs.

And yet, as the week progressed, he was more and more tempted to include Laura in the mess of his life—and ask her to accompany him to Shropshire that weekend. He imagined the look of stunned delight on his mother's face when he finally brought someone home. And he liked the idea of having a whole weekend with Laura, facing the farm with her by his side, although admittedly it meant her seeing his weaknesses in all their unprepossessing glory.

But as the week had gone on, he realised he actually wanted that. Well, sort of. He wanted her in his life, whatever that looked like. Whatever it meant. He wanted to take things to the next level, even if that was risky and hard.

And so, on Thursday evening, when they were watching a movie at Laura's and there wasn't any more time because he was expected in Shropshire tomorrow evening, he asked her, with his heart in his mouth and his voice coming out in something like a squeak so he had to clear his throat. Twice.

"You want me to come with you?" Laura looked so flummoxed that it was hard for him not to cringe inwardly. Did she have to be *that* surprised?

"That was the concept I was going for, yes."

"To meet your family?" Now she was the one squeaking, in incredulity. Great.

"Again, yes, that is the idea. Is it so terrible?"

"No, I'm just surprised. I mean…that's big. And I haven't even told my kids yet."

"Are you going to?" He tried to sound interested rather than aggressive, or worse, hurt, but the secretiveness of their relationship still annoyed him. They'd been in each other's pockets this last week but Laura had been reluctant to get a drink at The Three Pennies together, in case someone saw them.

"Well, yes, at some point. We've been spending just about every day together, haven't we?" Except when he'd had a dentist appointment, and when she'd wanted to work on her CV.

"Yes, I know." She bit her lip. "It just feels like a lot. Won't…won't your family be horrified by me?"

"Horrified?" He stared at her in dismayed surprise. "Why would they be horrified?"

"Because I'm so much older than you. And I have two children already."

"So?"

She shrugged. "You said they were traditional…"

"What does that have to do with anything? Besides, you're a perfectly respectable widow." He gave her what he hoped was a teasing smile. "They'll love you." *As I do.* Thankfully he didn't go that far. He wasn't ready to make that kind of declaration, even in the quiet of his own mind.

Still, Laura hesitated, enough to make James backtrack. Perhaps he was jumping the gun a little. Coming across too strong.

"Look, it's fine if you feel it's too soon," he said, trying for an offhand tone but speaking too quickly. "It probably is too soon. In fact, I'm sure it is. This is more like a six-months-in thing, isn't it? I do get that, believe me. It's just that the timing seemed right since your kids weren't here and I don't actually get out to the farm that much, but—"

"James." Laughing, she pressed a finger to his lips. "Enough. I'm sorry I was so surprised. I wasn't expecting it, but I've got used to the idea now. So, yes. I'll go with you. Thank you for asking me." And smiling, she leaned over and pressed a kiss to his mouth.

Chapter Eighteen

THE DRIVE FROM Wychwood-on-Lea to the outskirts of Shrewsbury took a little over two hours, up the M5 from Birmingham and then westward, towards the Welsh border where James's family had their farm.

As Laura gazed out at the pleasant green fields glinting with rain puddles in the fragile February sunshine, she tried to untangle the knotted jumble of emotions that had been lodged within her ever since James had asked her to accompany him home last night.

Her initial surprise—total shock, really—had soon been replaced by a flattered gratification, along with a very real and deep apprehension. The last week had been lovely, *so* lovely, just the two of them painting walls, walking in the wood, watching movies, chatting, laughing, and best of all, kissing.

It had felt more like a fairy tale than a holiday, with no intrusions of real life save for the occasional text from Maggie or Sam, assuring they were having a brilliant time, or at least that was what Laura inferred from the comments they made about the food, the hot tub at their chalet, and, from Maggie, the fit ski instructors.

For the last week she hadn't had to think or worry about *anything*, and the freedom had been glorious. It hadn't made her completely worry-free, of course, since she was prone to a bit of a panic, but now that a new reality was galloping towards them at a very brisk clip, Laura realised just how relaxed the week had been.

Since James's invitation, questions had been running through her mind on a constant, anxiety-inducing reel. What would his family think of her? What did this mean for their relationship? How could she tell her kids about him? How would they react?

And then, on the heels of all that, even more enormous issues reared their demanding heads. If they were seriously dating now, did they need to talk about the future in a concrete and practical way? What if James wanted children, coming from a large family himself? Could she have another baby, or even two? Did she want them? How could they even talk about babies when they'd gone on their first date less than a week ago, not counting that coffee in Tea on the Lea?

Her brain felt as if it might explode. It was a wonder she wasn't hyperventilating. Laura slid a glance at James; he had seemed preoccupied and a bit withdrawn since they'd got in the car over an hour ago, and they'd barely spoken since they'd left Wychwood, something that added to her anxiety.

It reminded her of Tim's dark moods, the way he'd

sometimes emotionally withdraw so much it almost felt as if he wasn't physically present, or worse, like he was, but only as some grim, looming shadow. But it wasn't fair, Laura reminded herself, to cast James in Tim's likeness. And anyway, he was allowed to have his own weaknesses and worries, since she had a whole shedful to deal with.

That was what real relationships were about—not some week-long idyll where reality never intruded, but battling through the muck and mire of life together, holding each other up, working through the problems.

Which made her wonder if she even wanted that, or if she was ready for it.

She'd already had an epic conversation with Chantal about it all last night, after James had asked her to come for the weekend, and in a moment of romance-fuelled optimism Laura had said yes. As soon as James had gone home she'd called Chantal to tell her everything that had happened, and then she really *had* started hyperventilating.

"I'm too old to start a serious relationship," she'd told Chantal in a voice that was almost shrill with panic. "I have two children to think of, two emotionally needy and de-manding children who have been recently bereaved. Plus I've got my own grief, which sometimes feels as if I've barely got a handle on. I can't deal with someone else and all their issues."

"James doesn't exactly seem like someone with a lot of issues," Chantal had remarked dryly, to which Laura had snapped,

"He's *human*. He has issues. Everyone does. And he deserves to have someone who can handle whatever he's dealing with. I'm not sure I can."

"What has actually happened, to make you think you're going to have to deal with all these so-called issues?" Chantal asked. "Because you're talking as if James has just told you he's got cancer or something."

"I don't know," Laura had admitted after a pause. "There isn't anything specific, per se. It just feels as if it's all become very *real*."

"Well, it has, and that's a good thing, Laur," Chantal told her bracingly. "You can't play-act at a relationship, at least not for long, and that wouldn't be very satisfying, anyway. Think of *The Velveteen Rabbit*. Real is good."

"Real is painful," Laura shot back. "And hard. And doesn't the rabbit end up being burned to death?"

"No, he's left out in a rubbish bag and the fairy makes him real," Chantal replied patiently. "*I* know that, and I don't even have kids. But the point of the story is that being real means being loved, becoming shabby, being worn to bits."

"It's been a while since I read it," Laura muttered, but she took her friend's point. If she cared about James, then she'd want their relationship to be real—not just flirting in the schoolyard, or Monday night dinners, or a week spent in each other's pockets.

But it felt scary. Very scary. And even scarier because as they turned onto the road to Little Hawes from Shrewsbury, James had started looking incredibly grim, in a way she'd never seen before, his usually smiling mouth in a foreboding downturn, his hands clenched on the steering wheel, his eyes narrowed as he drove down the single-track lane.

"Looking forward to going home?" Laura asked, pitching her tone somewhere between teasing and downright sarcastic.

James grimaced. "Can you tell I'm a little unenthused?"

"Yes, actually, which is making me nervous. Not to blame you or anything, but why did you ask me to come again?" She let out a little laugh to mitigate the accusation she'd heard in her voice.

He glanced at her, smiling, although his eyes looked serious. "For moral support?"

Laura bit her lip. She wasn't being supportive right now, was she? Goodness, but this was *hard*. "Sorry. I get this is hard for you."

He shrugged. "I know it's mainly my issue, and no one else's. I just need to get over it." He sighed. "Do you know how many times I tell myself that?"

"Hundreds?" Laura guessed. "We all have our patterns and pitfalls, don't we? You might have noticed I have a smallish tendency to panic."

"What?" James raised his eyebrows in mocking incredulity. "No."

"I know." Laura nodded solemnly, relieved he seemed to be coming out of his dark mood. "Crazy, isn't it? Admittedly I usually hide it quite well."

"Except when you start to hyperventilate." He reached for her hand, brushing her knuckles briefly with his own before he returned his hand to the wheel. "You're right, though. Everyone's struggling with something."

"It'll be okay, James." At least, she hoped it would. She paused, needing to ask, to know, although she suspected he wouldn't appreciate the question. "Did you tell your family I'm older than you? And that I have almost two teenaged kids?"

James gave her a smiling glance. "Sam's only eleven, and no. They didn't ask for details, and I didn't volunteer them. But my mum was thrilled I'm finally bringing someone home."

"She might feel differently when she sees me," Laura couldn't keep from saying, and James let out a little sigh of exasperation.

"Laura, the age thing matters so much more to you than it does to anyone else, I promise."

"You can't know that," she said as reasonably as she could. "Since they don't even know yet."

"What I know," James replied evenly, "is that you're making a very big deal of it."

With a little frisson of panicky surprise, Laura realised they were actually almost arguing. There had not been a single cross word between them since they'd first met, and now they were starting to snipe at each other? Her stomach soured at the thought. Instead of the beginning, this could be the end of everything. Everything was too new and fragile to be tested this way, with family dynamics and her panicky paranoia and James's issues with his dad. What had she been thinking of, agreeing to come?

"I'm sorry," James said after a moment. "I don't mean to snap. I always feel a bit tense when I come home, as you have sussed out, which is probably making you dread meeting my family. They're all actually lovely, I promise. This is much more about me than it is about them. I know I've said that before, but it really is true. I just need to get over myself."

"Easier said than done," Laura replied with a sympathetic smile. "I'm sorry for overreacting." She wanted to be as grown-up about this as he could be, even though she still felt panicky. "I'm tense, too, which isn't helping you at all, is it?" She drew a steadying breath and let it out slowly. "Why is this about you? What do you mean by that?"

"Just my old insecurities rearing up yet again," James replied with a shrug. "Issues around my dad, and feeling less— well, valued, I suppose, than my brother." He gave her an unhappy grimace of apology. "This makes me sound rather pathetic, I realise, at my age."

"No more pathetic than anyone else," Laura returned. "It's just hard to imagine. You seem so confident to me. As well as insanely gorgeous." That coaxed a small smile, at least, although it didn't reach his eyes. With a pang Laura wondered whether this weekend would really make or break them. Whichever it was, she had a feeling it would change things, and she didn't think she was ready for that.

JAMES WAS STARTING to seriously regret inviting Laura on this weekend. What had seemed so lovely when he'd asked— the prospect of having her company, of showing her off— now just felt like a minefield of dangers. Why not just invite her to view all his insecurities, all his weaknesses, everything about himself that he didn't like? Why not make a list? *This is what you signed up for*, except they'd only been dating a week and going home to meet the parents was, like he'd said, more like six-month territory.

He had a very bad feeling about this. Laura had seemed panicked since they'd got in the car, and frankly he couldn't blame her. He hadn't exactly talked his family up, had he? And he couldn't keep his mood from taking its usual nosedive when he headed home. He enjoyed seeing his sisters, and yes, even his brother, and his mum would fuss over him in a way that was both irritating and flattering, but what about his dad?

David Hill was a salt of the earth type who won people's respect if not their hearts. Generous, gruff, unyielding and hardworking. And he and James had never seemed to be able to agree about anything.

Get over it already, James told himself, as he had a thousand times before. Easier said than done, it seemed, judging by the way he was feeling now. He took a deep breath and let it out slowly. There was the farm ahead of them—rolling fields dotted with cows and sheep, the corrugated iron of the barn roof glinting in the sunlight, the square, stolid farmhouse of dark grey pebbledash standing like a sentinel on the top of the hill.

"Here we are," James said as cheerfully as he could. Laura reached over and placed her hand over his on the gearstick. She gave him a smile that was part sympathy, part encouragement, and James didn't know whether it made him feel better or worse.

Dogs erupted from the house as he pulled up alongside his father's ancient, mud-splattered Land Rover, and his sister's smarter estate, squaring his shoulders as he stepped out of the car.

"James!" His mother came forward, wreathed in smiles, her arms outstretched. James hugged her briefly before she pulled away to look with eager expectation at Laura, who was shyly emerging from the passenger seat of his car.

"And you must be Laura."

James didn't miss the slightly knitted brow that accompanied this statement, and he knew Laura, didn't either. Perhaps he should have warned his mother that Laura was older than him, but really, what did it matter? It was the last thing on his mind right now.

"So lovely to meet you, Mrs Hill," Laura said, and shook hands.

"Oh, call me Janet, please," his mum insisted. "And yes, a pleasure." She'd recovered from her surprise, although James could tell she was still a bit taken aback. "I hope you don't mind dogs," she added, for one of the springer spaniels was circling around Laura and sniffing with intent.

"No, not at all. We have a golden retriever at home. He's being watched by a friend for the weekend."

"Come inside, come inside," Janet urged. "The kettle's boiled."

James placed one hand on Laura's lower back, anchoring himself to her, and her to him, as they headed into the farmhouse, which sometimes felt like falling back in time. His mother's decorating taste was decidedly twenty years out of date, with so many antiques that it might as well be fifty or even one hundred. Not that he minded; there was something comforting about the dark, heavy furniture that had never once been shifted, the black-and-white photographs of his unsmiling grandparents and great-aunts and uncles on the walls. Comforting, but also stifling.

The kitchen had always been the heart of the house—a big, square room with an ancient and temperamental Rayburn taking up most of one wall, a large, rectangular table of scarred oak in the centre, and a jumble of Welly boots and plus-fours cluttering the corners.

James's older sister Mhairi was sitting at the table holding baby Hannah, with her two older ones pounding Play-Doh at the other end. James introduced them all, and to her credit Mhairi didn't bat an eyelash at seeing Laura for the first time, or when Laura greeted his two little nephews, and made a point of mentioning her own children.

"It's been a while since mine have played with Play-Doh," she said quite deliberately, James thought, and his mum paused in pouring the tea.

"You have children?" Her tone was an attempt at being neutral, with more than a whiff of scandalised.

Laura's smile was bright and determined, if a little brittle. "Yes, Maggie is fourteen, Sam eleven. James is Sam's teacher, actually. That's how we met."

"Oh, I see."

An awkward silence ensued before James did his valiant best to bridge it. "Where are Dad and Jack?"

"They're out in the shed," his mum answered. "Lambing season, you know." This for Laura's benefit, James supposed, since he certainly knew when lambing season was. "Jane's at work—that's Jack's wife." Again for Laura's benefit. "Elin is arriving later today, and Bella is out with friends but she promised to be home for dinner. Gwen is on her way home from uni. Her train gets into Shrewsbury at six."

Janet started handing cups of tea around. "So, Laura," she said brightly. "Tell us about yourself."

"I'm not sure how much there is to say," Laura answered with an uncertain laugh. She glanced at James and then continued a little stiltedly, "I used to be a history teacher, but I stopped when my children were little." She paused, giving James another uncertain glance before continuing, "I only moved to Wychwood-on-Lea in January. Before that I lived in Suffolk… My husband died in a car accident just over a year ago." This last was said in a rush, and his mum blinked in surprise.

"Oh, my dear, I'm so sorry," she said, and James detected a thawing in her voice and manner. No doubt she'd assumed Laura was divorced, a black mark in her book. He sighed inwardly, and Mhairi, no doubt wanting to deflect attention from Laura, held Hannah out to him.

"How about a cuddle from Uncle James?"

"All right." He scooped the baby up in one arm, an old hand now that he had five nieces and nephews. He loved babies, something that made him feel as if he were a bit soppy, but he didn't care. He brought Hannah up to his chest and pressed his lips against her downy head, breathing in that lovely milky baby smell that seemed to him a comforting mixture of laundry detergent and toast.

Mhairi eyed him affectionately. "You really are a natural."

"It's easy when you don't have them twenty-four seven."

"Yes, remind me when you were offering to babysit for a weekend?" Mhairi half-joked. "So Rob and I can get away?"

"A whole weekend?" James feigned alarm, but actually he wouldn't mind. "My house is a construction site at the moment, as Laura can attest to, but when it's ready to receive very small visitors, I'll be more than happy to have them." He rocked Hannah gently. "You know that, Mhairi, right?"

His older sister eyed him with her distinctive brand of tolerant affection. "Yes, I do."

James rocked Hannah a bit more as she started to grizzle, and eventually, reluctantly, he handed her back to his sister before turning to his nephews who looked as if they were trying to kill the Play-Doh rather than mould it, although Tommy, the younger one, was also trying to eat it.

"Easy there, kiddo," James said as he rescued a disgustingly squidgy piece of damp Play-Doh from his nephew's chubby fingers. "It's for playing with, yeah?"

He glanced up at Laura, meaning to share the humorous moment as well as to check how she was coping with all this mayhem, but to his surprise, for a second, she looked utterly stricken.

James felt as if his heart were leaping into his throat at the look on her face—what on earth could be so wrong? But then it cleared, and she smiled at him and said lightly, "Why is it that children find Play-Doh so delicious?"

The conversation moved on easily enough, but James was left with the lingering and uneasy sense that this weekend was about to send him and Laura right off the rails.

Chapter Nineteen

THE NIGHT AIR smelled of coal smoke and cow as Laura tramped through a dark, muddy field with James at her side. With the farmhouse full to the rafters—she was sharing a bedroom with teenaged Bella—a walk in the dark was their only chance for any privacy.

It had been a happy and chaotic afternoon and evening, with people coming and going, a dozen different conversations seeming to happen at once as Laura did her best to try to remember who everyone was—Mhairi and Rob with their three children Ben, Tommy, and Hannah; James's brother Jack with his wife Jane and their two boys Brody and Gethin; Elin and her husband Rob, and then Gwen and Bella, plus Janet and David reigning over it all, and the three dogs whose names Laura couldn't remember on top of everything else.

It had all been a lovably jumbled mess, and Laura had taken to the homely warmth of the farmhouse, so many things happening at once, the deep and abiding sense that everyone loved one another, and yet there had been undercurrents.

Laura had felt the beginnings of them with Janet's diplomatic silences and unable-to-be-disguised surprise at the sight of an obviously older Laura; she'd felt their strength when James's father had come into the house with his brother Jack, both tall, strapping men with cold-reddened faces and a taciturn manner. David Hill's only greeting for his second son had been a nod and a grunt.

The talk over the evening meal in the fusty, old-fashioned dining room had been varied, but David's contribution had only been to address Jack about the lambing. When Elin had asked James how he was finding Wychwood Primary, David had snorted once, the sound not quite one of derision, but almost.

Laura had learned over the course of the meal that all of the Hill children were involved in farming in some way save for James. Mhairi and Rob ran a farm shop in Cheltenham that was supplied locally, including by the Hill farm, and Elin worked for Natural England, advocating to the government on behalf of farmers. Gwen was studying land management at uni and Bella was thinking of doing the same. Jack worked the farm with his father, and he and his family lived in a house they built themselves half a mile away, on the other side of the property.

As the meal progressed, Laura could see why James felt like an outlier, and she knew every deliberate silence on his father's part was felt like a wound. It made her ache, and yet she couldn't even be truly angry on James's behalf, because it was obvious that everyone loved him, if with a sort of bemused confusion about some of his life choices, and his father was simply the man he was, no more, no less. Laura didn't think he meant anything unkindly; it was more he couldn't understand what made his son tick. That realisation, however, made James's unhappiness no less.

Although as they tramped through the fields, stumbling over the tussocks in the darkness, it wasn't James's family that Laura was thinking about, but rather her own. Or lack of it. The future that felt as if it just raced up to smack right into the present.

"Was this a mistake?" James asked, his voice seeming disembodied in the darkness, after they'd been walking in silence for a good fifteen minutes.

"I like your family," Laura said, which was true enough.

"But?" James turned to look at her, no more than a gleam of eyes and teeth in the starless night. "Because I have been sensing a but from you all evening."

"It's a lot to take in," Laura said slowly. She didn't want to have this conversation, and yet it now felt inevitable.

"What is a lot to take in? My family? Or me?"

"You?" Laura wished she could see his expression, because his tone had sounded a bit bitter. "What do you mean by that?"

He shrugged, his hands dug deep into the pockets of his waxed jacket. "Coming home doesn't exactly cast me into the most flattering light. I know that."

"James, you told me on the way here that the issues you had with your family were more about you than them. You haven't been cast in an unflattering light at all, trust me." She paused, doing her best to keep her voice gentle. "I think you feel that way, but no one else does. I certainly don't. You're still the amazing, insanely gorgeous guy I fell for when I first met him." She kept her tone light even though the admission made her feel so very vulnerable. "I promise."

He sighed, barely seeming to take in her words. "I can barely paint a wall, and my brother built his own house. It's hard not to make the comparison."

"I didn't agree to go on a date with you because I thought you could build me a house," Laura joked, but judging by James's lack of response it fell flat. "Why does this bug you so much?" she asked softly, and he sighed again, a sound of aggravation, as he drove one hand through his hair.

"Honestly? I don't know. I know I shouldn't let it. I'm thirty-two years old, after all. I'm way past this. I should be. And mostly it doesn't bother me. It's just when I come home, and I feel about fifteen again, and never measuring up. It brings everything back."

"Is that how your dad made you feel? Like you weren't enough?"

"Not deliberately, which is almost worse. It's like I...I *baffle* him."

"And yet you were still strong enough to make your own choices and live life on your own terms," Laura returned. "That takes strength and confidence, James. It's admirable."

"Thanks." He let out another weary sigh before he turned to her with a smile she saw as a gleam of teeth in the darkness. "So what's been bugging you this evening?" he asked. "Or do I want to know?"

Laura hesitated, feeling as if she were edging towards a precipice that she felt like running away from. They'd only been dating a *week*. And yet seeing James cradle his niece that afternoon…it had crystallised an unwelcome knowledge inside her. If their relationship wasn't going anywhere, it wasn't fair to James to keep it going. Yet how could either of them make that decision now? But there wasn't enough time to deliberate or dither. It put them in an impossible situation, and yet it was one she had to address.

"Do you want children?" she asked abruptly. "Children of your own?"

James was silent for a moment, no doubt absorbing the sudden shift in their conversation. "Yes," he finally said. "Ideally. But it's not—it wouldn't necessarily be a deal breaker for me, Laura, if that's…if that's what you're thinking about."

The painfully wobbly note in his voice made her fear otherwise. "It feels far too early to have this conversation," she said after a moment. "And yet I don't know how we can *not* have it, considering."

"Considering what?"

"Considering I'm forty-one, James. I know you don't like me to keep rabbiting on about the difference in our ages, but it *matters*, whether we want it to or not. I'm forty-two in April. If I'm going to have another baby, it would have to be soon." She flushed, cringing inwardly at her own reckless-ness. To talk about having a baby together when they'd barely begun dating…! What was she thinking?

"Do you want to have another baby?" James asked after an interminable silence. He sounded so guarded, so Laura had no idea what he thought about the concept, or this whole conversation. Everything in her was cringing with mortification. Why had she gone there, so soon? She'd been so reckless, so stupid, and yet she didn't know how she could have kept herself from it.

"I don't know. After I had Sam and Maggie, I was hop-ing to have another, but Tim wanted to stick to two, which seemed sensible financially. And now…well, it was absolute-ly off my radar for a long time. In a way, it still is. And I hate that we have to talk about this, when we're still just getting to know one another. It feels way too soon, like I'm forcing something that might make or break us."

"That's what I did this weekend though, isn't it?" James sighed dispiritedly. "I almost wish I could put back the clock. Go back to last night when we were canoodling on the sofa and I never even mentioned coming home."

Laura was silent, unsure how to feel about that futile

wish. "I feel like we're both in an impossible situation," she said miserably. "I haven't even told Sam and Maggie about us. I have no idea how they'll take it. And what about you? If—if things were to progress, do you want to take on the raising of two teenagers? You'd practically be their stepdad." She closed her eyes briefly. "Please believe me when I say I know how crazy this all sounds, but it matters."

James reached for her hand, lacing his cold fingers through hers. "We're both borrowing trouble, aren't we? I'm thinking too much about the past, and you're thinking too much about the future. Perhaps we should just enjoy the present." He tugged on her hand and she came towards him willingly, gladly, because at least here, with his arms around her and his lips brushing hers, the world righted itself. She believed things could work out. She realised she wanted them to, desperately.

But would that be enough? *If wishes were horses, beggars would ride.* It was an old-fashioned phrase her mother had used to say, and with a pang of bittersweet longing, Laura wished she had her mum around to give her advice. She'd died when Laura had been only twenty-four, pancreatic cancer, diagnosis to death in just six months.

Laura let out a shuddery sigh as James enfolded her in a hug and she pressed her cheek against the corduroy lapel of his jacket, closing her eyes against the world and all the uncertainty she feared they both still felt. At least they were here now, together, arms around each other, lips on lips, finding each other in the darkness.

"I LIKE HER."

Elin gave James a wry smile that he returned, albeit with a bit of effort. It was six o'clock on Saturday morning, and he and Elin were alone in the kitchen. His dad and Jack would already be out in the barn; his mother would bustle in soon, ready to make a full fry-up for the whole family. Everyone else was understandably asleep. Still a farmer's son, James had never got out of the habit of getting up early.

"I do, too," he said as he poured himself a cup of coffee. The kitchen was full of pale morning light, the only sound the comforting rumble of the Rayburn and the gentle snoring of the dogs sprawled out on the floor.

"Much more than Helen," Elin continued. "She was always looking at you as if she was thinking of ways you could improve. Laura seems real. Genuine, I mean."

"Yes," James agreed briefly, taking a sip of his coffee.

Elin cocked her head and gave him a considering look. "Why don't you seem more pleased?"

James hesitated, unsure how to answer. He was pleased, of course he was. He was *thrilled*. But last night had thrown up way too many questions. Part of him just wanted things to be simple—he liked her, she liked him. Easy. But then Laura had started talking about babies and him being a stepdad and James's mind had gone into overload.

Yes, he wanted children, he always had, but he hadn't thought about the *specifics*. Like Laura having his baby, a prospect that filled him with both physical and emotional yearning, but also scared him half to death.

And what about being an actual stepfather? He hadn't considered *that* angle before. He saw himself as more an uncle or even big brother kind of guy, a buddy, but if he and Laura…if he and Laura stayed together, actually *married*, then yes, he needed to think about those kinds of things…which blew his mind.

"It's complicated," he told Elin.

"Every relationship is complicated," she returned. "Because every relationship has two human beings in it."

"Still."

"Still what?" Elin raised her eyebrows in challenge, as if she suspected he was the one dragging his feet.

"It's not what you think," he explained a bit tersely. "Laura's the one who is cautious. Her husband died just a little over a year ago, and she has her kids to think about. I understand that." Even if he didn't completely like it. Even if he was feeling a little cautious now, too.

"And you're ready to sign on the dotted line?" His sister's features softened with sympathy, making James grimace. Why was he the one who was ready to commit, who wanted to go all in? Except did he even want to, anymore?

"I suppose I'm a bit naïve when it comes to relationships," he told his sister on a sigh. "Or maybe just simplistic.

I think if two people like each other, that's it, no problem. Everything can be worked out." Except when it couldn't.

"That's a good way to be, James," Elin told him.

"Even if it hurts and I stay single forever?" he only half-joked.

"Laura being cautious is one thing," she answered after a moment, her eyes crinkled in concern. "But do you feel like this weekend has been too much for her? It's making her rethink the relationship? I know we can be a bit full on."

"I hope it hasn't," James answered frankly. Even with all the questions Laura had fired at him last night, all the possibilities, responsibilities, uncertainties…he still wanted to keep going. He knew that absolutely, and it both fired him with purpose and made him afraid.

The last week had been just about the best of his life. He wasn't ready to throw it all in just because it might get a bit tricky, or even a *lot* tricky. He knew that, and he was willing to fight for her. For them.

But what if Laura didn't feel the same?

BY SUNDAY AFTERNOON, when they were driving back to Wychwood, James was tense and exhausted and also relieved to be going home. Nothing terrible had happened, fortunately, but then nothing terrible ever did. His family didn't fight or even shout. There were no falling-outs or arguments. Everyone got along, no matter what, and silence was the preferred indication of disapproval, although so rarely acknowledged.

His mum and sisters, at least, had made Laura feel welcome, although Janet Hill had looked at her with the same sort of affectionate bafflement she regarded her son. As if they both were unusual specimens, creatures from another universe who didn't live and breathe by the farming calendar.

His father and brother had been a bit less welcoming, although not intentionally so. At least, James didn't think so. They just were who they were—strong, silent men whose conversation revolved around the farm and not much else. James sometimes wondered how Jack had managed to date and marry a woman like Emma, who was also from a farming background but charming and sociable, and then he wondered why, if Jack could, he couldn't.

Still, he and Laura made it through—three meals a day with the whole family, a tour of the barns and lambing sheds on Saturday afternoon followed by a trip into Shrewsbury with his sisters, church on Sunday, an enormous roast dinner, and then another tramp through muddy fields. Laura had been game for it all, always friendly and interested, chatting to his sisters, engaging as best as she could with his parents, but James couldn't help but feel as if a veil had come down over her eyes, her heart, if that wasn't being too fanciful. He felt like he didn't know what she was thinking about anything, including him, and that made him feel vulnerable in a way he really didn't like.

A gusty sigh of relief blew through him as they turned off the single-track lane onto the main road to Shrewsbury. "So," he made himself ask. "How bad was it?"

"What a question." She was looking out the window so he couldn't gauge her expression, not that he could really look, as he was driving. "Do you want to try rephrasing that?"

"Or you could just tell me." Where had that faint edge in his voice come from? They were finally alone, away from the farm. He didn't want to pick anything close to a fight. He wanted to commiserate, to grow closer together...if they could.

"I think it was far worse for you than me," Laura said quietly, her face still to the window. "I actually had a nice time, James. Your family is lovely, just as you said."

That simple statement, made so sincerely, should have brought relief, the tension bracketing his shoulder blades finally starting to loosen. But it didn't. Instead that perverse irritability sharpened to a honed point. So *he* was the problem, was he? Well, he'd known that all along.

Fortunately he still possessed the self-control and maturity not to reply with his hurt feelings. He kept his gaze on the road as the silence between them stretched on.

This trip had been a big, big mistake. And he was kicking himself all over the place for having so stupidly suggested it.

"When do Sam and Maggie get back?" he asked when they'd passed Shrewsbury.

Laura glanced at the clock. "Their flight lands at Heathrow at seven. They'll be tired for school tomorrow."

"Happy to be home, though."

"I hope so."

Silence. When had it become so hard to talk to each other? "I'm sorry," James said after another fraught fifteen minutes had passed by. "I feel like I messed up this weekend."

"Oh James, you didn't." Laura reached over to place a hand on his arm, and her warm smile felt like the best thing he'd seen all day. "You didn't," she said again, and he waited for more, braced himself for it. "It's just..." *Uh-oh.* "We've jumped into the deep end, haven't we? And I feel like I was emotionally ready to go about ankle-deep, if that." *Ouch.* "So it's hard to adjust to the...intensity. I'm not saying I don't want to, or that I don't care about you..." *Cringe.* "It's just hard." She sighed, defeated by her own explanation.

What could he say to any of that?

"I guess I know what you mean."

The smile he'd found so warm now held far too much sympathy. "I'm sorry, James. I wish I was ready to jump in with both feet or head first or whatever, but...just give me some time, okay? To get things straight in my head, before I give a relationship—our relationship—a chance." He swallowed, nodded, and she squeezed his arm. "Not oodles and oodles of time. Just…a bit. Time and space, to sort myself out."

Again, what could he say? What choice did he have? *No, I'm not going to give you any time. You have to decide right now that you love me and want to have my children.*

"Sure," James said, and managed a weak smile. "No problem."

Chapter Twenty

"COME ON, PERRY."

With a sympathetic smile for her tired dog, Laura looped the lead about Perry's head before setting outside into a crisp, sunny day that held the faint promise of spring. It was Monday morning, and Maggie and Sam had headed off to school, exhausted from both their flight home and holiday but mostly cheerful, and Laura was feeling at a distinct loose end.

It was hard enough having to process the weekend in Shropshire, something she wasn't even sure she was ready to do, but it was just as hard not to have a job to go to. She'd only been a teaching assistant at Wychwood Primary for five weeks, but she'd settled into a rhythm there, and having seven hours stretch in front of her so emptily made her feel a bit out of sorts. A bit lonely. Especially considering how she'd left things with James last night, when he'd dropped her off at Willoughby Close with an unhappy smile and a kiss on the cheek.

Laura wasn't even sure if anything had actually gone

wrong between them, but things definitely didn't feel right. The two and a half hours in the car had been suffused with a silent misery and tension that she didn't fully understand. What were they arguing about, really? Nothing, she thought, and everything. They'd backed each other into a corner, having to make or at least consider decisions neither of them felt ready for. She knew she didn't, and she didn't expect James was, either. No wonder things had felt fraught.

She'd asked for the old cliché of time and space, but she didn't know whether either would actually help straighten out her own head. Her feelings were in a ferment and she couldn't imagine them ever settling down. But one day, surely, with a little breathing room, a little perspective...

Her children's arrival back home had been a welcome distraction from thinking about all that; they'd both been bubbling with excitement about the trip, and yet had still managed to get into an argument within the first five minutes back. Laura had been both delighted and exasperated, suspecting they'd been on their best behaviour while with their grandparents and now needed to let off some steam.

"It seems like it was a really nice break," she'd ventured when she'd gone up to Maggie's room to have a private debrief.

Maggie was, as usual, on her phone. "It was all right."

High praise indeed, then. Laura had picked up a few dirty clothes from the floor before perching on the edge of her daughter's bed. "And how about things at school?" she'd asked. "Everything going okay there? You looking forward to going back tomorrow?"

Maggie had shrugged, eyes still on her screen. "Yeah, I guess."

"I love you, Maggie." It was, perhaps, a non sequitur, but one Laura felt compelled to keep saying. She had a feeling her daughter couldn't hear it enough, no matter how indifferent she pretended to be, and in truth Laura didn't have much other wisdom to offer.

Maggie had grunted in reply, and Laura had left it at that. Small steps, slowly moving forward. At least she hoped so.

Perry trotted faithfully after her now as she headed out of Willoughby Close towards the woods that flanked the manor house. They were due there on the weekend for a Sunday roast with Alice and Henry; when she'd seen Alice the other day, she'd assured her she could bring 'someone'—this said with smiling emphasis—if she liked. So word of her going on a date had clearly gotten around, which Laura supposed she should have expected it to. She told Alice she wouldn't be bringing anyone; she'd meant what she said about time and space and she certainly wasn't ready to tell either Sam or Maggie about James yet. Not until she knew her own mind, anyway, although who knew when that would be?

The wood was damp and green, the first tiny shoots visible on the trees, the ground carpeted with bright-headed crocuses. Laura let Perry off the lead so he could snuffle among the mulchy carpet of old leaves. In the shadows of the trees, the air was still decidedly chilly, and she hunched her shoulders against a breeze that was more winter than spring.

The sensible thing to do, she told herself as pragmatically as she could, was to have a reasonable discussion with Maggie and Sam about her the possibility of her dating in general, and see how they felt about it. Then she could mention James, making sure to reassure them that it didn't change their family dynamics, she loved them both utterly, and in any case it was very early days—something she needed to remind herself of, as well.

She could picture the chapter in one of the many books on grief and healing that she'd been given or recommended, although most had remained unread. It had simply been too difficult to relive her own experience through the pages of a book.

But really, would Sam or Maggie even object to her dating? Sam might be pleased, or even thrilled. And Maggie… A sigh escaped her as she considered her daughter. She really had no idea how Maggie would react. Two months on from discovering she'd been self-harming and taking her back to counselling and although she felt more positive than she had, she still wasn't sure how Maggie was doing. If only her daughter would open up to her a little. If only Laura could make her.

Perhaps telling her about James would help with that, make Maggie see it was possible to move on. But considering her own ambivalence, that didn't seem like the wisest thing to do. No, she couldn't tell Maggie or Sam about James until she'd decided for herself what future she could have with James.

But how was she supposed to do that? Flip a coin?

"Hey."

Laura stopped in her tracks as a figure loomed out of the forested shadows towards her. Perry's ears pricked although he didn't bother with a bark. As the figure came closer, she saw it was Ava's husband Jace.

"Hey," she answered with a smile. "How's life with little Zoe?"

"Great." He grinned, his eyes glinting with good humour. He had the same effortless sex appeal as his wife, Laura couldn't help but notice. Really, they both should be models or something. "If a bit tiring."

"That's to be expected, I suppose."

"How are you?" Jace cocked his head as his gaze swept over her in a way that felt both thorough and knowing. "Ava mentioned you'd been widowed. I'm sorry."

"Thank you." As ever, the exchange about Tim's death felt stilted. "It's been fifteen months now." She lifted her chin, unsure whether to smile or not. "I feel as if we're starting to get back to normal, if there ever was a normal. Or is one, after a death. I still don't know."

"There's a new normal, I guess. Learning how to relate to each other in new ways."

"Yes." This was quite emo, for a guy like Jace, a man's man who looked like he slept in his work boots. "That's true."

"It can be hard sometimes," Jace said slowly, "when you're not sure if you should have a second chance at everything. Life, love, the works." He gave her a lopsided smile. "Ava and I both got second chances, but I think we felt we didn't deserve them. It took a while to realise we could accept them anyway, through grace, whether we deserved them or not."

A blush scorched Laura's face as she absorbed his words. How did he know she was struggling with guilt? That she wondered if she deserved to be happy? How could he possibly tell, when she hadn't even fully acknowledged such feelings to herself? Unable to form a reply, she simply stared.

"Sorry if I'm offering advice that isn't wanted or needed," he continued. "I've just…I've seen that look on your face on Ava's, once upon a time."

"The look on my face?" Laura stared at him in surprise. She hadn't realised she'd been so revealing.

"A sort of stricken smile," Jace answered with a shrug. "Like you're putting a brave face on it all, but inside things feel really different. I get it."

"I know Ava was widowed," Laura said slowly. "But why didn't you feel like you deserved a second chance?" The question didn't feel nearly as nosy as it might have done, if Jace hadn't been so shockingly perceptive.

He hesitated, then said, "When I was out at the pub I got in a fight. I punched a guy and he hit his head and died. I spent seven years in prison for it."

Laura stared at him in shock. "Oh…"

Jace smiled crookedly. "Yeah. It happened to be Henry Trent's younger brother, in case it comes up in conversation. It usually doesn't, but you never know."

"Henry's…"

"Yeah, I know. He was a hothead, but so was I." Jace sighed and scuffed one boot through a drift of dead leaves. "Henry and I have managed to make it up, although I doubt we'll ever be each other's favourite people. But if I can have a second chance, so can you."

Quite suddenly Laura felt near tears. "Thanks," she said quietly. "I still don't really know how you knew I needed to hear that, but…thanks."

She hadn't even realised she'd needed to hear it. She hadn't let herself think too much about how guilty she still felt. But she was grateful that Jace, of all people, had managed to see in her face what she hadn't acknowledged was in her heart.

"HEY, MR HILL."

Sam's grin was as infectious as ever as he stood in front of James's desk at the end of the first day back after half-term.

"Hey, Sam. Looks like you got a ski tan. Did you have a

nice time?"

"Yeah, it was amazing." Sam nodded enthusiastically before hitting him with a direct stare. "Are you coming back for dinner tonight, after Minecraft Club?"

The boy's gaze was so guileless that James had a tough time to keep meeting it. It had been less than twenty-four hours since he'd said goodbye to Laura last night, and yet it had felt endless. He hadn't realised just how much he'd enjoyed catching glimpses of her throughout the day, how much he'd depended on those snatches of conversations, those passing smiles.

No, scratch that. He *had* realised. He just hadn't realised how much it would hurt, not seeing her, not knowing. Because he didn't know where they stood, and he couldn't stand the ignorance. She'd asked for time, for space, all those awful things he'd had to pretend to be cool with, but giving them to her was another thing entirely.

"Um, maybe?" he hazarded. "Your mum might have plans, Sam. I don't want to be pushy, you know?" Little did the boy know just how pushy he was tempted to be. He wanted to sweep Laura up in his arms, kiss all her doubts away, tell her he was sorry for acting like a spoiled kid all weekend—because he was afraid he might have—and beg her to take him back.

Although perhaps he was overreacting. They hadn't actually broken up...had they? Laura just needed to deal with some emotional stuff. That was totally expected, considering she'd been widowed just over a year ago. Maybe he just needed to chill. She was meant to be the panicker, after all, not him.

"My mum will be fine with it," Sam assured him. "She likes you."

Pathetic that an eleven-year-old innocent assessment gave him hope, but it did.

"All right, well, we'll see. I'll walk you home anyway," James said. At least he'd get a chance to see Laura, gauge her mood. And he wouldn't stay for supper if it was clear she didn't want him to.

THE HOUR-LONG CLUB that afternoon felt endless, although James usually enjoyed himself. Today he checked the clock above the classroom door about every three minutes, tapping his foot impatiently as he waited for time to pass. And finally it did; the club ended, parents picked up their kids, and he and Sam started back towards Willoughby Close.

The evenings were starting to get lighter, which was welcome after the dark winter, and James enjoyed the last of the sunlight streaking across the pale blue sky as they headed out of the village, Sam keeping up a cheerful chatter about skiing, school, and all things Minecraft.

As James glanced down at his rumpled dark hair, he had a sudden, piercing memory of Laura asking him if he could take on the raising of her two children. Could he be Sam's stepdad?

On one hand, yes, the answer seemed obvious. Sam was a good kid, and he reminded James of himself when he'd been that age. Slightly geeky, enthusiastic, sensitive, yet brimming with easy optimism. He knew how to handle Sam.

But what about Maggie? While some of her theatrics reminded him of his sister Bella, he didn't know how deep her anger or grief ran. He couldn't picture himself in some vaguely authoritative role, telling her that her skirt was too short like his own dad had with his daughters, or thundering that she was grounded for some infraction or other. Although maybe Laura wasn't looking for that kind of parenting. Maybe she'd want him to back off, because at the end of the day these weren't his kids and they'd had a dad they'd loved for most of their lives.

Like he'd told Elin, it was complicated. More complicated than he wanted it to be, especially at this early stage. They'd catapulted themselves into a what-if world, and he wasn't sure he liked it. He wanted to go back to the two of them teasing and flirting and kissing while they painted his living room wall a very nice shade of blue. *That* had been easy.

Shadows were beginning to gather as they headed into the close, and Sam flung open the front door of number three and barrelled inside, leaving James unsure whether he should follow.

"Mum, Mr Hill is here," Sam sang out. "He can stay for

dinner, right? Like he always does?"

When always was about three times. James remained on the doorstep, feeling woefully uncertain, hoping Laura didn't think he'd pressured Sam into begging an invitation.

"Hey." She came to the doorway, a faint flush to her cheek, nibbling her lower lip as her gaze swept quickly over him.

Since no invitation was forthcoming, James stumbled to fill the silence. "Hey. I don't need to stay for dinner. I mean, I understand you wanted a little space…"

"I don't know what I want," she admitted in a low voice. James had no idea how to respond, or how to feel about that. Was that a good thing, or not so much?

"Okay," he said at last.

"I'm sorry." She shook her head. "You're going to despair of me."

"No—"

"Come inside." She opened the door wider. "Sam will be disappointed if you don't stay."

But he didn't want to stay just for Sam's sake. Trying not to feel the sting of her words, James started inside, only to stop at a screech from the courtyard.

"Laura!"

They both turned at the sound of the voice; James blinked bemusedly at the sight of a six-foot-tall women hurrying towards Laura, her left hand raised as if it was injured.

"Lindy," Laura called in greeting, sounding almost as bemused as he felt.

"You'll never guess! You're the first person we've told."

Belatedly James registered the tall fortyish man walking behind Lindy at a far more sedate pace.

"Told what?" Laura asked.

"We're engaged." Lindy held her hand out for Laura's inspection, and James realised she'd been holding it up to show off her ring, a beautiful diamond sparkler.

"Oh…!" Laura sounded both delighted and stunned. "Wow. That was quick."

"Yes, it was," Lindy agreed happily. "But when you know, you know, right?" She gave James a meaningful glance, and he managed a smile back.

"How long were you guys dating?" he asked.

"Since just before Christmas."

Whoa. That was less than three months. "Wow," James said a bit weakly. "That's great."

"Neither of us is getting any younger," Lindy said with a loved-up look for her fiancé. "So we figured we needed to get our skates on, especially if we're going to have children." She blushed becomingly at this, while James tried not to tug at his collar. The parallels that could be drawn felt screamingly obvious, and he didn't think either he or Laura needed to be making them right now.

"Have you set a date?" Laura asked. She still looked a bit gobsmacked, while Lindy was radiant, her fiancé quietly brimming with happiness. The fact of their obvious joy made something inside James twist hard. *He wanted that.* He wanted to feel that. And he wanted Laura to, as well.

"Not yet, but we're thinking springtime," Lindy said.

"This springtime?" It was already March.

"Well, yes, like I said, we're not getting any younger. And we'd like Roger's mum to be there, if she can." Lindy slipped an arm around his waist.

"She's in hospice, with cancer," Roger explained. "So we're thinking April, actually."

"Wow." Laura shook her head slowly, and then smiled. "Wow. Well, congratulations. Like you said, when you know, you know."

"Yup." Lindy grinned at Roger. "You certainly do."

After they'd left to go celebrate, James followed Laura into the cottage. She gave him a wry smile as she closed the door.

"Well, that's one way to do it, I suppose."

He couldn't quite gauge her tone, but he knew she'd made comparisons, just as he had. "Yes, I suppose it is."

"Lindy's only thirty-six." She glanced away from him. "Five years younger than me."

"I am a primary schoolteacher," he joked. "I can just about do the maths."

"James…" There was no disguising the unhappiness in her eyes, and he couldn't bear it.

"Look, there's no need to rush things just because they

are," he said quickly, keeping his voice low so Sam, sprawled on the sofa, couldn't hear. "Okay? Right now I'm here as Sam's teacher, nothing more. Let's not panic."

She nodded, her gaze still troubled, and James didn't think she was convinced by his argument, and that made *him* feel like panicking. He was falling in love with Laura, and he had a horrible feeling she was thinking about breaking up with him.

Chapter Twenty-One

LAURA DIDN'T REMEMBER much about the dinner. Everything seemed to be happening from a distance as if she was underwater, or perhaps everyone else was. She kept seeing Lindy's beaming smile and sparkling ring, and then James's unhappy look. Half of her wanted to run into his arms, and the other half wanted to run away.

Why did it have to be so hard?

Of course, she knew the advice she should give herself. To relax, first of all, and just breathe. Chill, as Sam or Maggie might say. Stop thinking about babies and marriage when they'd been officially dating for little over a *week*. And yet it was hard not to think about those things, when Lindy was spouting off proclamations about how *when you know, you know and we're not getting any younger*.

She and Tim had dated for two years before they'd got engaged, and then they'd had an eighteen-month engagement because Pamela had wanted such a big wedding for her only son. How could she be contemplating something serious with James after so little time? It made her head spin and her heart beat faster, and yet…and yet…

"Mum?" Sam stood in front of her, a frown wrinkling his forehead. "You are, like, seriously spacing."

"Sorry." She snapped back to attention, giving the table a general smile while somehow managing to avoid James's gaze. Why? If only she could get things straight in her own mind, but she didn't even know how to begin.

"I should probably go," James said as he started to rise from the table. They'd only just finished; the table wasn't even cleared yet, never mind about coffee on the sofa, as had been their habit.

"Already?" Sam's face fell. "But I wanted to show you my new world on—"

"Another time, Sam." James laid a hand briefly on his shoulder before he reached for his jacket. "Thanks for dinner. Delicious as always. Shepherd's pie is actually one of my favourites."

"You always say that," Maggie said, smiling, which heartened Laura. Her daughter so rarely smiled.

"Because they've all been favourites," James replied. He shrugged on his jacket, meeting everyone's gaze but Laura's, just as she'd been doing to him since he'd come into the cottage. What a pair they were. "Bye, everyone. See you tomorrow, Sam."

"I'll see you out," Laura said hurriedly, because she couldn't leave it like this, an hour of painful awkwardness. James didn't reply and both Maggie and Sam sloped off without removing a single dish from the table. Laura wasn't about to nag them now.

"I'm sorry," she blurted as soon as they were outside. It was lighter in the evenings now, and she didn't have the cover of darkness to hide her blushes.

"You don't need to be sorry for anything, Laura." James sounded sad, and that tore at her heart. She was hurting him, and she couldn't bear it. How had it come to this?

"I still am," she said in a low voice. "I don't even know what's happened, but it feels like everything is unravelling between us."

"I'm still here. I'm not going anywhere." He paused, his clouded gaze scanning her face. "If you don't want me to, anyway."

Laura hesitated, and James nodded slowly in understanding. "I'll see you later."

"James…"

"It's okay. You asked for time and space, and I really do want to give it to you. Coming to dinner tonight was probably an ill-judged idea, but with Sam…"

"I'm glad you stayed." Her throat felt thick and she had to force the words out. James nodded again, and then he started walking out of the courtyard.

Why did it feel as if he were walking out of her life? And she was letting him?

She needed, Laura thought miserably, to call Chantal. She needed someone to talk her down from this ledge she hadn't even realised she'd clambered up on. Maybe she wasn't even on it; she just felt as if she was. She didn't know anything anymore. With a raggedy sigh she watched James disappear around the corner, and she turned back towards the house.

"Why were you out there so long?" Maggie asked sharply as Laura closed the door behind her. She stiffened at the suspicion in her daughter's voice and found herself prevaricating. Again.

"I was just saying goodbye."

"You guys aren't, like, *friends*, are you?" The disdain, and even the disgust, was audible. Maggie stood at the bottom of the stairs, her arms ominously folded, while Laura busied herself with clearing the table.

"Yes, we're friends. We worked together for six weeks, after all. Can you help clear, please, Maggie?"

Grudgingly Maggie took a single glass to the sink. "But not, like, really friends," she stated.

Every parental antennae was twanging unbearably as Laura strove to keep her voice light. "What does that mean?"

"I mean…you're just friends because you have to be. Because of Sam and school and stuff."

"We like each other," Laura said carefully, knowing it would be worse to lie. Her heart had started to thud; she felt as if she were defusing a bomb. "Why are you asking?"

She forced herself to meet Maggie's gaze; her daughter was staring at her hard. "What do you mean, you *like* each other?" Her voice was now edged with something like panic, and Laura felt the situation slipping out of control. She felt instinctively that to lie when asked point-blank would be worse than not telling at all, and yet this seemed far from the perfect moment, with Maggie aggressive and James having just walked away with his heart in his eyes.

"We like each other," she stated again, a bit desperately. "It's…" She meant to say no big deal but somehow she couldn't make herself.

"You're not…" Maggie swallowed convulsively. "You're not…like…*dating*, though." There was a pleading note in her voice that reminded Laura of when she'd been a child, asking her to check under the bed again before she turned the light out at bedtime. Maggie had once had a deathly fear of under-the-bed monsters.

She took a deep breath and let it out slowly. "Maggie…"

"You *are*." She sounded horrified. "I can't believe it. How long has it been going on? Why have you been keeping this secret?"

"Not very long," Laura said quickly. "Just since you've been away skiing. I was going to tell you when the moment was right—"

"You guys were shacked up together while Sam and I were skiing?"

"Maggie, no!" Laura's voice came out sharply. "Of course we weren't *shacked up*. For heaven's sake. We went on a date." Or twelve.

"But he's like, fifteen years younger than you—"

"Nine, actually, and yes, I know there is an age difference."

Maggie glared at her, and then her face started to crumple. "What about Dad?"

Laura drew a careful breath. "What about Dad?" she repeated quietly.

"He's only been dead a *year*."

"Fifteen months, Maggie, and—"

"Oh *well*, then, that makes it all right." Maggie rolled her eyes, her expression both fierce and heartbroken. She reminded Laura of a wild animal, trapped and terrified, lashing out.

"I know this is a shock," Laura said carefully. "I didn't want to tell you this way."

"When were you going to tell me?" Maggie demanded.

Laura shrugged helplessly. "Soon. We've only just started dating, and I'm not even sure…" She paused, deciding now was not the time to go into it. "It's all very new, and the truth is I was worried, Maggie." Worried that she'd take the news exactly as she was. "Dating James doesn't mean I didn't love Dad," she said hesitantly, unsure if that was even the angle that upset her daughter. Maggie's reaction seemed over the top and yet at the same time completely expected. "And it doesn't have to change anything between us. It *won't* change anything between us—"

This was clearly the wrong thing to say, because Maggie

let out a strangled cry and then raced upstairs, slamming her bedroom door so hard the sound reverberated through the whole house. Laura let out a shuddering sigh.

That went well. Not.

"Why's Maggie so upset?" Sam asked as he came downstairs, iPad in hand, hair sliding into his eyes.

Laura released a slow breath. "I told her that Mr Hill and I are—are seeing each other." Although she wasn't even sure if they were anymore. James had looked so resigned as he'd left the close, and she'd said she wanted time and space, neither of which she seemed to have. Everything felt confused.

"You are?" Sam's face lit up. "Cool."

Laura almost laughed out loud at her son's simple response. "You're okay with it?" she asked, just to check, and he shrugged his assent.

"Sure."

Well, that was something, Laura supposed. She tousled Sam's hair and told him to do his homework while she headed upstairs. She knocked once on Maggie's door, but her daughter's muffled 'go away' made her reconsider trying for a reconciliation so soon. She'd give her some time to cool off, and meanwhile she could have a much-needed talk with Chantal.

She hadn't had the time or energy to call her and debrief her about the weekend in Shropshire, although she'd managed a text saying things were complicated, to which Chantal had fired back that everything was, accompanied by an inexplicable aubergine emoji.

Needing privacy, she told Sam she was going to give Perry a quick walk, and headed outside with a bewildered dog in tow, to find the best place on the property for mobile reception.

The first stars were coming out in the sky like twinkling pinpricks as Laura huddled on the lawn in front of Willoughby Manor, a morose Perry at her feet, and dialled Chantal's number.

"Finally," her friend exclaimed as soon as she picked up. "All I get is one lousy text telling me it's complicated in over twenty-four hours? You do know I'm living vicariously through you, right?"

"Sorry." The word came out on a tremble and Chantal immediately dropped the jokey tone.

"Laura, what happened?"

"I don't even know. It's all seemed to go so wrong, so quickly."

"Start from the beginning."

And so she did, telling Chantal about the weekend in Shropshire, the tension James had with his family, the unhappy conversation about babies and stepfathers and getting serious, and then how she had asked for some space.

"And then tonight when I said goodbye after dinner—he always comes on a Monday because of Minecraft Club—Maggie jumped on me. She asked me outright if we were dating and it felt worse to lie about it, so I told her the truth and she flipped, Chantal. I know she's a moody teenager but it seemed over the top, even for her. It makes me wonder if something else is going on, and if something else is going on, then how can I possibly date James…"

"Okay," Chantal said after a moment. "Let's take this one thing at a time."

Laura nodded, relief flooding through her at her friend's sensible approach. "Okay."

"First of all, going with him to Shropshire was a bloody stupid thing to do."

Laura let out a huff of outraged laughter. "He *asked*—"

"I know, and if I was talking to him, I'd tell him he was being bloody stupid. The family test is not one to take after a week, Laura. For heaven's sake."

"I actually liked his family. He was the one with the problem, not me."

"Well, of course he was. They're his family. He's had thirty-two years of dealing with the drama. You had forty-eight hours. Cut him some slack."

"I did—"

"You might have seemed like you did, but I sense a little judgement. What, did you think it was a bit immature, how he got riled by his dad, at his age?"

"Maybe," Laura admitted, surprised at this notion. She hadn't realised she'd felt that way until Chantal spelled it out. "I suppose it made me a bit extra sensitive about our age differences. I mean…I gave up on trying to win my father's approval a long time ago." After her mother died, she'd stopped making much of an effort with her dad. Her father was friendly enough, but he was happy to keep their visits to once a year, if that, and brief, sporadic phone calls. He'd never needed more, and so Laura had chosen not to, either.

"Yes," Chantal agreed, "and as a result you barely see him. At least James goes back home. He tries."

"That's true." Laura hadn't considered that angle before. "I didn't even realise I felt that way, Chantal. I doubt James picked up on it."

"As if. He probably knows he's being a bit immature about it, but he can't help himself."

Laura thought of the apologies he'd made about just that and winced. "Maybe."

"Second thing. The conversation you started about having his baby. I mean, really? You thought that was a good idea?"

"No, I didn't," Laura returned with some defensiveness. "But it felt necessary. I'm forty-one—"

"So? You think it would be a better idea to rush into a relationship, a marriage, and pop his baby out in the next six months?"

"It takes nine months, actually."

"You know what I mean. I know you feel the age difference, Laura, but you can't rush things, especially when you're still grieving. You shouldn't have had that conversation, especially on top of the tension you were already experiencing."

"I know," Laura said quietly. "I just…panicked."

"As you often do." Chantal's voice softened. "I get that. This is scary and new."

Laura closed her eyes. "Maggie was so upset, Chantal. It made me feel so guilty."

"You've felt guilty for a while, haven't you?" Chantal replied quietly.

"You know I have."

"Maybe Maggie feels guilty, too."

Laura's eyes flew open. That was something she'd never, ever considered. "But Tim had a great relationship with both Sam and Maggie. He was Mr Fun with them." She thought of him building the zip wire in the garden, or going running with Maggie. Sprawling on the sofa with the three of them while they binge-watched *Dr Who* or *Merlin*. Tears crowded in her throat and gathered behind her eyes as the memories slammed into her. They'd all been so happy. Once.

"He was," Chantal agreed, "except when he wasn't. I know you might have picked up on his moods a bit more than the kids, but Maggie's perceptive, and as far as I can see, something is eating her up now. She wasn't like this before he died, and it feels like more than grief to me. I think you need to get to the bottom of it."

Laura's heart bumped inside her chest. "How?"

"Talk to her."

"Chantal, she won't talk to me—"

"She will when she's ready, but you might need to be the one to start the conversation. Ask the hard questions." Laura gulped at the thought. She'd thought she'd been doing her best, but maybe that wasn't good enough. She'd shied away from asking hard questions because, she realised, she wasn't sure she wanted to hear the answers. But maybe Maggie needed to give them.

"I'm sure this is all in a parenting manual," Chantal mused. "Maybe I should write one myself. *How to Parent Well, written by a non-parent.*"

Laura let out a trembling laugh. "I think it would be a bestseller. Thank you, Chantal. You've been amazing through this all. I feel so selfish, focusing on my problems all the time—"

"Now don't go adding to your guilt," Chantal cut her off sternly. "Because I don't think you're selfish at all. We've talked about this, okay? Remember last year, when I moaned about that bad break-up for about six months?"

"Brian," Laura recalled. "Yes."

"You've been there for me. I'm here for you. That's how relationships work, Laur. And maybe you need to think about that, when it comes to James. But," Chantal added, her tone turning severe, "you are setting me up with that head teacher, right? Because that's what friends are really for."

LAURA WAS SHIVERING from cold by the time she walked back to the cottage. Sam had finished his homework and was sprawled on the sofa with, surprisingly, a book rather than his iPad.

"You're reading?" Laura said, practically doing a double take.

"Yeah, this cool book about a boy having to survive in the wilderness with only a hatchet. Mr Hill recommended it."

"Great." Something else to thank James for. Even though she'd only seen him a few hours ago, she already missed him. She missed what they'd had together. "Where's Maggie?" she asked. "Still in her room?"

"Nah, she went outside a while ago."

Laura stilled by the stairs. "She did?"

"Yeah."

"But where would she go?" It was pitch-dark out, nearly eight o'clock at night.

"I dunno."

Laura reached for her phone and dialled Maggie's number, her heart starting to thud. Again. Just when she'd been determined to deal with a situation, it got worse. Maggie's phone switched immediately to voicemail, which made Laura's heart thud all the harder. Her daughter never switched her phone off.

She took a deep breath, willing her panic to ease. She was overreacting as usual, fearing the worst because it had happened once. Maggie might have gone for a walk or even a run, to clear her head. Switching her phone off in such a situation was perfectly natural. There was absolutely no need for Laura to panic. Yet. Except of course she was.

An hour crawled past with Laura pacing the downstairs of the cottage, checking her phone every few seconds, and then ringing Maggie, whose phone was still switched off.

At half past eight, Pamela had called, and Laura had had to bite her lips to keep from asking if Maggie was with her in-laws. She didn't know how Maggie would have made it all the way to Burford, but she couldn't bear to admit to Pamela she didn't actually know where her daughter was.

"I just thought you'd like to know how the ski holiday went," Pamela said a bit coolly, and Laura knew immediately this was code for being disappointed that she hadn't called and rhapsodised about the trip already.

"Sam and Maggie were telling me all about it," she said, trying to inject a note of enthusiasm in her voice and most likely failing. "It sounded brilliant. Thank you so much, Pamela, and Steve, as well. You're both so very generous."

"Well." Pamela sniffed. "We try."

After ten interminable minutes Laura managed to get off the phone with her mother-in-law, and was reaching for her coat, ready to search the mean streets of Wychwood for Maggie herself, when her phone rang again. It was James.

She hesitated, because if he wanted to have it out in some heart-to-heart, this was definitely not the moment. And yet…

"Hello?"

"Laura? It's me." His voice sounded as warm and comforting as ever, like a blanket she could wrap herself up in.

"James—"

"I didn't want you to worry. Maggie's here with me."

Chapter Twenty-Two

"TISSUES," JAMES SAID briskly. "And tea." He handed a mug of tea and a box of tissues to Maggie, who was curled up on his sofa, red-eyed and sniffling. When she'd shown up at his door, looking both furious and heartbroken, he'd been completely gobsmacked. He didn't even know how she knew where he lived, never mind what she was actually doing there.

"Maggie—" he'd said. "What…"

"My mum told me you were dating her." This was hurled as an accusation, and then she marched inside, while James, still gobsmacked, closed the door behind her, having no idea where this conversation might be going, or how he was supposed to handle it.

"Does your mum know you're here?" he asked as Maggie stood in the centre of his sitting room, dwarfed by her huge parka, looking very young and lost and alone. His heart ached for her and all the difficult emotions she had to be grappling with. Yet why had she come to him, of all people? And how could he help?

"Noo, of course she doesn't," Maggie said with a lip curl of contempt, as only a teenager could do.

"How did you know where I lived, out of interest?" James kept his tone friendly even though her presence alarmed him. How had Maggie found out about him and Laura—if there even was a him and Laura anymore? After walking away from Willoughby Close just a few hours ago, he wasn't sure there was. But far more importantly than anything to do with his dating life, was why this sprite of a girl was looking so devastated. He hoped he could help her.

"You can find out anything on Google," Maggie told him with a shrug. "It was in one of the school's newsletters, when you first moved to the village."

"My address was?" he asked, startled, thinking he needed to have a word with Dan Rhodes about the level of personal information given in newsletters, but Maggie shook her head, his assumption incurring even more disdain.

"No, 'course not. They just mentioned you were doing up an old cottage on Chapel Lane. And this place looks like it needs doing up."

"Wow." He shook his head slowly. "Perhaps you should consider a future career in the MI6. Or maybe cyber security."

That earned him a flicker of a smile before she threw herself down on a sofa, drawing her knees up to her chest.

James perched on the chair opposite, knowing this needed delicate handling. "So why are you here, Maggie? How can I help?"

She didn't answer for a long moment and James decided to wait her out. He did the same thing with his students, whenever something was clearly bothering them, making them sulk or sigh or twitch. Silence could be golden.

"I can't talk to my mum," she said at last.

"Why not?"

She burrowed her chin into her knees, her gaze lowered. "Because." Again James waited. "I don't want to hurt her," Maggie said in little more than a whisper, and then she started to cry in earnest, hiccupy sobs that both alarmed James and made him ache.

That's when he decided on tea and toast, the two cure-alls his mother had always put forth, and it also gave Maggie a bit of space. While in the kitchen he rang Laura, as he expected she had started to panic.

"Wh...what?" Laura had stammered, sounding as gob-smacked as he had been when he'd opened his front door. "I'll come there—"

"I'm not sure that's a good idea just yet," James had said, his tone both hesitant and gentle. "Maybe in a bit."

"Oh." Laura had sounded nonplussed, and James wondered if he was overstepping. This really was fraught. "Okay," she finally said. "I'll give it a little while. Is she...is she talking to you?" Again he couldn't quite discern her tone. Was she hopeful, resentful, a bit of both? James would understand either of those feelings.

"Sort of," he told her. "But not really. Not yet." Yet perhaps she would. For whatever reason, Maggie had chosen him as her confidant. James wasn't sure how he felt about that, but it was a trust he didn't want to betray. It seemed this stepdad gig was happening sooner rather than later. After ending the call with Laura, he headed back into the sitting room and Maggie, who had stopped crying and was sipping her tea rather morosely.

"Somehow I don't think you're this upset because I'm dating your mum," James announced, and again he was treated to that specific and skewering brand of teenaged scorn.

"Of course I'm not."

"Right."

She sighed heavily and slurped more tea. "I know my mum has to move on," she said slowly, her gaze fixed on her mug. "I'm not angry about that. Not really, anyway, although you are loads younger." She eyed him doubtfully. "I mean, not to be weird or anything, but you could pull a younger woman, you know?"

Pull? James didn't think she meant the opposite of push. "I like your mum," he said firmly. "But that's not what this is about, is it?"

"No, not really." She looked up at him, tears trickling down her face. "It's because...I feel like I can't move on. And she doesn't understand that. She can't understand it, because she's obviously moved on, no problem." She gave him a knowing look, which James chose to pretend to ignore.

"Okay," he said slowly, absorbing this astute confession. "Why do you feel like you can't?" He paused, feeling his way through the words. "Did something happen with your dad? Before he died?" He knew all about unspoken fractures in that particular relationship, and how the fault lines could go on and on, getting deeper with time, even as they were never spoken about. "Something that is making it hard for you to grieve?" he guessed quietly.

Maggie was quiet for a long time, and it took effort to simply let the silence stretch on, expanding and filling the room. Giving her space to think...and to speak.

"Yeah," she finally said, her voice little more than a whisper, and she buried her face in her knees so James couldn't make out her expression at all.

He was out of his depth, but somehow, strangely, that felt okay. He was glad Maggie had come to him, and even though he had no idea how to handle this moment, the fact that it was even happening at all encouraged him. Maybe he could, in time, manage the stepdad thing. Maybe he and Laura didn't have to freak out about the future, because, as his mum liked to quote from the Bible, every day had enough trouble of its own.

Then the wheeze of the elderly doorbell startled them both.

"That will be your mum," James said, because he figured

Maggie deserved a warning. "I called her to let her know you were here. I didn't want her to worry, and I don't think you did, either."

Maggie didn't so much as look up but she still managed a nod, her head moving against her knees. James rose to answer the door.

"She's here?" Laura asked breathlessly as soon as he'd opened it, her face pale and pinched with anxiety. "How did she even know…"

"That's what I wondered. She's an expert at an internet search, apparently." He wanted to pull her into a hug but she seemed too tense, almost breakable.

"What has she said…?" Laura asked in a whisper.

"Not much. Just that she's having trouble grieving Tim. I think she feels guilty, or perhaps just conflicted. I don't know. But if you want to talk to her, I can make myself scarce."

"I left Sam alone…"

"Why don't I go hang out with him? You can stay here with Maggie."

Confusion and something else, something deeper and more hurting, clouded Laura's eyes. "I'm sorry, James. We're dragging you into our mess…"

"I don't mind." He laid a hand on her arm, needing her to see and believe his sincerity. "I really don't, Laura."

"I know," she whispered. She looked as if she wanted to say something more, but then she just briefly clasped his hand, still on her arm, before heading into the sitting room—and Maggie.

James grabbed his jacket and went outside. It seemed he had some Minecraft to play.

LAURA STOOD IN the doorway of James's sitting room, everything in her aching as she saw Maggie curled up on the sofa, her knees to her chest, her head to her knees, so she was no more than a tangle of dark hair and a pair of jeans.

Yet as she stood there silently, Laura felt as if she were seeing her daughter with new, clearer eyes. She saw a hurting little girl rather than a rage-filled, defiant teenager. She saw someone in need of love and acceptance, patience and care, in a way she hadn't quite been able to before, when Maggie's anger had made her wary and despairing even as she'd kept trying. Now, strangely in this moment of crisis, she felt a new, fragile hope.

Silently she sat down next to her daughter and without saying a word, Laura put her arms around Maggie and drew her into a hug. And to her amazement, gratitude and joy, Maggie came, burrowing into her like she had as a little girl, as she sobbed against Laura's chest.

Laura murmured soothing words and stroked her hair, letting that be enough. She wasn't so naïve that she thought a simple hug could cure everything, or even anything, but at least it was a beginning. She hoped.

After what might have been ten minutes or half an hour, Laura couldn't be sure, Maggie pulled back with a big sniff as she swiped at her still-streaming eyes.

"I'm sorry, Mum," she mumbled.

"You don't need to be sorry, Maggie. For anything."

Maggie looked up at her, her eyes like dark pools. "I've made your life so difficult. I know I have."

"It's okay. I can handle it."

Maggie looked dubious, which made Laura smile. "But what's really going on, Mags? Because James said you'd told him you were struggling to…to grieve for Dad." She studied her daughter's face, the familiar guarded expression, the tremor of vulnerability. "Is that true?"

Maggie was silent for a long moment. Laura waited, longing more than anything to get to the bottom of whatever was troubling her daughter. "You can tell me," she said softly, when she sensed that Maggie was struggling to confide in her. "Whatever it is. Whatever you think it means, or however you're afraid I might react."

Still more silence, while Maggie nibbled her lip and Laura waited, wondering what on earth had been tormenting her daughter for so long.

"I was angry with Dad," Maggie finally blurted. "Before he died."

"You mean right before?" She'd been angry, in a simmering sort of way, for months before he'd died. That picked at her now, although she did her best not to think of her own feelings, but rather her daughter's.

"Yes. We got in a fight." Maggie bit her lip hard, her eyes filling with tears once more. "He said he was going out and I asked him if he could drop me off at the Costa in town, to meet some friends. He said no, he couldn't. He didn't give me a reason, and I got mad at him and said he was really unfair and mean and stuff." A tear slipped down Maggie's cheek and she dashed it away.

"Oh, sweetheart." Laura reached for Maggie's hand and clasped it in her own. The details of that last morning for her were both hazy and terribly clear; there were hours Laura couldn't remember, and moments that, over a year later, remained in stark clarity.

Tim rolling out of bed in the morning; neither of them speaking as they got dressed. They hadn't argued the night before, but they had been existing in a frozen sort of silence, because once again money was tight and Tim was frustrated by his lack of work.

It had been a Saturday, a clear, cold day with a brisk wind off the sea, just a few weeks before Christmas. Laura couldn't remember eating breakfast or waking up Sam; she did remember snatching her keys off the worktop to drive him to football practice. Tim had been slouched in an armchair in the sitting room, scrolling on his phone. His immobility had annoyed her, although she hadn't said anything. She never did, but maybe she should have. Maybe if they'd talked through their problems, they wouldn't have loomed so large.

When she'd returned from dropping Sam off, both Tim and Maggie had been gone. She'd texted them both, asking them where they were. Maggie had texted back right away to say she was walking into town; Tim had never replied.

It must have been about an hour later—an hour Laura couldn't really remember—when the phone rang, and life changed forever.

"Dad knew you loved him, Maggie," Laura said quietly. "Even if your last words were harsh ones. He would have always known that."

"I know." She sniffed. "I just wish it had been different."

"I know. I do, too." Laura drew a shuddery breath. "The truth is, Dad and I were having some problems too. Nothing big, we weren't going to separate or anything like that, but I don't even remember if I said anything to him that last morning. I don't know what my last words to him were." Perhaps something about making coffee, or who should take Sam football, although those were just guesses. Had she actually said *anything* to him that morning? She couldn't remember. She might never know.

"Mum…" Maggie's voice was achingly hesitant. "Why wouldn't Dad drive me that morning? Where was he going?"

Laura stared at her in blank confusion. "I don't know, darling. Something for work, perhaps." He'd been driving on the road out of town, towards the industrial estates where he got most of his equipment.

"But…" Maggie licked her lips nervously, her eyes wide and dark. "Don't you think it's strange, that he crashed into a tree on a straight stretch of road? The *one* tree, and it was on the other side?"

Laura's insides seemed to hollow out as she kept her gaze on Maggie's pleading one. "They think he must have skidded. He could have been distracted. On his phone." Tim had had the annoying and dangerous habit of occasionally checking his phone for work texts while he was driving.

"But what if he wasn't?"

"What are you saying, Maggie?" Laura's voice came out more harshly than she intended, and she pulled her daughter into her arms once again as the implication reverberated through her. "Are you afraid he…he did it deliberately?" she asked quietly, barely able to form the words even though they felt carved on her heart. In the fifteen months since Tim's death, she'd never let herself consider this possibility, and yet it had loomed large all the same, skulking in the shadows. The police had asked what Tim's state of mind had been at the time of the accident, and although they'd ruled it out, Laura knew she never had, although she'd tried. It was, she knew now, the reason why she'd suppressed her own emotions, just as Maggie had.

"He'd been so down," Maggie said against her shoulder, her voice thick with tears. "I know he tried to hide it from us, but I could tell. He was worried about work and I think he felt guilty for moving us to Woodbridge just for his job when it wasn't working out."

"Yes, that's true. Your dad struggled with depression sometimes." Laura had urged him to go to the doctor, get a proper diagnosis or some antidepressants, but Tim had refused, scornful of it all. Another reason she felt guilty... Should she have pushed him more to seek help?

And what if he had done it deliberately—a single tree, a straight stretch of road, a moment of madness or just deep despair. It was, she knew with a terrible, leaden feeling, possible.

"So do you...do you think he killed himself?" Maggie asked, pulling back to look up at her with eyes that were heartbreakingly wide.

"I don't suppose we can ever know for sure, Maggie," Laura said slowly, struggling to keep her voice level as the emotion she'd been holding back began to rush through her. Guilt. Regret. *Grief.* "I'd like to believe he wouldn't have done that, not even when he was feeling depressed. But even if he did..." She swallowed hard, trying not to cry herself as she realised afresh how much she'd been holding back. "He loved you and Sam, and me as well. He wouldn't have wanted to throw all that away, even if in that moment he might not have been able to see past the sadness he felt."

"So you think he did?"

Maggie wanted confirmation, and Laura could understand that, but it wasn't hers to give.

"I honestly don't know, Maggie. Dad might have been

on his phone. You know how he was, checking work texts. It's possible. It's what the police thought. But…" She made herself say it. "He did get down. Really down. I thought he hid it better from you and Sam but I guess he didn't. I haven't let myself wonder if he did it on purpose, but that thought has been there, in the back of my head." She drew her daughter into another hug. "I wish I'd spoken to you about this before. I should have been more honest about my feelings. Maybe then you would have been able to be honest about yours."

"I didn't want to upset you," Maggie confessed with a sniff.

"Likewise," Laura admitted with a wobbly laugh. "What a pair we are." Gently she gave Maggie a squeeze. "The important thing to remember is, he loved you. That I know absolutely, a thousand per cent. And if he was depressed or down or anything like that, it was not your fault. It was never your responsibility."

And yet…like Maggie, she'd felt guilty. Guilty for not being a better wife, for getting so frustrated when she knew Tim was struggling, for feeling he was selfish when he was trying so hard.

And guilt kept you from being able to grieve. That was why both she and Maggie were stuck, terrified of the future, unable to let go of the past. She and her daughter had far more in common than she'd realised, and yet it had been that very guilt that had kept them apart, isolated by the torment of their own feelings.

"None of it is your fault, Maggie," she stated firmly as she gave her daughter another hug before easing back. "Even if Dad did crash deliberately, and we don't know that he did, it's not your fault. I know you wish your last words with Dad could have been better, and heaven knows, I wish the same for mine. But we didn't know they would be our last words, did we? I suppose it is a lesson to us to make every moment count, but it's also a lesson not to tie yourself in knots with guilt. Dad knew you loved him, and I think you know he loved you. A lot. That's what matters."

Maggie nodded, gulping as she wiped the tears from her cheeks. "I'm sorry, Mum. I'm sorry for being such a pain these last few months."

Could she have that on record, Laura wondered wryly, even as her heart suffused with love. "None of this has been easy," she said, "and that's okay."

"I just felt so angry all the time. Angry with Dad…and angry with myself."

Laura nodded her understanding. "I've been the same."

"Maybe you should see a grief counsellor," Maggie said with a reproving look, and Laura smiled.

"Maybe I should." Actually, she knew she should. She'd had enough of trying to deal with her feelings by pretending she didn't have them. She needed to get it all out in the open, as hard and painful as that might be.

They sat in silence for a few moments, letting it breathe

around them, turn into something more hopeful. Saying it all out loud really did help.

"So, are you really dating James?" Maggie finally asked, her eyes still reddened and watery, her skin blotchy from crying even as she smiled. "Because, I have to say, Mum, *phwoar*. He's pretty, you know, hot for an old guy. Not as old as you, though, obviously. And I mean, *I* don't fancy him or anything. Because...*ew*."

Laura laughed and hugged her again. "Thanks, sweetheart, for the thumbs up. The truth is, I don't know where James and I stand. I've come to realise I have a lot to deal with, and I need to get my head straight before I jump into a relationship."

"Maybe he can help you with that," Maggie suggested. "You don't have to do it all on your own, Mum."

"Wise words," Laura answered with a smile, and Maggie grinned.

It was going to be okay, she realised. Sometimes life was a long, hard slog, but it was going to be okay. Maggie was going to be okay. So was Sam, and she was, too. In time. With patience and trying and love.

And as for her and James...well, Laura realised, they needed to talk. Properly. Honestly. In time. She wasn't ready yet, and she might not be for a while, but she was definitely going in the right direction. She just hoped James was a patient man.

"Shall we head off?" she asked Maggie, and her daughter

nodded, giving her a fragile smile that broke Laura's heart and bound it up all at once.

Smiling back, she reached for her hand and helped her up from the sofa. It was time to go home.

Chapter Twenty-Three

THERE WAS MORE than a hint of spring in the air as James released his Year Sixes to the world. They emerged leaping and howling from the classroom like a band of wild dogs; that was what a little sunshine and warmth did to the eleven-year-old psyche.

It was early April, and the first day of the year when you could go outside without a coat. When the sun felt properly warm, and the daffodils were showing off their bright yellow heads; the flowerbeds lining the village green were bursting with a ridiculous amount of colour.

It had been almost a month exactly since Maggie's meltdown. Laura had returned to Willoughby Close where James had been sitting on the sofa with Sam, watching him play Minecraft and counting the minutes. He'd sprung up as soon as she'd opened the door, and she'd smiled tiredly at him. Maggie had shot him a look of hesitant apology and then scurried upstairs.

"Is everything…" James had asked, not even knowing where to begin, and Laura had nodded.

"Yes. At least, it will be. That is, if you were asking if everything is okay, which I suspected you were."

He nodded his affirmation as he reached for his coat. Laura looked exhausted. "I should go."

"Thank you, James, for everything."

That had sounded rather horribly final. "I was glad to help. If I did help, that is."

"You did."

She saw him to the door, and stepped outside with him just as she had earlier that night, which already felt like a million years ago. Then, to his surprise, she stepped close to him and put her arms around him, resting her head against his shoulder.

James's arms had closed around her automatically, and he'd savoured the sweet feel of her body against his before she'd let out a sigh that seemed to come from the depths of her being.

"I still need time and space," she'd said, "but I'm getting there. I really am. I have things I need to deal with. Grief I haven't let myself feel." Her voice choked a little. "I will explain it all to you at some point, I promise."

"I can wait," James told her.

"Can you?" She pulled away to look at him frankly. "Because I said before I wasn't a good bet, and I still feel that way. There have to be women out there who are less complicated and messed up than I am."

"No one is a good bet, Laura," James said gently. "And

in any case, that's not what relationships are about. I care about you. I'm willing to wait. And if, when you've got your head straight, as you like to say, you realise you're not ready to be in a relationship, or you don't want to be in one with me, well, I can accept that. I'll be disappointed, admittedly, but I want what's best for you." As he said the words he realised he meant them. This wasn't about him feeling rejected the way he had with Helen. This was about loving Laura enough to let her go, if that was what she needed. To be at peace with the prospect, even if it hurt.

She hugged him again, her arms wrapped around him tightly. "Thank you," she whispered. He hugged her back silently, knowing that for now at least, there were no more words to be said.

As he let her go, she stood on her tiptoes to brush a soft kiss against his mouth. It had taken everything James had not to try to turn it into something more, but simply accept what she'd had to give with gladness.

And he was glad—glad that they still had a chance, that Laura was looking to heal. It made him realise that perhaps he needed to put a few things in order, as well. And so, a few days later, with much trepidation and grim resolve, he'd called his father.

David Hill had been nonplussed, to say the least, by his call. He was a man who only used the phone for emergencies; he'd never bought a mobile, and never would. Having a heart-to-heart conversation on a telephone was beyond him, but then it had seemed so was having one in real life.

However, to his father's credit, he listened to James's halting explanations of how he'd felt inferior because he wasn't a farmer, and how he knew that was on him more than it was on his dad, but he wanted to do better. He wasn't even sure what the point of the conversation was, except that it was stuff he needed to say.

"I suppose I always knew you felt that way, at least a bit," his dad said gruffly when James had finished his stilted lament. "I never meant you to, though, lad. I hope you know that."

James didn't think he'd ever heard his father say so much before. So much about feelings. "I think I did," he said slowly. "It's just we're really quite different."

"That we are." His father gave a dry chuckle that made James, improbably, smile. "You ought to come home more, James," he continued, his voice as brusque as ever. "I know you're not one for farming, but it's in your blood whether you like it or not."

Which had made James realise that perhaps his father had felt the same sort of rejection he'd felt, over him choosing teaching rather than the farm...not that David Hill would ever say as much. But maybe he didn't need to.

"Okay, Dad," he said. "I will."

"We'll get you sheering a sheep yet."

He'd shorn plenty of sheep during his teenaged years, when his Easter holidays had been nothing but helping on the farm. Still, he kept quiet about that. "Sure, and maybe I'll get you reading a book."

His father was strictly a newspaper only man.

He gave another rasp of a chuckle. "Who knows, maybe you will," he answered. "One day."

All in all, it had been a good conversation, and it had given James hope, even as the weeks of not seeing Laura had felt like agony. No glimpsing her at school any longer, no chats in the schoolyard, no Monday night suppers, no texts, even. He'd kept his word, and he hoped she'd keep hers, and that one day—one day soon—they'd talk.

The last of the school's pupils was trickling through the gate and into the bountiful spring sunshine when he saw her. She was standing by the gate, wearing a bright purple jumper and a darker scarf, her hair pulled back into a messy bun, the expression on her face, even from this distance, one of both hope and hesitation, making him feel the same.

James took a step into the schoolyard. "Laura…?"

"Is this a good time?"

He had thirty math notebooks to mark, and parent-teacher conferences next week, but yes, this was a good time. It was a perfect time. "Sure."

She smiled, and James turned back to the classroom. "Let me just close up." He turned off the lights, deciding to leave his jacket and bag to fetch later. The day still held the benevolent warmth of spring, and it really was one to go without a coat.

He fell in step with her as they walked out onto the lane. "Up or down?" he asked, nodding towards the high street. "Or we could do both, like we did before. A parade of sorts."

"As tempting as that suggestions is, let's go up," Laura answered with a laugh. "I'd like to see the river on a day like today. It must be rushing so fast."

They walked in silence towards the bridge at the top of the village. James didn't want to press and Laura seemed deep in thought. What if she was going to break up with him? He hoped she wasn't; she didn't look sad, merely preoccupied, but still. He wondered. Worried, because even though he'd told her he'd accept whatever decision she came to, that didn't mean he'd like it.

Well, he told himself, if she broke up with him, then he'd take it like a man. Relationships didn't work if only one person was invested. He'd learned that before, and he felt it now. He was falling in love with Laura, but it was no good if she wasn't falling in love with him. He couldn't force that kind of feeling, and he didn't want to. He'd learned that, too.

Finally they reached the little wooden bridge that spanned the Lea River, which was burbling and splashing in a torrent down the hill, miniature crystalline waterfalls tumbling and splashing over the rocks. The banks were bursting with daffodils and crocuses and the golden stone of the village buildings practically sparkled in the sunlight. It was a scene worthy of the quaintest postcard.

Laura took a deep breath and turned to him. "Thank you," she said, "for being patient."

"It was the least I could do." James paused, feeling his way. He couldn't tell anything from Laura's expression, which looked...tranquil. Like she'd come to a decision, but what? "How is Maggie?"

"Good. Getting there." She let out a little sigh, a sound of acceptance rather than impatience or defeat. "I could beat myself up for not getting to the heart of what was going on earlier, but I'm not going to. That's something I've learned, at least."

"Good."

Laura glanced at him for a moment, her expression serious and more than a little sad. "Maggie thought Tim had killed himself," she stated quietly. "Driven into the tree on purpose."

James absorbed this silently, realising he wasn't as surprised as he expected to be. "Do you think he did?"

"I don't know." She let out a breath. "I've been seeing a counsellor for the last month, and I've hashed out a lot of things, but I realise there's no real answer to that one." Her gaze moved from him to the river, rushing onwards. "I suppose the fact that I don't know is an answer in itself. He *could* have, and I've had to come to accept that. So has Maggie. It's hard to make peace with something when you're not sure if it's even true, but...we have. At least, we're in process."

"I'm glad." He wanted to touch her, even if to just hold her hand, but he kept himself from it, for now. "I'm so sorry, Laura."

She nodded slowly. "Thank you." A silence that he waited out. "I realised I needed to process a lot of stuff that I'd just kept pushing back," she said slowly, "because I told myself I needed to be there for my kids. But I couldn't exactly be there for my kids when I wasn't dealing with my own issues." She let out a self-conscious laugh. "Which might sound like a lot of touchy-feely psychobabble, but it's the truth."

"I believe you." He hesitated, wanting, *needing* to ask about them, even as he told himself to let her set the pace. "Has it helped?" he asked instead, and she nodded.

"It has. I've cried a lot. And raged a lot. And generally just emoted." She gave a wobbly laugh. "After an hour-long therapy session, I'm pretty wrung out, to tell you the truth. But it really has helped."

He nodded slowly. "Good." And now he couldn't keep himself from it. "And have you come to any…conclusions…about us?" He felt as if he were offering her his heart on a platter. *Here. Take it. Stamp on it, if you like. Please, feel free.*

"Yes." She smiled wryly. "Quite a few, actually."

"Okay."

"First off, I've realised that we both were, as my friend Chantal said, bloody stupid for rushing into talking about things like babies and all the rest after so short a time together. I'm sorry about that. I never should have put that sort of pressure on you."

"I'm sorry, too," James said, meaning it utterly. "Taking you back home for the weekend, considering everything else that was going on, was probably not a good idea."

"It wouldn't have been a terrible idea," Laura allowed with a laugh, "if I wasn't such a ridiculous overthinker. A panicker. And I panicked."

"Understandable. I think I did, too."

"Also understandable."

They lapsed into a silence and James wasn't sure what it meant. Was Laura letting him down gently, explaining why she wasn't ready to date? It seemed that way, and yet...

He still hoped. He *had* to, because the alternative felt too bleak. A month of separation hadn't dimmed his feelings for Laura in the least.

"So I want to go back," Laura told him with a shy smile. "That is, if you do, too. If you're willing to."

"Go back?"

"To the beginning. To having only dated for a week. To having things be very exciting and different and, well, *new*." She let out another self-conscious laugh. "To when we have dinner or go for a walk or a movie, and get to know one another properly, without thinking about the future or the fact that I'm almost forty-two." She regarded him seriously. "Which I know could be a big thing, for you especially, if things do get serious and it's too late for…well, look, here I am, talking about the big stuff again." She shrugged helplessly. "I can't seem to resist. But can we do that, James? Can we just…date? For now? Just have fun and get to know each other and see where it goes?"

"Yes, of course we can." Relief was rushing through him, making him buoyant, his heart ready to float right up to the sky. "Of course we can. That sounds very sensible."

"And hopefully a little romantic, too?" She raised her eyebrows. "Because when things are new, they can still be romantic, right?"

"Definitely," James assured her, and he took that as his cue to kiss her. With a smile he reached for her and she came gladly, fitting into his arms, against his body, in a way that felt like both a relief and an ache. How he'd missed this. Her. In his arms, snuggled next to him, and with hope in his heart. Hope for the future—their future. Because they had one, wherever it led. Whatever happened. He'd been guilty of jumping the gun just as Laura had. Taking it slow sounded just about right, even if he'd never felt more sure of his feelings for Laura than he did now.

With Laura in his arms, he could take it very slow indeed.

A CHILL HAD crept into the afternoon air as Laura stood on her tiptoes to kiss James one more time before they headed back. She'd missed kissing him. Missed being held by him. Missed everything about him, actually, which was a good sign, even as she had to keep reminding herself to take it slowly. Enjoy the moment, because you never knew how many you would have.

The last month had been hard but good, as Laura had finally confronted her own grief. There had been ugly crying sessions with her counsellors, and even uglier ones with Chantal, as she'd poured out emotions and doubts and fears she'd suppressed for too long, and come to peace with them one by one.

There had been help from new and unexpected quarters too—a heart-to-heart with Harriet over coffee, an emotional discussion about the nature of grief with Lindy. And fun times too; she'd had to totter home after a night at The Three Pennies with all the Willoughby Close gang—Ellie, Harriet, Ava, Alice, Olivia, Emily, Lindy, and her. All the residents, past and present, together under one roof, knocking back wine.

It had been a wonderful, riotous evening, and even that had been part of her healing. She still had a long way to go, but she was getting there. Slowly. And that was a good thing.

She'd learned not to rush the process…not with her grief, and not with James.

"If you rush," Chantal had told her quite sensibly, "you miss things. All the little details. All the fun bits."

And Laura knew she didn't want to miss anything, when

it came to her and James.

Hand in hand, they crossed the bridge and started towards home.

Epilogue

Summer, two years later

COLOURFUL BUNTING WREATHED Willoughby Close, with printed signs directing visitors to all the areas of the estate—the close, the manor, the gardens, and even the old gatehouse, where Jace and Ava had once lived.

A table had been set up at the entrance to the close, for interested parties to register and collect a nametag and paddle. None of the former Willoughby Close residents had been able to resist getting one of each, although they hardly needed the paddle. Today was a banner day, a poignant day, and they couldn't help but exchange bittersweet smiles as the crowds coming in from the village headed towards the great lawn, where the auction was to be held.

Willoughby Manor, and all of its surrounding estate, including the close, was to be sold by auction that very morning. The announcement, made several weeks ago, hadn't been as much of a shock to the former residents of the close as some of the residents of Wychwood-on-Lea had felt it was; the close had been empty of tenants for over six months, and Alice and Henry Trent, the lord and lady of Willoughby Manor, had decided to relocate their charity, Willoughby Holidays, to a purpose-built complex a few miles away. The upkeep on the manor had simply been too expensive, and Henry in particular had felt he couldn't justify the expense when they were running a charitable organisation.

"I can't believe this day has come," Ellie exclaimed as she hugged Harriet in greeting. Ellie was now a viscountess, and had her own family estate to deal with. Her husband Oliver had retired from his lectureship at Oxford to run the estate full time, with Ellie's help. Abby, Ellie's daughter from a previous relationship, was heading to university in the autumn.

"It is strange," Harriet agreed. "I have such happy memories from this place. Happy but hard."

"Yes," Ellie agreed. "We were all going through something or other when we lived here, weren't we? And we all got through in one piece, more or less. It's all making me feel a bit nostalgic." She let out a soppy laugh and gave a slightly shamefaced smile while Harriet pulled her into a quick hug.

"I know, I'm feeling it, too." Her youngest, Chloe, was now finishing up at primary school, and her oldest, Mallory, was heading to university. Life marched on for all of them, whether they liked it or not.

"No one had better cry," Ava announced as she strolled up to them in her languid way, "or then I will, and I'm wearing far too much mascara for that." Jace stood behind her, holding William by one hand, and Zoe, now an angelically chubby toddler, by the other. Ava had gone back to work a year ago and her charity to help women into business was taking off wonderfully. They had moved out of the caretaker's cottage and bought a house in the village last year; Jace had set up his own carpentry business, which had been a great success, thanks to all his connections in Wychwood.

"It does feel like the end of an era, doesn't it?" Harriet said, doing her best to be pragmatic, although her eyes were suspiciously bright. "I wonder who on earth will buy the place? Who can afford it?"

"Alice mentioned there was an American who was interested," Ellie said, and a laughing voice called out:

"Who said what?"

"Didn't you, Alice?" Harriet asked as Alice came up to their little group, eighteen-month-old Harry balanced on one hip. He had the most adorably impish smile, although Ava had remarked he could look as stern as Henry when he chose, his pale eyebrows drawing together in a ferocious scowl.

"An American? Yes, there was some interest, but it's all very mysterious. We don't have the name of a person, just one of an investment bank."

"I hope it's not some Hollywood star, looking for a British bolthole," Harriet said. "There are enough airs and graces around here, as it is."

"Maybe they'll turn it into a hotel," Ellie suggested a bit gloomily. "Or a golf club. It seems such a shame, not to have a family here, filling up all the rooms."

"That would take a lot of children," Ava remarked dryly, and everybody laughed.

"I don't know what will happen," Alice said, "but I hope it goes to the right person." She glanced up at the manor, its impressive frontage glinting in the summer sunshine. "It holds so many happy memories for me."

"And some sad ones, as well," Ellie remarked quietly. They were all silent for a few seconds, remembering Lady Stokeley, Henry's great-aunt who had lived in the manor when they were all resident in the close. Regal, imperious, wise, and terminally ill, she had affected each of their lives powerfully, and a sense of her presence still lingered to this day.

"I thought I'd find you all here," Olivia announced with a laugh as she came up to the group. Married to Simon, they had bought a tumbledown cottage one village over and were doing it up slowly. Olivia had sold Tea on the Lea to a couple from London who were relocating to Wychwood, and she and Simon were hoping to start up an arts and crafts workshop that offered lessons for children and adults alike, along with Olivia's signature scones.

"I wonder what it will go for," Ava remarked with a nod towards the manor. "Someone has got to be seriously loaded to take this place on."

"All the proceeds from the sale will be going to the charity," Alice felt compelled to remind them. "So frankly I hope there's a bidding war!" She nodded towards a couple strolling towards them. "Look, there's Emily and Owen. Isn't she blooming?"

Emily was six months pregnant, and it suited her well. Her skin was glowing, and she radiated happiness. She and Owen had been married for just over a year.

"I see we all have paddles," Emily said with a laugh as she waved her own. "And yet somehow I don't think any of us will be bidding!"

"Not unless it goes for a tenner," Ava joked. "Look, there's Lindy. We're almost all here." She took a bottle from the hemp bag looped around one wrist. "I brought a bottle of bubbly to toast the manor and of course the close. But we need all the residents together!"

"I can't miss the bubbly," Lindy teased as she came up to them, Roger behind her, looking slightly incongruous with a baby strapped to his chest in a sling. Lindy had given birth to a little girl, Daphne, three months ago. After they'd married, she and Roger had moved to his cottage in the village. His mother, Ellen, had died soon after the wedding, but she'd been beaming for the whole ceremony, overwhelmed with joy.

"And here's Laura," Harriet said with satisfaction as Laura appeared with James by her side, Sam bounding out in front and Maggie slouching behind, giggling with a friend.

"Let me see that sparkler," Olivia said, and with a laugh

Laura waved her hand about. The diamond ring, flanked by two sapphires was duly admired; she and James had become engaged just a few months ago, after a long, slow, steady courtship. The wedding was going to be before Christmas, and they had plans to add to their family through adoption.

"Right, then. Let's get this party started." The cork came out of the champagne bottle with a satisfyingly loud pop, and Ava began to pass around papers cup of fizz. "To Willoughby Close, and all the happy memories made there!" she pronounced, her cup held aloft. "And may many more be made, whatever happens."

"Hear, hear," everyone chorused, and toasting paper cups, they drank.

A few minutes later, the auctioneer, a stern-looking woman from London dressed in a power suit of bright cerise and wearing a pair of stilettos that sunk into the grass, came to the front of the lawn.

"It's about to begin," Ellie whispered excitedly, and rather unnecessarily. Everyone was rapt as the woman went through the rules of the auction. A fair crowd had gathered, many of them significantly well-heeled, all armed with paddles. Already there was a buzz of expectancy in the air, a hum of excitement. Then the auction started.

All eight women listened and watched, spellbound, as the bids flew from one end of the lawn to the other and the price of the estate climbed higher—one million and a half, two.

"My goodness," Emily murmured. "It feels a bit like a game of Monopoly, doesn't it?"

After two million, most of the bidders dropped out, leaving only two—a dark-haired man in his thirties who looked louche and slightly bored, raising his paddle languidly, and a woman in a polka-dot sundress who couldn't yet be out of her twenties, her auburn hair pulled up into a high ponytail, looking fresh-faced and bright-eyed with determination as her arm shot out, holding her paddle high.

"I *like* her," Ava whispered. "But who on earth is she and how can she possibly have so much money?"

"They might just be agents," Harriet said knowledgeably. "Acting on behalf of some rich old biddy somewhere."

It was at two and a half million, two and three-quarters… Without realising they were doing so, everyone had started to hold their breath.

A look of annoyance had crossed the man's face, as if he felt this whole business was being drawn out unnecessarily, while the woman's eyes shone brighter. Every single Willoughby Close resident was transfixed by the drama as the tension ratcheted higher and higher, the whole crowd gathered on the lawn captivated by the bidding war raging between the two.

"Three million two," the auctioneer called out. "Who will give me three million two?"

"That is *so* much money," Olivia whispered, scandalised, and they all watched as the woman hesitated, her face a mask of hesitation, while the man, who currently had the highest bid, started to look smug.

"He *can't* win," Lindy exclaimed, a bit too loudly, and a

wave of titters rose and fell around them.

Then, with her chin lifted proudly, the young woman raised her paddle high, to a few raggedy cheers from spectators who had clearly taken sides.

The auctioneer continued, unfazed. "Three million three. Who has three million three?"

A scowl had darkened the man's features as he tossed the paddle aside, shaking his head.

"She won," Harriet exclaimed incredulously. "She actually won. Who is she, do you think? And what on earth is she going to do with this huge place?"

"I suppose we'll find out eventually," Ava remarked. "One day."

"Sold," the auctioneer called out triumphantly, "to bidder number twenty-four, the lady in the polka-dot dress!"

As one, all eight residents turned to glance at the young woman who now owned Willoughby Manor. She was smiling widely, yet she also looked slightly sick.

"I think," Ava said with a note of profound satisfaction, "this is going to get *very* interesting."

Stay tuned for the next chapter
in the world of Willoughby Close!

Want more? Check out Lindy and Roger's story in
Christmas at Willoughby Close!

Join Tule Publishing's newsletter for more great reads and weekly deals!

If you enjoyed *Remember Me at Willoughby Close,* you'll love the other books in the....

Return to Willoughby Close series

Book 1: *Cupcakes for Christmas*

Book 2: *Welcome Me to Willoughby Close*

Book 3: *Christmas at Willoughby Close*

Book 4: *Remember Me at Willoughby Close*

Available now at your favorite online retailer!

More books by Kate Hewitt

The Willoughby Close series

Book 1: *A Cotswold Christmas*

Book 2: *Meet Me at Willoughby Close*

Book 3: *Find Me at Willoughby Close*

Book 4: *Kiss Me at Willoughby Close*

Book 5: *Marry Me at Willoughby Close*

The Holley Sisters of Thornthwaite series

Book 1: *A Vicarage Christmas*

Book 2: *A Vicarage Reunion*

Book 3: *A Vicarage Wedding*

Book 4: *A Vicarage Homecoming*

Available now at your favorite online retailer!

About the Author

After spending three years as a diehard New Yorker,
Kate Hewitt now lives in the Lake District in England with
her husband, their five children, and a Golden Retriever. She
enjoys such novel things as long country walks and chatting
with people in the street, and her children love the freedom
of village life—although she often has to ring four or five
people to figure out where they've gone off to.

She writes women's fiction as well as contemporary romance
under the name Kate Hewitt, and whatever the genre she
enjoys delivering a compelling and intensely emotional story.

Thank you for reading

Remember Me at Willoughby Close

If you enjoyed this book, you can find more from all our great authors at TulePublishing.com, or from your favorite online retailer.

TULE
PUBLISHING

Made in United States
North Haven, CT
08 February 2023

32226107R00205